THE
REGENCY
DETECTIVE

THE REGENCY DETECTIVE

DAVID LASSMAN & TERENCE JAMES

The
Mystery
Press

To Michael.

Map opposite courtesy of Bath in Time, Bath Central Library.

First published 2013

The Mystery Press is an imprint of The History Press
The Mill, Brimscombe Port
Stroud, Gloucestershire, GL5 2QG
www.thehistorypress.co.uk

© David Lassman & Terence James, 2013

The right of David Lassman & Terence James to be identified as the
Authors of this work has been asserted in accordance with the
Copyright, Designs and Patents Act 1988.

British Library Cataloguing in Publication Data.
A catalogue record for this book is available from the British Library.

ISBN 978 0 7524 8610 9

Typesetting and origination by The History Press
Printed in Great Britain

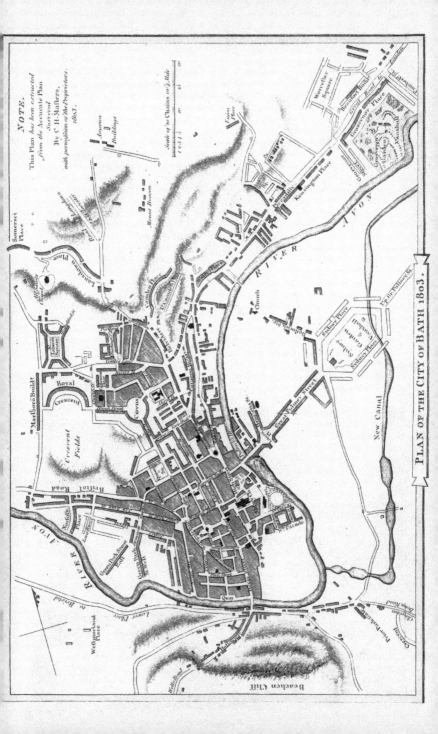

PLAN OF THE CITY OF BATH 1803.

VOLUME I
SWANN'S WAY

PROLOGUE

'Again?' asked the man.

The boy nodded.

'All right, but watch carefully this time.'

The man's fingers hovered over the three inverted wooden cups and then, with a dexterity borne out of practise, began shuffling them – two at a time – around one another on the table. The deliberate staccato rhythm of each separate action merged into a blur of movement, much to the awe and delight of the watching boy; his wide-eyed amazement belying an intense concentration.

The shuffling stopped.

'So,' said the man, 'which cup is the pea under?'

Without hesitation the boy pointed to the middle one. The man's right hand remained poised above the chosen cup momentarily, as if building suspense for an imagined audience, before lifting it to reveal – nothing! Affectionate laughter accompanied the revelation but the boy was too preoccupied to notice, staring incredulously at the empty space left by the cup.

A noise came from elsewhere in the house and the laughter ceased.

'The master must have returned early. Stay here son.' The man then smiled. 'And don't touch the other cups while I'm gone.'

The man stood up, ruffled his son's hair and after checking his own appearance in the reflection of a large copper pan hanging on the wall, left the kitchen.

The boy remained seated at the table, his gaze transfixed at the upturned cup which had been his choice. It lay with its opening facing toward him. An opening he had come to view as a gateway to another world; one he did not yet fully understand and so could therefore not enter. The only way to enter this world was through the 'solution', which his father had promised to reveal when he thought the boy ready.

Against his father's wishes the boy now tentatively lifted the second cup, the one to his left ... but again, nothing! There was no solution to it he told himself, no answer to the game, other than watching the cups more closely, more intently, as they were being shuffled. It was the speed of the hands against the quickness of the eyes. And if the physical skill of one could be learned, so could the other. He would therefore practice observing over and over and not just with cups but anything capable of movement, until finally he would be able to choose the correct cup on the first attempt rather than the last. He reached his hand over, this time lifting the remaining cup with a more determined grip and stared in disbelief at what was underneath.

Crash! A vase smashed in the hallway.

'Father?'

The boy stood and went to the kitchen entrance. For a couple of seconds, as he watched from the doorway, he saw his father entangled in a ferocious struggle with another man, a man he did not recognise, before they fell, still grappling with each other, into a front room and out of sight. By the time the boy reached this entrance, his father lay on the floor, one arm outstretched, his hand inching closer to the fireplace, with the intruder's arms entwined around his legs trying to stop him. But then, in one swift action, his father gripped a cast-iron poker and thrust the pointed end into the intruder's right cheek. As the red-hot metal made contact there was a piercing scream, the smell of scorching flesh, and a pitiful but loud cry of a man's name: 'MALONE!'

From elsewhere in the house Malone now appeared in the hallway, pushing the boy roughly aside and onto the floor as he rushed past in to the front room. And it was from this position, lying on the hallway floor, that the boy witnessed the images which seared themselves into his memory, scarring him as permanently as the poker on the stranger's flesh: the glinted blade … the raised arm … his father's gesture of capitulation … the brutal kick to the head … and then, the callous, calculated thrust of the knife which … but before the final image could play itself out the boy always let out a primeval *Noooooooooooo!* and the nightmare would mercifully end.

CHAPTER ONE

As the Royal Mail coach sped along the Great Bath Road the small market town of Calne was left rapidly diminishing in the background. The overnight journey from London had been mostly uneventful and so its scheduled arrival in Bath, in a little over two hours time, now seemed certain. Nevertheless, the driver, ever mindful of potential delays on this stretch of road – a herd of cows on their way to milking and a fallen tree the most recent examples – snapped his whip twice and the newly tethered, four-horse team obligingly increased their pace.

Inside the distinctive black and maroon carriage Jack Swann awoke with a start from his nightmare and glanced around the interior. The other passengers – two women and a man – were still dozing, oblivious to his startled awakening. He turned his gaze to the countryside becoming visible in the reddening dawn sky and stared at it pensively as the wretched melancholy that always accompanied the aftermath of his nightmare enveloped him fully. At these times he found a little solace in a poem remembered from childhood – though its title and author long forgotten – which in some way he equated with his own situation. It concerned a ship bound for an undiscovered land, but blown off course onto jagged rocks by a storm, leaving the vessel holed but not wrecked. Forever cursed, as the poet had concluded, to flounder in troubled seas like a maritime Prometheus, never to sail calm waters again. And so it was that Swann felt cursed within this life of bad dreams and the melancholic gloom on waking from them, never to find a peaceful mind. He felt this disposition even more acutely this morning, travelling as he was for the funeral the next day of the woman he had called mother for the past twenty years; ever since she and her husband had adopted him at the age of twelve.

Mrs Gardiner had been a kind, caring woman who bestowed unconditional love on all members of her family and Swann reciprocated with feelings which would have been reserved for his real mother, had she not died in childbirth. Likewise, his sibling affections were easily and naturally imparted to his new 'sister', Mary, herself an only child. Regrettably, however, Mr Gardiner had been a different matter. Although as considerate and nurturing in his own way as his wife and daughter, he could never replace Swann's father – the man who raised Swann single-handedly to the threshold of manhood – and so a distance existed between them, neither able to completely benefit from the paternal bond the elder man was willing to offer 'the son he always wanted'. It was twenty years since Swann's real father was murdered, while attempting to protect the Gardiner's property, but not a day went by without his thinking of him.

Through this remembrance of his father, Swann's mind turned inevitably to his work and a case he had just concluded in his consultancy role for the Bow Street Runners – the law-enforcement organisation created some fifty years earlier by the novelist Henry Fielding and whose name derived from the London street where it was based. The case concerned a victim of blackmail that had resulted from his patronage of brothels and his specific requirements there. The practice of entrapping gentlemen in high office or powerful positions by criminal gangs, in collusion with disreputable brothel keepers, was rife in the capital, as no doubt elsewhere, yet the unsuspecting politician had blissfully walked straight into this well-honed trap. Unsuspecting? Swann considered the word and found it erroneous. When one held duties and responsibilities, professional and personal, as this married minister had, perpetual vigilance and constant awareness became foremost, especially with licentious temptations and extortionist activities being such easy bedfellows in the criminal underworld. Too much injustice already existed and far too many perpetrators roamed the streets unpunished to allow oneself, an upholder of the law, to become the hapless quarry of the criminality prevalent throughout the city. Unsuspecting or not, the minister had become entrapped. Realising, however, that recent ill-advised speculation on the stock market meant he would not be able to pay the blackmailers, and so making a public scandal certain, the minister had risen early on the previous Saturday, hired a hansom cab to Putney Heath and, after dismissing the driver, discharged a bullet through his own temple. After being informed of this news, Swann had spent the remaining weekend calling in favours from several newspaper owners to ensure, for the sake of the dead man's family, that reports regarding the politician's demise in that morning's papers lay the blame squarely on the fluctuating stock market and not on the more insalubrious aspects of the case.

From the beginning to the end of the case Swann had been able to do very little, other than put on a disguise and pursue a couple of tenuous leads to the heart of London's underworld. Indeed, ordinarily Swann would have politely declined the case, if it had not been for a name linked to one of the brothel keepers. It was a name he knew only too well, as it was the name cried out on that murderous night and which summoned the man who so callously ended the life of Swann's father: Malone. So, whenever a possible clue to the killer's whereabouts arose, however slender, a sense of responsibility to his father's memory dictated Swann follow it. As it transpired, the name turned out to be a false one and the petty criminal using it far too young. But then, it was always like that: a promising lead, an investigation and a disappointment. The obligation he felt to investigate each one, however, would continue until his quest was at an end; through his father's murderer finally being brought to justice, or else details surrounding his death authenticated.

The sun had now fully risen and the reddened sky turned blue when the coach entered a slight dip surrounded by trees. The semi-darkness caused the window to act as a mirror, revealing Swann's reflection. He looked tired, but not just the kind of tiredness expected from overnight travel; in fact, the journey had proved less arduous than anticipated. No, there was a deeper tiredness, one borne out of prolonged exposure to London's criminal fraternity. The circumstances were not as he would have wished but Swann was grateful for the few days they would afford him out of the capital.

And it would be good to see Mary once more. Dear Mary, her mere presence in a room was enough to lighten Swann's darkest mood. From the moment she had put her hand into his on the day of his adoption, knowing she now had a brother, a special bond, strong as any blood tie, had developed between them. Swann had given himself the role of his sister's 'protector' as they grew up. In reality though, he became more an observer, watching in admiration on returning home from boarding school and later university as Mary blossomed into a strong-spirited, independent-minded woman. Her sharp wit had developed in tandem with her artistic talent, most markedly shown on the pianoforte. And what she lacked in original composition, she made up for in her interpretation of others: most notably Bach. If she did have a slight imperfection, or rather a feminine Achilles heel, perhaps it was that at times she could show a naivety where matters of the heart were concerned. In the past, it had twice led her to the threshold of imprudence, although thankfully on both occasions fortuitous circumstances had conspired to bring her reputation through safely intact.

Mary was now twenty-four years old and still unmarried, which in certain households might have given cause for concern. Her financial independence, however, meant that she did not have to rely on finding a husband to secure a future. Nevertheless, Swann would be comforted to see her at least betrothed in the not too distant future and although not wishing to cast himself in the role of match-maker, there was a lawyer acquaintance who had expressed a wish to be introduced to Mary when Swann brought her back from Bath to live with him in London ... but that was moving too far ahead. There was the funeral to attend first and putting his adoptive mother's affairs in order.

There was, of course, the other reason Swann was coming to Bath and which would occupy part of his stay. If there had been one positive aspect to the case he had just completed back in London, it was that when he had been visiting one of the several disreputable public houses seeking information, he had overheard a conversation; the details of which he had hastily written down afterwards. As the coach came out of the tree-lined dip and into open countryside once more, he tapped the notebook secured in the breast pocket of his jacket, aware the hastily scribbled notes, written three nights ago, contained the next possible lead to finding Malone. Swann looked outward to the western horizon, beyond which the city of Bath was beginning a new day.

CHAPTER TWO

In 1702, and again the following year, Queen Anne visited Bath and it is true to say that the city never looked back. Her royal patronage prompted the rich and powerful elite of British society – Goldsmith's 'people of distinction' – to do likewise and this one-time medieval textile centre, located ninety-seven miles west of London, now found itself the most fashionable resort in the land. In turn, the middling classes followed the elite and throughout the eighteenth century the economic prosperity this brought with it resulted in a sustained programme of building and rapid population expansion rarely witnessed anywhere in Europe beforehand. By the start of the nineteenth century, however, the elite, as is always the way with fashionable and ephemeral pursuits, had now bestowed their patronage elsewhere, on spa towns and health resorts such as Cheltenham and Brighton.

Yet the middling classes, with their domestic entourages in tow, still kept coming in ever increasing numbers and alongside them came a multitude of shopkeepers, tradesmen and skilled labourers who flocked to the city to provide for their every need. But with this influx of the middle, lower and skilled classes, the city also attracted the underclass – the impoverished section of society drawn to places of wealth and abundance, ready to take their share in whatever way they were able. These were the beggars, pickpockets, con-artists, prostitutes and other nefarious characters that saw in Bath a place ripe for plunder. And where crime becomes rife, organised gangs and iniquitous leaders quickly emerge to control it. In Bath the undisputed criminal boss was an Irishman called Thomas Malone, a one-time barek-knuckle fighter who it was said had killed at least two men during his 'career'. He had arrived in the city several years earlier and in a relatively short space of time ruthlessly intimidated and brutally murdered his way to take control of the city's underworld. He had held that top position ever since and during that time had seen off at least three major rivals for his territory and survived as many attempts on his life. At present there were several, less powerful, gang leaders in and around the city with their sights set on seizing power but in reality there was only one serious contender: Frank Wicks.

Not long after midnight, as Swann and the Royal Mail coach were somewhere between Maidenhead and Reading, events connected to the scribbled notes in his notebook were unfolding in Bath; the consequences of which would trigger more far-reaching effects than anyone involved could ever have imagined.

The warehouse door slid open and Thomas Malone stepped through into the building, swiftly followed in single file by several of his men. His eyes scanned the semi-darkness until they stopped at the solitary figure of Richard J. Kirby, standing on the loading platform at the far end. Malone gestured for his men to wait as he walked across the uneven earthen floor towards the waiting man.

'So, what's that important it couldn't wait 'til morning?' Malone sneered, as he ascended the few wooden steps to come level with the other man.

'I am terminating our understanding Malone – and I am aware you desire to receive disagreeable news immediately.'

'We don't have an "understanding" Kirby,' Malone replied, contemptuously. 'I pay you and you do as I say.'

'However you wish to describe our situation, it is over. And from now on you call me Mister Kirby.'

Malone stepped forward, bringing their faces only inches apart.

'Now you listen to me, *Mister* Kirby. I own this city and not you or anyone else tells me what to do.'

'I'm sorry you feel like that Malone, but then you leave me no choice.'

In one sudden movement Kirby raised a small wooden truncheon from behind his back and struck the side of Malone's head, knocking him unconscious. On seeing their leader fall to the floor his men rushed towards the platform but from the shadows a larger group appeared and surrounded them. The fight between the two gangs of men was brief but brutal and in the aftermath all of Malone's men lay dead or dying. Two of the victorious group now came up onto the raised platform and after a gesture from Kirby hauled the unconscious Malone to his feet. Kirby slapped the other man's face several times and slowly Malone's eyes opened. Looking around he saw his gang decimated on the warehouse floor.

'I will kill you for this, Kirby, and send your body down the Avon.'

'That's no way to speak to an associate of mine, Malone,' said Wicks, as he stepped out from the shadows to face his rival.

'Wicks! You'll join him too.'

'And what makes you sure it isn't you ending up in the river?'

'I know people in London,' said Malone, still defiant.

'That's interesting, because your "people" have already sent word they'll not interfere. It seems they're having doubts about you and I have to agree.'

'What d'you mean?'

'Well, there was a time you'd never have walked into such an obvious trap as this, at least not with so few men. No, your time in this city is over, Malone.' Wicks took another step forward and as he did so drew a large cutlass from its scabbard attached to his belt. For the first time, fear appeared in Malone's eyes.

'Wicks, now wait a min …' but he didn't get a chance to finish his words, as the cutlass was driven deep into his midriff by Wicks, who watched with malicious pleasure as the blood spurted from his adversary's mouth. Wicks then gave the blade a victorious twist as it reached its hilt, before drawing it out unhurriedly, savouring every moment of his triumph. As Malone slumped to the ground dead Wicks turned to his own men.

'Right, finish off any of Malone's men still alive and get rid of all the bodies. Dump them in the river. That'll show people who's in charge now.'

Wicks turned to his 'associate', still standing next to him.

'You've done well, Kirby. I won't forget this.'

'I am glad to be of service,' Kirby replied.

They glanced at Malone's body as it was being dragged away.

'This city is mine now,' said Wicks, 'and there's no one to stop me.'

CHAPTER THREE

In May 1760 it was decided by 'The Corporation' – the self-regulating, self-appointed body of men who controlled everything in the city from municipal policy to granting sedan licences – 'that the Town Hall be newly built in a more commodious place, and a committee formed.' This conclusion being drawn from the realisation that the current building had not only outgrown its original purpose but through its location in the middle of the High Street, which happened to be the main thoroughfare, had become a fairly substantial obstruction to the ever increasing volume of traffic entering the city. And so began one of the most controversial and convoluted episodes in Bath's architectural history. The saga dragged on for seventeen years until the old building was finally vacated (and unceremoniously pulled down soon after) and the Mayor and council officials made their way across the street to take up residence in the new Guildhall. And in the quarter century which had elapsed since then, the building had become the symbol of corporate authority in Bath and its seat of justice.

Inside the main courtroom the early session was reaching the culmination of its first case of the morning: a private prosecution brought by Theodore Evans against one Mr Tyler with local magistrate Richard J. Kirby presiding. Kirby banged his gavel, bringing his court to order. He did not look any the worse for his nocturnal activities as he turned to address the all-male jury.

'Gentlemen of the jury,' Kirby began, 'you are now in possession of the facts in this case, including what I believe to be a key character testimony by Mr Wicks, the defendant's employer.'

Wicks nodded approval from his seat in the front row of the public benches.

'It is therefore your task to decide whether the defendant, Mr Tyler, is indeed such an immoral man as suggested by his prosecutor and if so to sentence him accordingly, or whether, in fact, he is the victim of a malicious vendetta intent on destroying his name.'

Evans rose angrily to his feet. 'This is an outrage, sir! You are engaging in blatant coercion of the jury. This man is a habitual pickpocket, a thief and no doubt worse and everyone in this courtroom knows it.'

Kirby furiously banged his gavel.

'Mr Evans, may I remind you that whilst your standing in this city is beyond reproach, this is my courtroom and if proper respect is not forthcoming you will give me no choice but to nullify your prosecution and hold you in contempt of this court.'

Realising he had no other choice, Evans bowed his head and sat back down. 'I am sorry, your honour.'

Kirby nodded his acceptance of Evans' apology and returned to the jury. 'Now gentleman, please begin your deliberation.'

∞

Meanwhile, not far from the Guildhall in traffic-congested Cheap Street, Mary Gardiner stood in the morning sunlight staring absentmindedly into a shop window; her black attire in stark contrast to the vibrant clothing on display in front of her. She had been there for a couple of minutes when her name was called from behind. She turned and across the busy street, at the end of Union Passage, saw a woman in her mid-twenties waving to her. It was an acquaintance, Isabella Thorpe, an unstoppable force of social climbing whose sole ambition in life was the marrying of a wealthy man; if he also happened to be attractive so much the better. The traffic was ceaseless but with the impatience of a spoilt child Isabella stomped across the street, causing a small gig to swerve to avoid her; its driver cursing her as he drove off towards Westgate Street.

'I do declare this street becomes more odious every year,' said Isabella, before greeting Mary with a kiss on either cheek. She now took a step backwards and with as much empathetic sentiment as she could muster, said, 'Oh my dearest Mary, you poor creature, how are you? I returned to Bath last evening to be told the sad news about your mother. The season will not be the same without her.'

'Thank you Isabella, your sentiments are most kind.'

'Is your brother here?' asked Isabella, glancing around with a predatory instinct.

'No. I am waiting for him now.'

'I still cannot quite believe it,' exclaimed Isabella, 'a financially independent bachelor and his first time in Bath. I wish I could stay with you and meet him but there are people in the Pump Room awaiting my company. You must promise to introduce me to him at the earliest opportunity though.'

The nearby Abbey clock struck the half hour.

'I must leave or I will be unsociably late,' Isabella said, and in another moment had disappeared around the corner and through the archway leading to the Pump Room. Mary remained standing by the shop front, feeling somewhat exhausted by Isabella in the way one did after a brisk walk in a strong breeze.

Mary's thoughts now turned to her brother and the imposition of having to be introduced to Isabella.

She undoubtedly knew that he would give her no more than a polite response and a diplomatic brush-off but unfortunately by meeting her it would, she feared, strengthen her brother's distain for what he believed to be the more frivolous nature of the city. Hopefully during his stay though, and with Edmund's assistance, her brother might experience more of the cultural side and then persuading him to stay permanently might prove that much easier. But that would have to wait until after the funeral.

Mary had deliberately omitted any mention of Edmund in her last letter to Jack as she wanted her brother's first impression of her new suitor to be in the flesh and not through the limitation of mere words, however flattering to his person she would have made them. Edmund's light manner had been a comfort to her in the days immediately after her mother's death and although he was presently in London on business, he would be at the funeral the following day.

∽

Back at the courtroom the foreman of the jury, a man of around forty-five with thinning grey hair and a dutiful expression on his face, stood facing Kirby.

'Sir, have you good gentleman reached your verdict?'

'Yes, your honour, we have,' said the foreman.

'And how do you find the defendant?'

'We find the defendant not guilty, your honour.'

Evans was immediately to his feet again. 'The law is being made a mockery.'

'Mr Evans, I will not warn you again,' said Kirby, banging his gavel once more to enforce the point.

'May I say I concur with you gentlemen in that I believe you have reached the right decision,' Kirby told the jury, before turning to the triumphant defendant. 'And let me on behalf of the court, Mr Tyler, apologise for your incarceration while waiting to appear here in court. You are now free to go.'

Kirby exchanged a brief, furtive glance with Wicks and then left the court, little realising the chain of events he had now set in motion.

CHAPTER FOUR

On reaching the outskirts of their next scheduled stop the uniformed guard brought the elongated coach horn to his lips and sounded the three long blasts signifying their imminent arrival to the city's inhabitants ahead. This included the postmaster who was to be ready and waiting with any parcels for loading; there was no delaying the Royal Mail. As the noise of the final blast died away in the crisp morning air the driver stridently announced the destination for the benefit of the quartet of passengers inside: 'Bath approaching!'

The combination of horn and voice was enough to stir the three slumbering passengers and their reaction on waking told Swann much about them. The two females reacted with girlish exuberance as they craned their necks out of the coach window to get a glimpse of the city; this unladylike conduct seeming to suggest this was their first visit. The gentleman, meanwhile, looked slightly amused at his companion's contorted positions, though not embarrassed, while his indifference to the buildings on view outside showed either a distinct lack of interest in grand architecture, of which some of the finest examples in Europe were on display, or else a familiarity with them which had resulted in apathy.

Swann turned his attention outward and immersed himself in the Palladian splendour of the buildings which lay in front of him. From what he had recently read, the fact Bath had achieved its place as one of the finest architecturally designed European cities in only a few decades was remarkable enough, but even more so as it was through the vision of one man. John Wood's proposal for this 'new' city, to be built upon and extended out from the old medieval one, was to create a harmonious and symmetrical urban metropolis uplifting to the casual eye. On a deeper level, however, he envisaged the views to transcend the secular world in order to bring its observer closer to the glory of God. The terraces and crescents Swann could see from the carriage gave ample enough evidence of the successful fulfilment of this vision but with the holy trinity of the King's Circus, Royal Crescent and Great Pulteney Street as yet unseen, the pinnacle of this achievement was still to be savoured.

The sense of awe-inspiring delight at the vista before them was now mirrored in the expressions on the two female faces but whereas Swann's focus was on the outer structures and the finely carved details upon them, their feminine eyes were firmly fixed on what was inside. As domestic dwellings gave way to commercial properties so their gazes darted from shop window to shop window and the superfluity of clothes and other items on display there. The city may have earned its reputation as a spa and enhanced its cultural significance with its architecture, but for many visitors it was the self-proclaimed title of the shopping centre of the South-West which they had come to experience.

In the years since the British had successfully supplanted the Dutch as the busiest merchants in the world, all manner of luxurious and exotic goods had found their way to English shores from numerous foreign ports. The result being that the act of shopping, which at first had been a fashionable activity for society's elite, had become a national obsession. And from what he was now seeing of the city, Bath not only welcomed this obsession but with its tempting window displays, advertising boards and the array of merchandise lining the pavements, aggressively encouraged it. For Swann, however, he could only perceive opportunities for crime: the free-standing, unattended tables laden with valuable goods; the rows of unguarded gold jewellery in shop frontages; and the chance to orchestrate, no doubt, various protection schemes to 'guarantee' that traders' contents and buildings remained intact during non-trading hours.

And then it struck him – if Malone had gone anywhere, Bath was an obvious choice. There had been a rumour that he had fled London after Mr Gardiner put up the large reward for his apprehension and whether or not he came directly to the city at that time, if details of the overheard conversation proved correct, he was certainly here now. Why Swann had not considered Bath before perplexed him momentarily, but as the coach entered the city centre a more overwhelming emotion gripped him: a feeling of anticipation at perhaps finally tracking down his father's killer and administering the justice he had sought for so long.

The coach neared the Guildhall and as it did so a man emerged from inside and stood on the steps surveying the scene, intently watching visitors and residents alike as they went about their business of generally 'seeing and being seen'. He immediately caught Swann's attention and as the carriage passed the building their eyes met. It was only for an instant but with both men well versed in the art of observation for their own means, each felt within that brief moment to have gauged the measure of the other. For Swann, he could recognise a man outside a judicial building with no other reason for being there than as a malefactor. His clothing may have suggested an ordinary resident, a witness perhaps, but the penetrative stare of the eyes revealed his predatory nature and the coldness therein, the detachment from morality when carrying out criminal activities.

To Tyler, standing on the Guildhall steps, he saw in the man looking out from the Royal Mail coach, his first 'mark' of the day, another rich visitor with a bill-purse full of money which he, Tyler, would acquire in the near future. The fact he was travelling on the Mail no doubt confirmed his wealth and instinctively, as he descended the steps, Tyler moved the fingers on either hand, limbering them up in anticipation.

Inside the coach Swann was now heading along Cheap Street, passing the shop window into which Mary had so recently been looking. The driver turned into Stall Street and their destination: the Three Tuns Inn. No sooner had the carriage stopped outside the building, than the postmaster appeared with several parcels.

Swann gestured for the women to alight first but they did not move.

'We are all bound for Bristol sir,' said their male companion. In reply Swann nodded politely, tipped his hat slightly to the women and stepped out. As he did this, he was watched by the gentleman who continued to observe as Swann was greeted by an attractive woman in her early twenties. On seeing the woman's face as she turned, however, the gentleman quickly sat back in his seat out of view.

After greeting one another fleetingly, Swann manoeuvred his sister away from the ensuing maelstrom which always accompanied the Royal Mail's arrival, to a more conducive spot further up the street where they could converse easier.

'Dearest Mary,' he said, 'I am so sorry I was not able to be here sooner.'

'Do not concern yourself Jack. I understand you have your work but it is good to have you in Bath now.' It was not a complete lie Mary told, more a half-truth. Her brother's belated arrival had been a major source of disappointment to her, but over the years she had become accustomed to his ways and now accepted them without either recompense or rebuke.

'Have all the arrangements been made?' Swann asked.

'Yes, the service is to take place at eleven o'clock tomorrow morning.'

'I hope this has not been too much for you, having to organise everything by yourself,' said Swann, with a genuine regretful tone at his absence.

'A family friend has seen to the majority of the arrangements,' Mary replied.

Swann felt somewhat relieved at this information.

'He did mention the possibility of being here to greet you Jack, but I know he is a busy man.'

At that moment though, with the Royal Mail seen off on its way to Bristol and the area outside of the Three Tuns clear once more, Mary spotted a gentleman making his way up Stall Street.

'There is Henry now,' she said.

Strolling up the street at a leisurely pace was Henry Fitzpatrick, a fairly rotund man in his early forties. If early ambition had been irretrievably thwarted, then later life had given him a pastoral demeanour he was constantly putting to good use within this urban setting.

Fitzpatrick saw Mary and waved. As she reciprocated, Swann was bumped into from behind. The man immediately apologised and strode on. Although Swann only caught a glimpse, he instantly recognised the man from the steps outside the Guildhall. His gaze followed the man as he carried on down the street and towards Fitzpatrick, who was now by the entrance of the Three Tuns. Instinctively Swann already knew exactly what was going to happen and as he watched he saw the man 'bump' into Fitzpatrick, gesture another apology and then hasten off down a side street opposite the inn.

'Stay here Mary,' said Swann, 'I believe your friend has just been robbed.'

Before she could respond her brother was already striding down the street on the pickpocket's trail. On reaching Fitzpatrick, who stood blissfully unaware that anything untoward had just occurred, Swann asked, 'Do you still have your bill-purse, sir?' Fitzpatrick felt his inside top left pocket. 'No, it is gone!' Swann nodded and began running into the street the thief had made his escape along.

At the far end of Beau Street, Tyler intuitively turned and saw the man from the Royal Mail coach coming after him. He calculated he had a ten second headstart, as he too began running, but that was all the time he needed.

On reaching the spot where the thief had become aware of being chased, Swann carried on and followed the man's trail around to the left, emerging out at one end of Westgate Buildings. This was now in the lower town, as it was known locally, and stood on the boundary of a more run down and decrepit area called the Avon Street district; a squalid part of the city deliberately omitted from guidebooks. This was where the thief was heading towards. In turn, Swann also crossed over the road and entered Peter Street, a shop-lined thoroughfare beyond which was the River Avon.

As Swann made his way down the street, the stark contrast between the parts of Bath he had witnessed from the coach and the area he was now entering became ever more apparent and, with the latter, came a palpable sense of foreboding at each corner and an undertone of menace oozing from every building and alleyway. But this did not deter Swann, as he had witnessed this contrast between poor and prosperous many times in London. One minute the vista in the capital could be that of fine squares, dignified thoroughfares and magnificent houses and the next, if taking an ill-advised turn, a stranger might find themselves in a warren of badly lit, stench-filled alleyways, overcrowded with squalid dwellings, and with the risk of losing everything from one's valuables to one's life. Over the years Swann had come to know both these contrasts well though and that was why what lay ahead of him now held no fear.

Amidst the bustle of street traders loudly hawking their wares, Swann caught sight of the pickpocket once again. Believing he had found sanctuary within the Avon Street district, which was his domain, the thief had stopped running and was now conversing with one of the numerous stall holders whose produce-filled carts lined either side of the lower half of the street. Swann continued his pursuit but his quarry, now realising he was still being followed, began running towards the end of the street before ducking out of sight into an alleyway. As Swann ran between the stalls, the man the thief had been talking to stepped out into Swann's path and 'accidentally' got in his way. Unable to avoid him, Swann went crashing into the next cart along, causing its contents to be spilled onto the filthy sewer encrusted and vermin-infested ground. He was only momentarily put off balance, however, and swiftly resumed his quest, accompanied for a short while by the cursing of the cart's owner. Swann reached the alleyway but now found the entrance to a complex warren of passageways. The thief was nowhere in sight. The bill-purse, however, had been dropped and was lying on the muddy ground in front of him. As he moved closer, the grubby hand of a street urchin reached out from a doorway to pick it up but Swann stepped forward and put his boot on the bill-purse.

'I will take that,' he said, bending down to retrieve it. As he did this though, several lowlife types appeared threateningly from other doorways and corners. In response, Swann opened his jacket and revealed a pistol. As he gestured to remove it, the mob reluctantly dissolved back into the shadows.

Ten minutes later the wallet was back in the hands of its rightful owner, who had loyally remained alongside Mary at the Three Tuns and had shared the same expression of visible relief as her on seeing an unharmed Swann returning back down Beau Street.

'I followed the miscreant into an unwholesome area across the road from Westgate Buildings,' Swann said, on handing over the bill-purse, 'but I am afraid he had the advantage over me there, in both geographical knowledge and assistance from acquaintances.'

'Oh Jack, I had hoped you would leave your work in London. I cannot bear to think what might have happened to you in that place of notoriety.'

'Your sister is right,' said Fitzpatrick. 'If I had known that was where you were bound, I would have persuaded you otherwise. The whole of the area is a notorious haven for the criminal element and the retrieval of my bill-purse was not worth the risk to venture in there.' Fitzpatrick held up the retrieved item. 'Nevertheless sir, I had given it up for lost. I am in your debt.'

Before Swann could respond, Mary made the formal introductions. 'Henry, may I introduce my brother Jack Swann. Jack, this is Henry Fitzpatrick.'

The two men bowed to each other.

'Considering the support you have recently provided my sister,' Swann said, 'I believe it is I who am indebted to you, Mr Fitzpatrick.'

'I am just pleased to have been of some humble service at this unfortunate and sad time. Are you planning to be long in Bath after the funeral, Mr Swann?'

'A few days only, I think. London criminals do not respect the grief of others.'

Fitzpatrick nodded in resigned agreement.

'As you witnessed,' he said, 'it is the same in our city, but let me not detain you further. You and your sister must have much to discuss. I will see you both tomorrow at eleven o'clock.'

With that, Fitzpatrick bowed and strode off up the street and turned the corner at the top of Stall Street.

'Fitzpatrick seems to be under the impression that we are both attending the funeral service.'

'He is right to be so inclined,' replied Mary.

'I am not certain your presence tomorrow will be wise – it is not the usual convention.'

'Whether it is wise or not, it is my wish to attend.'

'And what does Fitzpatrick think of your intention?'

'Henry was of the same opinion as you, Jack. That is, until I reminded him that when father passed away both mother and myself were advised not to attend the funeral, due to the same convention, and until her dying day mother regretted her absence.'

'Very well,' said Swann, seemingly now accepting his sister's decision as well. 'By the way, this Fitzpatrick, what is his profession?'

'He is a local magistrate.'

Swann was keen to know more but Mary deliberately ignored his inquisitive expression and said instead, 'Come Jack and let me show you the house.'

CHAPTER FIVE

After escaping into the warren of alleyways he'd known since childhood, Tyler recovered his breath and readied himself to carry on his day. He was angry to have dropped the bill-purse, a costly mistake as its heaviness suggested a lot of money. Its owner looked vaguely familiar, although he could not put a name to the face. He knew most of the marks he pickpocketed by sight and it made sense to remember them all. There were those who had been unaware of his presence when he stole from them and therefore would not recognise him when they met again, so allowing him the chance to rob them anytime their paths crossed; while the ones who might have seen his face or where others had raised the alarm, as with his last dupe, he would not deprive them of their valuables again for at least a month.

As for the man who had chased him, he was different. Tyler knew they would instantly know each other the next time they met, even within a large crowd, and however much time had passed. It was the passenger from the Royal Mail coach, the one he had marked as he stood on the Guildhall steps. Even as their eyes had met, however, something in them told him the man might be trouble, but having been in jail for nearly a week he was too desperate for money to heed the warning. His attempt to relieve him of his belongings had been to no avail though, as Tyler had been left empty-handed. He could not understand it. Even in the few seconds the two of them had made contact, Tyler was able to search all the man's pockets but had found nothing there. What was even more of a mystery was that he had not felt a weapon about his person either and yet on realising he had lost the other mark's bill-purse and having retraced his steps, he then saw the man produce a pistol to disperse the Corn Street gang. He now briefly remembered the weight of the bill-purse and for a moment imagined how much money was inside, but then chided himself for such wasteful thinking. It was gone and there was nothing he could do about it.

Tyler's thoughts now turned to his 'round', the weekly collection of money from street traders, shop owners, brothel keepers and pub landlords which they paid Wicks to keep their premises intact and themselves from having 'accidents'. It lightened his mood, after the loss of the bill-purse, to choose to come down extra hard on those that could not pay this morning. His patch was the 'triangle', the area enclosed by Avon Street, Corn Street and Peter Street and he was a day late. This gave him the added satisfaction of knowing his 'regulars' would have been anxious since then. In the protection racket there was security in routine and the fact he had not appeared as normal the day before would not have been taken as a sign of reprieve, but a cause for concern.

Wicks would normally have sent someone else to collect the money but he had not done so this time as he was preparing to kill Malone. It had been planned for a while but for whatever reason Wicks had waited until last night. It was just bad timing, Tyler thought, that he had been in jail and missed it, as there had been several old scores he would liked to have settled personally with a few of Malone's men.

Now Wicks controlled the whole city Tyler might get a better patch. Malone had thought the Avon Street area too poor and so concentrated on the wealthier parts of the city and the upmarket tradesmen. And he was right. There was little Tyler could skim from currently but with another, more substantial round, he might manage a decent cut without his boss knowing. He might also have to collect from that shopkeeper, Evans, and he could exact revenge for what he had just been put through by his attempted prosecution. He would try and raise the subject when he saw Wicks later that day and, as it had been Tyler who had brought him into the gang in the first place, his boss would hopefully see he deserved it.

Wicks had appeared in Bath more than a year ago and yet had quickly risen through the criminal world to assume total control of it, helped in no small part by Tyler himself. It was said he had arrived in the city to kill a man who had double-crossed him, that he had spent time doing hard labour on a prison ship, and that the cutlass he always carried with him had been taken from a guard on board the ship returning from Botany Bay, after Wicks had strangled him with his bare hands. But Wicks never talked about his past. Tyler was certain his boss looked familiar though, as if they had met before, a long time ago. When he had asked Wicks about it, the other man had said no and Tyler quickly found out that if he said no to anything, you didn't ask again.

Another reason Wicks had probably not sent anyone else to do his collecting was that he knew Tyler would be free today, as he now had Kirby in his pocket. It was good to have the law on one's side, he thought, laughing to himself. Tyler was involved in the trap that Wicks was going to use to blackmail the magistrate but in the end he had needed no persuasion to defect from Malone. From what Tyler knew, Kirby was so corrupt he didn't care whose side he worked for, as long as he got a share of the money and his regular supply of child prostitutes.

Fitzpatrick! That was the second mark's name. He remembered him now. He was a magistrate just like Kirby. In fact, Wicks had approached him sometime earlier but as they had nothing on him to use as blackmail, he had refused. Tyler was certain it was only a matter of time until they discovered a weakness though, or else he got in their way and had to be dealt with. And with that thought, Tyler felt the cosh he had retrieved from its hiding place, a cavity behind loose stones in a nearby wall, and entered the first premises on his round.

CHAPTER SIX

'The house is certainly well appointed and spacious,' said Swann, as he gazed out from the drawing room window onto the street below, 'but perhaps a little too spacious now?' He looked across at Mary to gauge any reaction, but none was forthcoming. Before Swann could continue introducing the idea of his sister moving to London, Mary's personal maid entered the drawing room carrying a tray of beverages. Swann remained silent as Emily went about her business and returned his gaze to the street outside.

When Great Pulteney Street was completed in 1793, linking the city centre with the new developments east of the river at Bathwick, it immediately became one of the most sought after addresses in Bath. At eleven hundred feet long and a hundred feet wide the street not only gave an appearance of a grand Parisian boulevard, but brought with it the accolade of being the widest street in Europe. Although the prestige it offered its residents was not a major factor in Mr Gardiner's decision to buy the house on his retirement to the city seven years earlier, nonetheless he had always derived a certain agreeable satisfaction on seeing people's expressions when informed where he lived. Sadly, he had only enjoyed this pleasure for two years. On his passing, his wife and daughter, Mary, had stayed on at the property. Now it was only Mary.

On returning home with her brother after meeting him off the coach they had enjoyed a breakfast consisting of toast, tea, fresh rolls and cold meats; although Swann had requested coffee instead of tea. After being suitably refreshed, Mary had then given him a tour of the family home that Swann, although several invitations had been given over the years, had never visited before. In the majority of aspects it was a traditional Georgian townhouse and typical of those in Great Pulteney Street; being spread over six levels, with the top floor – the garrets – assigned to domestic staff. The two levels below the garrets contained the main bedrooms, with the dining and drawing rooms on the ground floor; located there for their close proximity to the basement kitchen. The final level of the building was the cellars, part of which extended out under the street itself.

Where the house differed from others, however, was in its balance between male and female styled rooms. Although on originally taking over the house the existing equilibrium had been maintained, since the death of Mr Gardiner the house had seen an ascendancy of the feminine, with only the library on the second floor – which had been converted by Mr Gardiner from a guest bedroom – retaining the masculine mark of its former main occupant. This modest but satisfactorily stocked library had been the room of most interest to Swann, even if he did not openly show it, and he was pleased to learn he would be sleeping in the bedroom next to it.

The most elegant and striking example of the feminine style was on display in the drawing room, the pride of place in any self-respecting Georgian family. And it was here, after the tour of the house, Mary had brought Swann. As Swann had walked over to the trio of tall windows, Mary sat down at the pianoforte and began to play the opening aria from

Bach's *Mit Verschiedenen Veraenderungen*, known in English as the *Aria with Diverse Variations*. This was her brother's favourite piece and he smiled on recognising it. Mary had just finished playing it when Swann had made his remark about the spaciousness of the house.

Emily put the tray of beverages down on a table, curtseyed and then withdrew from the room.

'I know it may seem soon,' Swann now continued, 'but have you thought about what you will do?' On seeing his sister's bemused expression, he tried to clarify his thoughts. 'Well, I assume you will not be staying in Bath now, a woman alone.'

'A woman I may be, but I am certainly not alone here. There is Emily …'

'That is not what I meant.'

'I know what you meant Jack, but mother and I coped well enough without any male presence in the house after father's death and we certainly did not feel like vulnerable women when out in the city. There is always Henry, who you have met,' said Mary, pausing for a moment before adding, '… and of late, there has also been Edmund.'

'You have not mentioned this suitor in your letters,' replied Swann, instantly realising the nature of the relationship from the tone of Mary's voice.

'It has all happened very recently,' she said. 'His name is Edmund Lockhart.'

Mary began to play the aria again, only this time slightly faster. 'But if you are that concerned about my welfare and having a male protector in the house,' she said, with more than a hint of mischievous delight at this opportunity to broach the subject so soon, 'then why do you not move to Bath? You would find the cultural life here most agreeable and I am certain Edmund would be your guide to the more male-orientated premises.'

'My work is my life and that work is in London, Mary. You know that,' said Swann, having suddenly found himself on the defensive.

'As you observed earlier,' continued Mary, rising to the challenge, 'we have criminals in Bath too.'

'Yes, but here they are mere pickpockets, opportunists and petty thieves. In London there are organised gangs run by ruthless killers.'

'You paint a most inviting picture of our capital.'

'Look Mary,' said Swann, realising he had to seize the initiative, 'the truth is that I have already started to make arrangements.'

Mary stopped playing at this revelation, her surprise being quickly replaced by defiance. 'I am more than happy in Bath and do not wish to leave now or at anytime, especially for such a dangerous place as you have just described.'

'It will be for the best, sister.'

'Now you listen to me Jack Swann,' defiance turning to annoyance, 'how dare you interfere in my life here, you have never visited in all the time we have been in Bath and after everything is said and done, you are not even my real bro …' she stopped, an expression of horror on her face. 'Oh Jack, I did not mean what I said. I am so sorry.'

'Do not be upset,' replied Swann. 'It is already forgotten.'

Swann opened his arms wide as Mary stood up to be embraced. 'We are both upset about mother's death,' he said, as their bodies met, 'and it was perhaps inappropriate of me to raise this matter at this time.'

'I do think of you as a brother, Jack, and it does not matter if you visited us or not, what is important is that you have come here now especially for mother's funeral. That means so much to me.'

They held each other tightly for a few moments and then moved apart. Swann smiled at her as he said, 'So, when am I to meet this beau of yours?'

'Tomorrow,' replied Mary, harmonious relations now restored. 'He will be at the service. I know you will find him most agreeable Jack. I know it.'

CHAPTER SEVEN

Swann had kept a journal since the age of thirteen, when the Gardiners had given him an elaborately bound volume for his birthday. He had written in it religiously every day and quickly filled it up, the present one being the forty-eighth; his copious entries necessitating a new journal each five or six months.

Bath, Tuesday 18th October, 1803
It was most pleasing to be with Mary today but it pains me to think that there was disharmony between us this morning, however brief it lasted. I cannot but regret introducing the subject of her moving to London then. It was too soon. What is worse though is that she was so appreciative of my presence here. What hurt would it cause her then, to learn that it is my father's murder which is the motivating reason behind why I have come to Bath at this time and not because of her mother's death.

It has been twenty years since my father's murder and nearly fifteen years since I became old enough to avenge it. And yet, after all this time, I still imagine myself in a bad dream and that one day I shall wake to find myself as a young boy once more, sitting opposite my father at the Gardiner's kitchen table. The reality, though, is that I am alone and I, alone, have assumed responsibility to seek the justice for his death. The task has been all-consuming, but if it was not I, then who would discharge this obligation? My adoptive father undertook what he was able to but once the trail had grown cold and with other things to concern him … well, I do not blame him for bringing the matter to a close in his own mind, even if I could not within mine.

At the age of eighteen I began the quest to track down my father's killer and like Odysseus' wanderings through the Grecian isles in search of his homeland, these long years have seen my course set by the winds of fate that have sent me, through the promising leads they provide, in whatever direction they deem fit. It is an odyssey which has demanded immense sacrifice during these years but I have accepted this, exiling myself from family life and friendships.

And now, even my relationship with Mary is tainted with the knowledge that she is deceived by my actions in coming to Bath. But I cannot allow emotion to overcome duty. Did not Odysseus's own son, Telemachus, conceal the truth surrounding his father from those he loved for the sake of the greater plan? And so I must continue to do likewise now I have reached my own Ithaca, for that is what I believe Bath to be. And having landed upon 'these shores', I must remain focussed and determined as I make my way to the 'palace of iniquity' in order to enact the final confrontation.

There is, however, something which troubles me. The feeling I became aware of this morning, when entering the city, has stayed with me throughout the day and remains as a bedside companion while I write this journal entry. It possesses a strange quality, carrying within it an anticipatory sense of final release and yet simultaneously auguring that which lies beyond. I have experienced this feeling before, although only ever fleetingly, and at those times it has led me to a moral questioning of my actions and to whether I act as judge or executioner? In the moment of retribution, I ponder, will divine justice be served or will it be simply the act of a man taking the old law – an eye for an eye – as his own decree? For I know that when I find Malone I will strike him down as surely as he did my father. And my justification to this questioning is that I truly believe his sentence was passed at the fatal moment he stabbed my father on *that murderous night. And so, having already been judged, it is only for me to carry out his rightful punishment.*

With the feeling remaining for so long this time, however, I have been able to reflect on it more objectively and I can now see it for what it is; not a moral question on my actions but an empirical one, in so much as when this deed is accomplished, what is left? What awaits me: a place devoid of meaning? Is that why I have never before let Bath as a possible haven for him enter my mind all this time, as the thought of finally ending what has consumed me all these years would leave me not knowing what to do next. I could not envisage staying in Bath, yet do I remain in London now that I have tracked him down. Thinking back over these last fifteen years I realise that every case I have undertaken, except perhaps one, can all be linked to this quest in one way or another. So what will my life become now that the end has possibly come?

Am I being too hasty in my belief though, that after all these years of searching, he is in the city? I cannot feel his presence, as I know I will when the time comes, for I have felt it once before. It was when I was sixteen years of age and attending a large fair on the outskirts of London. As I stood in a crowd watching a magician, I suddenly felt a presence nearby. On turning, I saw him for a brief moment, at least the back of him. By the time I had raised the alarm he was gone. Perhaps though, the reason I cannot feel his presence is because he is already dead? Have the details of that conversation overheard in London already played themselves out here? And if this is the case, I wonder how I will feel knowing another hand has extinguished his life and fulfilled what I believed to have been my destiny.

Whether I can feel Malone's presence or not I know that this feeling augurs an ending of my quest one way or another, but whatever lies beyond is for another time and perhaps a future journal entry. So I will attend the funeral tomorrow (or rather today, as I observe the clock has reached midnight) and while there, create the opportunity to converse with Fitzpatrick to discover what he knows about Malone.

CHAPTER EIGHT

The boy sat on the bed he had shared with his father. He had not shed any tears at the funeral earlier that morning; these would come later, if at all. He had never seen his father cry and however hard it might be not to now, he wanted to follow his example. 'Leave that to the other sex,' his father had once joked. The loss hurt so much though that he felt numb from it and all he could do was sit and stare at the wooden chair across the room, on which a few of his father's clothes lay. He wanted to go over there and hold the clothes, to feel their familiar texture and his father's warmth once more. But he did not.

The boy did not know how long it had been there but he now became aware of something in his hands. As he continued to gaze at the chair across from him, he felt the heaviness and shape of the object and realised it was a book. It was the one he had taken off the bedside table when he first entered the room at the top of the house. The book was the latest that his father had been allowed to borrow from Mr Gardiner's library and which the boy and his father had taken turns to read aloud each evening. The boy ran his fingers down the book's spine and over the raised lettering that spelt out the title and author. The book was *Robinson Crusoe* by Daniel Defoe. It was a story about a man shipwrecked on an island far away, but who survived on it through his resourcefulness. They had reached a section, however, where Crusoe had become sick with bad dreams and in his sickness remembered his father. He had wondered whether his present situation was a 'just punishment for his sin'; his sin being that of going against his father's wishes and setting sail on the adventure which led to him being marooned on 'this island of despair', as Crusoe had called it.

The boy's thoughts turned to his own act of disobedience. He had gone against his father's wishes, lifting the cups after being told not to, and now wondered whether his father being taken from him was his 'just punishment'. If only he had not lifted those cups perhaps things would have been different, or else if he had actually tried to do something other than merely watching. Could he have done anything to change things that night? The images which had haunted his dreams ever since now invaded his waking state. This time, however, he saw his father receive the fatal blow and Malone, with evil intent still in his eyes, turning after toward the boy himself. But in that moment, the boy was already getting to his feet and by the time Malone was at the front door of the Gardiner's property, looking up and down the street for him, he had already hidden himself well enough in the neighbouring hedgerow to escape being found. The boy had then stayed there until he saw Malone and his scarred accomplice make their way down the street; the wounded man sobbing and racked with pain.

There was a knock on the bedroom door but the boy was too preoccupied in his thoughts to respond. The door opened and Mrs Hunter, the Gardiner's nanny, stood at the entrance. She saw the solitary figure on the bed and her heart went out to him, but she knew there was nothing she could do to comfort the boy over the loss of his father.

Mr Swann had been highly regarded both by the Gardiner family and the other members of staff that worked for them. He had been in the Gardiner's service for fifteen years and during the first three of those years had his wife beside him. When she died, the Gardiner's were initially against Mr Swann's plan of raising the newborn child himself, but when they saw how determined he was, they relented and helped all they could. A wet nurse had been hired and after the child was weaned, they had allowed the female staff in the household to take turns looking after the boy when Mr Swann was on duty. He had never forgotten their kindness and so Mrs Hunter was not surprised at the courageous act which had cost him his life.

There had been some debate as to whether the boy should attend the funeral but in the end it was decided he should and so had gone with Mr Gardiner and the male servants of the household. It obviously had been too much for him though, as he had slipped away from the men as soon as they had returned to the house. It was then that Mrs Hunter had been dispatched to find the boy and bring him back downstairs.

Mrs Hunter saw the boy holding a book. Mr Swann had taught himself to read and write and had been doing the same with the boy. He had adored his son and would always have such a look of contentment when talking about him. At least the boy's future was now set.

'Jack, they are waiting for you downstairs.'

Mrs Hunter went over to the boy and gently took his hand. He did not resist and accompanied her downstairs to the first floor of the house. They stopped at the two large drawing room doors and Mrs Hunter knocked reverentially.

'I have the boy here, sir, madam, as you requested,' she said.

'Thank you, Mrs Hunter, please bring him in,' replied Mrs Gardiner.

Mrs Hunter brought the boy into the room, to where Mr and Mrs Gardiner stood waiting, along with their four-year-old daughter, Mary.

'Jack, do you know why you are here?' asked Mr Gardiner, as he beckoned the boy closer toward him.

The boy shook his head.

'Well, in appreciation of your father's loyalty to this family, may god rest his soul, and as you have no living relatives that we know of, we are to adopt you.'

'You will now be part of our family, Jack,' said Mrs Gardiner. 'It means that Mr Gardiner and I are to be your guardians and Mary will be your sister.'

As Mrs Gardiner spoke, the girl moved closer to the boy and put her hand into his, holding it tight.

Mrs Gardiner had been true to her word and until her dying day had treated the boy as her own son. It was perhaps right then that Swann was at her funeral, whatever the original intention for his coming to Bath had been.

As he stood by the graveside, Swann now reciprocated his sister's childhood gesture and moved his right hand into a position where she could take it. She did so and squeezed his hand hard, as she fought to hold back her tears.

As the service neared its close, a gentleman arrived at the cemetery entrance. This was Edmund Lockhart. He made his way prudently through the gate and stood behind a clump of bushes for a few moments, assessing the situation. After deciding his course of action, Lockhart crossed a small path and discreetly took a place at the back of the mourners.

If one wished to be thoroughly pedantic, and there were plenty amongst Bath's social echelons that would wish to be so, then it could be held that the gentleman was inappropriately dressed for the funeral; the grey clothes he was so attired in being a colour normally reserved for the later period of half-mourning. In his defence though, he had only this very hour returned to Bath from his business trip and had no opportunity to change his apparel. He was embarrassingly late but would hopefully still be able to console Mary. And besides, no one had seen him enter, so he could have arrived at any time after the start of the service and merely choose not to interrupt proceedings, especially as he could see there was already a gentleman beside her, who he surmised to be the brother arrived from London.

Lockhart had been surprised when Mary had first mentioned she was going to attend the funeral and it had briefly crossed his mind to persuade her otherwise. On realising her mind was made up though, he decided instead to do all he could to support her. It was, after all, this spiritedness which had first attracted her to him. He was, however, late and there was no way around this fact. The coach he was travelling back to Bath in had broken a wheel and it had taken an inordinate amount of time to fix. Once he reached his destination, he had hailed a fast gig and come straight to the church on the outskirts of the city.

The service finished and the mourners began to offer their condolences to both Mary and Swann. Lockhart slowly moved forward to where they stood. As soon as she saw him he raised his arms in an apologetic manner.

'My dear Mary, my lateness is unforgivable,' Lockhart said, 'but my business in London detained me longer than I had expected.'

'Do not concern yourself Edmund, as it is good to see you here. Now, let me introduce you to my brother,' she said, as Swann finished talking to Fitzpatrick nearby. 'Jack, I wish you to meet someone.'

As Swann turned to be introduced to Lockhart, they instantly recognised the other as travelling companions on the Royal Mail coach the previous day.

CHAPTER NINE

Wicks looked out from the window at the top of the warehouse and surveyed *his* city. From where the building stood, on the Bristol Road, he could look back across the river and see the entire length of Avon Street and the surrounding district, known locally as 'the hate'. This was where Wicks had been born thirty years earlier and even at that time it had acquired the reputation for being the most notorious area in the city. His gaze now moved upwards, to the roofs and upper floors of the houses of the well-to-do that climbed in rows up the sides of the encompassing hills. Then finally, further up the slopes, to the crescents and mansions within which the real wealth of the city waited to be plundered.

It had taken Wicks eighteen months to attain this position of power; eighteen months since he had docked at the port in Bristol and returned to the city of his birth. The first thing he had done on his arrival in Bath was seek revenge on the thief-taker who had set him up and got him transported to Botany Bay ten years earlier. Wicks was prepared to take that length of time again to track the man down, but in the end found him in the first place he had looked; the pub in Walcot Street that the man had been known to haunt all those years before. The city was strange that way, Wicks thought; as much as things constantly changed, you could leave it for a decade, as he had done, and yet still find things the same on coming back.

The man who had convinced Wicks to rob a house, then arrested him on his way out in order to collect a reward, had not recognised Wicks when he entered The Bell. He had not recognised him either, when Wicks had sat next to him and engaged him in conversation. It was only in the moment before Wicks killed the corrupt thief-taker did he tell him who he was. After the two men had their fill of ale, they both staggered out and, at Wicks' suggestion, headed back to the centre along the river. But Wicks was merely acting and as his companion stopped to relieve himself, he readied himself for the kill. As the man turned back, Wicks looked him in the eyes and said, 'Remember me?' There was the briefest moment of recognition on the part of the thief-taker before Wicks stabbed him through the heart and the body fell backwards into the water. Wicks watched as it was carried away downstream, where it would be discovered a week later in a state of severe decomposition.

After he had taken his revenge, Wicks joined a gang based in the Avon Street district and waited for his chance. It came swiftly. Three months later, the leader of the gang had been murdered by Malone, after trying to seize power from him. Through a combination of force and quick wits, Wicks assumed control of the Avon Street gang and in a short space of time had made it the most feared and powerful in the city, after Malone's. He always stayed on the right side of the crime boss; not out of fear, but in order to bide his time. He had paid him to be allowed to operate his rackets in 'the hate', an area Malone believed beneath him and not worth the effort of exploiting. That had been his first mistake. Whatever reputation the district held, to Wicks it was at the heart of his successful rise, a place where the toughest fighters and most adept thieves could be recruited and where valuable information regarding Malone's operations could be gained from those who worked in the upper town but lived in the lower one.

And he maintained this control by knowing each of the men recruited to his gang inside out. He knew their strengths and their weaknesses and, when it was necessary, how to pit one against another. That was why he was going to keep Tyler where he was. Although it had been Tyler who had brought Wicks into the gang in the first place, he knew to 'promote' him would bring trouble. If Tyler was allowed to collect protection money from the upper town, he would become greedy and Wicks would have to make an example of him. And he did not want to lose such a good man through killing him. He had grown up with Tyler, had roamed the same streets as him, but the ten years away had changed Wicks beyond almost all recognition. Tyler had thought he recognised him but Wicks had denied it. The less people knew about you and your past the better, because in the criminal world you always had to keep alert and maintain an edge. It was a business after all. That was what Malone hadn't realised. He had become lazy and lost touch with what was happening in the city. You had to constantly watch your back, as there would always be others prepared to take advantage if you didn't, which is what had allowed the meeting between Wicks and Malone's London connection to take place right under his nose.

Wicks had been impressed that those in the capital had known all about his operation and in their opinion was the only man to take over from Malone. He didn't know what had happened to turn them against their former associate and he didn't ask, it was not wise to do that. Wicks had begrudging admiration for Malone though, especially for the fact that he had built up such a large network of spies and informers throughout the city, but either he had become greedy and been caught taking more than his share or else he had done something which had angered them. Whatever he had done, he had become a liability and Wicks had been approached to take care of it. Now that he controlled the city, he would not make a similar error.

The 'friend' from London, as the contact had referred to himself, was on his way down to meet Wicks again, the next morning. No doubt they would discuss his part in the criminal 'triad' that also included Bristol. All goods that arrived at the docks bound for London passed through Bath, by one means or another, and similarly the other way. And Wicks received a share from everything both ways. He had now moved into the big league, he was someone. The person that controlled the Bristol–London road, as everyone knew, held the power of the whole South West in his hands. And Wicks had big plans. Only the day before, a potentially lucrative scheme he had initiated and which involved all three points of this triangle, had been put into action.

And with Kirby in his pocket, he also had the law on his side! An addiction to gambling and child prostitutes had made it easy to get incriminating evidence on the magistrate and lure him away from Malone, although he had seemed only to willing to change sides and betray his former boss. Now that Wicks 'owned' him, Kirby would ensure that he oversaw any cases connected to Wicks and thereby secure the 'right' verdicts.

It all seemed too good to be true.

It was.

CHAPTER TEN

'Edmund, this is my brother, Jack Swann,' said Mary. 'Jack, this is Edmund Lockhart.' The two men bowed courteously to each other as if having never met before, although both had instantly recognised the other from the journey they shared the previous day from London.

'Mary has told me a great deal about you,' said Lockhart.

'Then you have the advantage over me, sir,' replied Swann.

'Edmund was detained on business in London until this morning,' said Mary.

'Indeed,' answered Swann.

'But I knew he would be here,' his sister smiled.

'Nothing would have prevented my being at your side in this time of great sadness, Mary,' said Lockhart. 'I must now, however, ask for your utmost forgiveness once more. I have an urgent business engagement back in the city and the man I am to meet there insists on punctuality. I have kept a gig waiting for me outside to take me there.'

'Then you must go, Edmund. I know how important your business is and I do not therefore wish to detain you any longer than is necessary. I will expect you at the house later today, as arranged, to collect me?'

Lockhart hesitated, aware of Swann's surprised reaction.

'Are you sure that is wise, Mary?' replied Lockhart.

'But Edmund, you were in perfect agreement before you left for London.'

'And so I was, my dearest, but since that time I have considered the matter more thoroughly and on reflection, believe it prudent if you do not attend.'

'Prudent or not, I know my own mind and therefore I will expect you at six o'clock. Please.'

Lockhart nodded reluctantly, made the customary farewells and left.

'You have an engagement this evening?' asked Swann.

'Yes, Edmund is escorting me to the Charity Ball at the Upper Rooms.'

'Mary, I am not a great advocate of many of the social mores prevalent today, as you know, but I am concerned about your reputation. Your presence at the funeral could be perceived as understandable,' said Swann, 'but to bestow your presence at a place of entertainment may be quite another matter entirely.'

'I think it shows spirit,' said a voice behind them.

They turned and saw Lady Harriet Montague-Smithson, a woman whose diminutive figure belied the indomitable influence she enjoyed throughout most of the capitals of Europe.

'Aunt Harriet,' said Mary. 'I did not realise you were here.'

'If I am honest, my dear, I only arrived slightly after the gentleman who has this very minute departed. My driver is new and became lost on our way here. I am present now though and I am very sorry for your loss, both of you. Your mother was a dear sister and although we did not agree on many topics, I will miss her kind-hearted demeanour and gentle ways. As for you attending the ball, my dear, I believe she would have approved most sincerely.'

'With Mary's best interest at heart, Lady Harriet, may I enquire as to why you believe it acceptable for her to deliberately flout established rules of etiquette and risk bringing her standing into disrepute?'

'If you are referring to those confounded rules laid down by that wretched man Nash, who had as much decorum as a French peasant worker, then I hardly believe flouting them would bring as much distain as you believe, especially as the man has been dead for the best part of forty years. Besides, when have you cared about society's opinion? I assume you to be first to applaud her action.'

'You would, of course, be correct Lady Harriet, if it was my standing at stake, but as the head of this family I believe I have an obligation to Mary and that is why I feel she should not attend this evening.'

'As Mary's closest remaining blood relative,' retorted Harriet, 'I believe I also have an obligation and I believe she should ... '

'Jack, Aunt Harriet, you converse as if I am not here,' interrupted Mary, 'or else I am still a minor in need of guardianship. I thank you both for your concern but I am quite aware of what I am doing. And please, let us not forget where we are and why we are here. Now, if you do not mind Jack, I would like a few moments to converse with Aunt Harriet on a certain matter.'

'Very well, I shall go over and resume talking with your Mr Fitzpatrick,' said Swann, who then walked off to where the magistrate diplomatically waited.

'That is the trouble with men,' said Harriet, a little exasperated. 'They believe themselves right even when they are so blatantly wrong.'

'Jack was only trying to protect me, Aunt Harriet.'

'I know you think fondly of your adoptive brother, my child, but he does not understand what you need. And as much as my sister, your mother, was dear to me, god rest her soul, we differed in our views regarding the raising of a female child.

I am sorry to be this forthright at her funeral, but this age upon us is not one for hesitation. Now that your mother is gone, I feel it my moral obligation to assume responsibility for your wellbeing and to educate you appropriately.'

'I do not wish to cause any offence Aunt Harriet, but I am twenty-four, not fourteen and my education was extensive and well-rounded. I was sent to …'

'My child, I know *exactly* where you were sent and I know *exactly* what you were taught there: facts, figures and all the other subjects that fascinate men. No, my child, the truth is that you have been educated like a man, but it is time to educate you as a woman. Your resolve to attend the ball this evening and your presence at the funeral show you have the right attitude. We just need to ensure it is developed properly and so, with that in mind, I wish to extend an invitation to my house tomorrow evening from eight o'clock. I am having a gathering of like-minded women and there will be a guest speaker. I believe you will find it most illuminating.'

Mary hesitated. 'I'm not sure whether Jack will … ,' she saw her aunt's reaction and smiled, '… yes; I would love to attend, Aunt Harriet.'

'Very good, my child, I will send my carriage for you at six. And you can tell Jack, if you wish, that you will be home by half past eleven.'

On the journey back to Great Pulteney Street, Swann and Mary quickly became lost in their own thoughts. For Mary, her emotions were in conflict. She felt sad but her mind was effervescent from meeting her aunt. In many ways, her relation had been abrupt and rude but Mary had found the forthrightness in her manner refreshing. There were no hidden meanings within what she said, no nuances one had to decipher. Her aunt said what she felt and you quickly knew exactly where you stood with her. Mary was already looking forward to Thursday and the gathering of 'like-minded' women.

From childhood onwards, Mary knew her aunt more by reputation than from actual personal experience. She had apparently moved to her present residence near the market town of Frome around two years earlier, but neither Mary nor her mother had received any invitation and her aunt had never visited them in Bath. The sisters had fallen out several years before, so Mary's father had told her once, and Harriet's name was thereafter rarely mentioned in the house.

And now there seemed to be animosity between Jack and Harriet, although she consoled herself with the notion that they were both only being protective of her; each in their own way. Hopefully she could go to her aunt's house the following evening without the need to justify her actions to her brother.

Meanwhile, Swann's mind was in turmoil from his encounter with his adoptive relative. He had only encountered Harriet on a handful of occasions but each time, including this most recent one, came away from their interaction feeling judged. In many ways Swann respected Harriet's outspoken manner and felt a kinship with her somewhat iconoclastic nature. Despite her title and standing she was known to hold extreme views and on more than one occasion, Swann had been told, had been the house guest of the radical William Godwin and his wife.

Harriet had married young but her husband had died not long afterwards and the inheritance she had received allowed her to indulge an independent lifestyle. She had written several pamphlets on a range of subjects and was an outspoken advocate on women's education. She had travelled extensively throughout the Continent until Napoleon had effectively cut England off from the rest of Europe.

Throughout her life, she had made as many powerful enemies as she had allies, but somehow the latter allowed her this blithe attitude toward her reputation. But whereas he respected her, Swann thought any association with Mary might be detrimental to his sister. He consoled himself, however, with the fact that this would hopefully be the last time they saw Harriet for a long time.

Swann now turned his attention to a more immediate dilemma to be dealt with – that of Edmund Lockhart.

CHAPTER ELEVEN

At the age of eighteen, fourteen years previously, Swann had embarked on the quest to bring his father's killer to justice by whatever means necessary. Even before then, however, he had begun to develop what he termed the 'System'. The System was a method of deductive reasoning that combined Socratic dialecticism and Hobbesian logic, but circumscribed by common sense. At its heart was the detailed examination of the various answers arising from any given question, in order to bring about a satisfactory conclusion. This exploration would continue to be applied until the truth, or as close an approximation of it as possible, was achieved. It had served Swann well on a number of previous occasions and so he decided to apply it to the matter of Edmund Lockhart and the coach journey they had shared from London the day before.

Swann thought back and recalled the information he always instinctively absorbed, even when it was not relevant to an investigation. On arriving at the Royal Mail coach's departure point in Lad Lane, Swann had been assured of three pieces of information. The coach would depart at thirty minutes after seven precisely, it would reach Bath thirty minutes after nine the following morning and, aside from the driver and guard employed to protect the mail box, he would be travelling alone. The initial piece of information had proved accurate, as had the next, despite a delay at their first stop – the General Post Office in Lombard Street – where congestion from a multitude of Royal Mail coaches bound for different parts of the country had held up the loading of their own mail box. It was the final piece of information, however, which had proved incorrect.

Five minutes before the coach had been due to start out from The Swan with Two Necks coaching inn, the trio of additional travellers entered the carriage. This had swelled its occupants in a single instance to the full compliment a Royal Mail coach was permitted to carry inside. Although Swann had been unperturbed by this intrusion at the time, a piece of information was a piece of information and the fact it was inaccurate told him one of two things; either the ticket officer who informed Swann of his sole occupancy not thirty minutes before was unaware of these extra passengers when relaying the information, or else the arrangements were made in the time that had elapsed since. If the former, this merely belied a lack of communication within the organisation and therefore this particular avenue of enquiry could be brought to a conclusion, as it could add no further dimension to the main question: what Lockhart was doing on the coach and why he kept silent about it at the funeral? However, if the latter, that the arrangements were made in the time that had elapsed since, then purchasing their tickets so close to departure suggested the decision to travel was almost certainly a recent one, as leaving it that late on an already predetermined journey did not seem likely. It also meant that the passengers were in some haste to arrive at their destination and possessed the money to pay for the privilege – the cost of a ticket on the Royal Mail coach being substantially higher than that of an ordinary stagecoach, one of which left later that evening.

Swann could have easily clarified any or all of these details through initiating a casual and seemingly innocuous conversation with the gentleman of the company – who he now knew to have been Lockhart – during the journey, but he had not done so as these details were not important at the time and he wished to converse as little as possible. In fact, the opportunity had presented itself not long after the trio boarded. After courtesy nods of acknowledgement, Lockhart had enquired as to whether Swann was travelling to Bath for the season. 'No,' Swann replied, adding, so as not to appear too rude, that it was 'for a personal matter.' Lockhart seemed keen to engage further, but Swann had averted his gaze outside the carriage to indicate the conversation ended.

There was also later, when he had studied his fellow passengers surreptitiously while they dozed. Nothing in their basic character profiles, assembled in his mind at the beginning of the journey, required any alteration – experience and disciplined observation had given him the ability to accurately gauge a person's temperament having just met them – except perhaps their ages. Lockhart's age, which Swann originally estimated to be close to his own, needed rising slightly, while the two women required their ages to be increased by a decade between them. Swann had placed their ages in the early-twenties and although they still held their looks, the life-lines earlier suffused by the darkness and deftly-applied powder on their faces could no longer be concealed within the elucidating dawn light.

Even then, however, there had been something about Lockhart that did not feel right to Swann. It was as if the man had stepped onto the stage in Drury Lane and assumed a role. One he was well-accustomed to playing, certainly, but a role nonetheless.

The three passengers were travelling together, he had concluded, but did not know each other especially well. There was certainly no romantic attachment between either of the women and Lockhart and he sensed the three of them had only met not long before the coach had departed; so in this way, it felt as if Lockhart was escorting the women to their destination, which he later discovered to be Bristol.

At the core of the System was what Swann termed 'givens' and 'assumptions' – one would be a predetermined fact, while the other the conclusion which might be drawn from it. Using the information he had recalled, he applied it to this particular situation. Given that Mary believed Lockhart had been due to return from London today, along with the lateness of the ticket purchases, it could therefore be assumed that Lockhart had not expected to travel to Bristol. But given the fact he had not mentioned this change of plan to Mary, it was further to be assumed, perhaps obviously in this case, that he did not want her to know about it. This assumption resulted in two possible outcomes; the undertaking of something underhanded within his personal life, or alternatively the matter was related to his business. Either way, Swann surmised, the women were connected with it, as given they had all entered the coach at the same time, it could be assumed they were travelling together. For it to be pure coincidence, all three of them would have had the same urgent need to travel to Bristol that evening and then arrived at the station to purchase their tickets at exactly the same time. Although this was a possibility, common sense dictated this was more than mere chance. And given there seemed to be no personal involvement, it could be assumed to be business related. If that was such, it could therefore be assumed that Lockhart was simply adhering to the existing convention that men did not concern women with matters of that nature.

By the time the carriage transporting Swann and Mary home had turned into Great Pulteney Street, Swann had reached his 'satisfactory conclusion', although he was not satisfied. He decided, therefore, as the driver pulled up outside the house, to investigate it further by contacting Fitzpatrick – who, although not able to offer much information on Malone through their conversation at the funeral, might be able to convey more on Lockhart – discreetly confronting Mary's suitor personally and, if Swann felt the right opportunity presented itself, to inform Mary herself.

CHAPTER TWELVE

On returning home after the funeral service, Swann and Mary had spent most of the afternoon in the drawing room, either in contemplation or reading books; *Robinson Crusoe* by Daniel Defoe and *Evelina* by Frances Burney.

Enthused at her meeting with her aunt, Mary had decided on the carriage ride back that she wished to begin reading more books about women's experiences which had been written by women. She had been a little disappointed to find her father had only male writers in his library, except for the Burney volume, and even that was only there, she assumed, because her father probably did not realise that it had been written by a woman. It was a first edition and had been published anonymously, the author's identity and gender not being revealed until several years after its publication. It was in the epistolary form – a novel based on a series of letters – and although not advocating any serious revolution in women's thoughts, nevertheless had caused a stir in its day.

The only other book in the house that had been written by a woman was *The Mysteries of Udolpho* by Ann Radcliffe, which her mother had been reading before she died. It had been borrowed from one of the four circulating libraries that she belonged to and would have to be returned. She had a feeling it was Pratt and Marshall in Milsom Street, but she would ask her brother to make enquiries. Her mother had adored gothic novels and in one month, she remembered, had devoured the following: *The Italian*, *Castle of Wolfenbach*, *Clermont*, *Mysterious Warnings*, *Necromancer of the Black Forest*, *Midnight Bell*, and *Orphan of the Rhine*. Mary had gone to take the bookmark out of the *Udolpho* book, when she had found it, but for some reason had left it in there and replaced it on her mother's bedside cabinet.

For whatever reason, and she could not think what that might be, Mary had never purchased any books while in Bath. With the contents of her father's library, albeit dominated by male writers, and the circulating libraries the family subscribed to, there never seemed to be any need. Nothing she had read from either source had made her want to purchase a copy of her own.

Swann had also chosen his book from the library, although there was no disguising the gender of its author. Daniel Defoe had been widely credited with creating the novel form, although he had already had a distinguished career as a journalist and pamphleteer before writing his first novel, *Robinson Crusoe*, at the age of almost sixty.

The previous evening, on his first night in Bath and before retiring to bed, Swann had made a brief study of the library and its contents. He had discovered the book and had taken it off the shelf. As he held it in his hands he felt the familiar binding, the familiar texture and the familiar lettering that spelt out the author's name and its title. After he had been adopted by the Gardiners he had returned the book to the library without reading any more. He always thought that one day he would finish reading it, but for one reason or another had not done so. He had searched for it on one occasion in the library at the London residence but could not locate it; the reason for that now clear. He could have bought a copy of the book for himself but there was something about wanting to read that exact copy. On discovering it, he had taken it out and decided that now was the time to finally finish it and so find out what had happened to this man stranded on his 'island of despair'. He had begun reading the book immediately, from the beginning again, and continued reading it during the afternoon. Crusoe had now established himself on the island and where he had been full of regret at the place where Swann originally stopped reading, he had subsequently come to terms with what fate had dealt him. When Swann had reached the place he had stopped, he paused for a few moments and thought about his father.

When Mary had retired to her room to get dressed for the evening ball, Swann had gone upstairs to the library to study the map he had noticed, which hung on one of the walls. It had been too dark the previous evening, but he now tried to trace the route he had taken when chasing the pickpocket. The area he had found himself in, however, was ill-defined and like most of the guidebooks on the city, it only concentrated on giving the details of the upper parts of the city. 'Too little detail,' he said to himself, 'and out of date.'

It was nearing six o'clock and Swann made his way downstairs. His intention was to intercept Lockhart on the street, before he called on his sister, so as to discreetly ask why he had not been forthcoming with the information regarding Bristol.

Meanwhile, Emily had just finished dressing Mary's hair when there was a knock on the main door. She left the room and went downstairs to answer it.

As Swann passed Mary's room, she called to him. 'Can you help me with my necklace, please?'

Swann reluctantly entered the room and went to the aid of his sister. The gold clasp of her necklace snapped shut easily with Swann's help and they both found themselves looking in the mirror for a moment at the pendant around her neck.

'It was a gift from Edmund,' replied Mary. 'I thought I would wear it this evening. Are you sure you will not attend?'

'You know how much I dislike those kinds of social occasions and I still do not believe that your attending is appropriate.'

Mary did not answer.

'So, how were you introduced to Mr Lockhart?'

'Through one of Henry's colleagues, a Mr Kirby.'

'And what do you know of this man?' asked Swann, with a hint of interrogation about his voice, 'other than the fact he is several years your senior.'

At this, Mary turned to gaze at her brother.

'I know that I am fond of him, despite the difference in our ages, and I believe that feeling to be reciprocated.'

Before Swann could say anything else, there was a knock on the bedroom door and Emily entered. 'Please madam, a note has just arrived addressed to you.'

Mary took the note.

'Thank you Emily, that will be all for now.'

As Emily left, Mary opened the envelope and began to read its contents.

'Is it from him?' Swann asked.

Mary did not reply but instead put the note down on the dressing table and began to undo the necklace.

'Perhaps it is better not to go out this evening, after all. Edmund has placed it within pleasing words but he now maintains his earlier conviction that it is not appropriate behaviour for me to attend the ball this evening and has decided to postpone our arrangement for, what he says, will be a more apposite time.'

Swann looked at his sister and feeling this was the right opportunity, spoke.

'Mary, would it surprise you to learn your Mr Lockhart was on the same coach as myself from London yesterday.'

Mary thought for a moment.

'Then why did I not see him alight with you?' she queried.

'Because he journeyed on to Bristol,' replied Swann, deciding at present not to mention anything about the two women who were travelling with him.

'Surely you must be mistaken?' said Mary.

'I am not,' replied Swann.

Mary was silent for another moment or two.

'Then there must be a rational explanation,' she finally said, 'of which we do not know.'

'If that is the case,' said Swann, 'then why did he not mention anything when he recognised me at the funeral.'

'You did not mention anything, either.'

'I wanted to protect you from a potentially embarrassing situation.'

'Perhaps Edmund had the same idea.'

'Mary, you are a strong, independent woman, and I have always admired you for that, but when it comes to matters of the heart I feel you are not so. My professional instinct tells me there is something about this man I find unsettling.'

'Well, my female intuition tells me otherwise,' said Mary, 'although I did not foresee not being able to attend the ball.'

They were silent for a few moments before Swann bent over and picked up the pendant from where Mary had laid it on the dressing table.

CHAPTER THIRTEEN

In any account of Bath's remarkable transformation in the eighteenth century, from mediaeval textile centre to fashionable playground of the upper classes, there are three names that need always to be included: Allen, Wood and Nash. Collectively known as the three 'creators' of Bath, the individual and distinctive legacies this triumvirate of self-made men left for the city, reverberated through the entire century and continued to do so at the opening of the next.

If Ralph Allen, one-time postmaster general turned property developer who discovered, developed and supplied the Bath Stone which would give the city its worldwide fame, brought the raw materials and the elder John Wood, who laid out designs for the city that gave it an enviable reputation as an architectural marvel, supplied the architectural vision, then Richard 'Beau' Nash contributed the social infrastructure and modes of behaviour which made Bath as famous as its stone and building style.

Nash was born into poverty but by sheer determination, audacity and charm rose to become one of the most powerful men in the city. He arrived in 1705, at the age of thirty-one and with his impeccable manners and affable nature swiftly made a name for himself within the burgeoning social scene. He acquired the moniker 'Beau' on account of his fine dressing – it was said that he would rather forego a meal than a prized item of clothing – and on attaining the position of Master of Ceremonies, was dubbed the 'King of Bath'.

With the power accorded his position Nash now set about 'cleaning' up the city both physically, through installing proper street lighting and paved walkways, and socially, by creating the 'Rules to be observed in Bath.' The latter being created to combat what he saw as people behaving in a 'rude and quarrelsome way.' The rules were vigorously endorsed and not even the titled could escape conforming to them. Yet how ironic it should be then, that when Beau Nash died, emblazoned on his tombstone was the inscription: *Beams ille qui sibi imperiosus*. Happy is he who rules himself. Yet the rules he created for others during the eighteenth century still remained intact at the beginning of the nineteenth, four decades after his demise; adhered to by all and enforced by the succeeding Master of Ceremonies.

Despite this ordered sense of regulation the previous ninety minutes had witnessed severe chaos, before a solution had been reached not long before the first guests arrived at the Upper Rooms for that evening's one-off special Charity Ball. A runner had been dispatched earlier to the residency of the current Master of Ceremonies, Mr Richard Tyson, only to find him ill in bed and in no fit state to perform his duty. With little more than an hour before the official start of the ball, a replacement had been sought. And so it was that a Mr Salter of New King Street was duly summoned and hastened forth to execute his duties. Having been in this situation twice before, however, Mr Salter was not overawed in the slightest and performed his duties admirably.

By the time Mary and Swann arrived, Mr Salter had announced a good three dozen revellers and after being given his instructions, Mr Salter did loudly, but clearly and without hesitation, announce: 'My Lords, Ladies and Gentleman, may I present Miss Mary Gardiner of Bath and Mr Jack Swann of London.'

Having only this temporary role and not being one to give or receive gossip in his ordinary daily business, the disapproving looks that accompanied his announcement, from several members of the already assembled company towards the newly arrived couple, left Mr Salter believing that any impropriety must reside in their bold statement of attachment, their arms interloped as one might undertake with a family member or spouse, rather than it being due to their abject display of non-conformity regarding the strict rules of mourning; a convention not actually laid down by Nash himself but one which he would have wholeheartedly agreed.

Mr Salter may have surmised about the mourning, due to the nature of Miss Gardiner's clothing, but as he had of late been in the presence of several women who had taken to the wearing of the colour black merely as a fashion statement, rather than as a resigned necessity, he reserved his right as the acting Master of Ceremonies to impart any judgement and he would not, even if asked, be drawn on any conclusion as to the disapproving glances. Therefore, always professional in his outlook and immaculate in his conduct, both in this function and his ordinary day to day behaviour, there was no expression of censure on Mr Salter's face and he bowed courteously as Mary walked by.

As Mary and her brother entered the main room, a wave of outraged, although hushed, whispering rippled around the periphery of the dance floor, alongside, however, another less powerful though still present, chorus of approval at her stand. As was the way, the disapproval was reserved solely for Mary, with her male companion being pitied for having, no doubt, been forced into such an overt display of social disobedience. Nevertheless, nothing was spoken outright to Mary's person and a victory, however small, had been won for those people to whom it meant something. Not that anyone present, even those who had voiced approval, would dare to mimic it, but the fact that it had been done, and most publicly seen to be done, was enough. Meanwhile, Swann, whatever his thoughts on the matter might be, merely held his head up high as he walked forward with his sister.

'Thank you for escorting me, Jack,' said Mary, 'it means a lot to me.'

'Do not mention it,' replied Swann. 'It is not often I have such beauty on my arm and the occasion to escort that beauty in public.'

Despite the voices of disapproval, the truth regarding the couple's relationship, that of siblings, and estimates of Swann's income – which fluctuated anywhere between five thousand and ten thousand pounds a year, depending on who was doing the recounting – soon drowned them out and a host of single women, including one Isabella Thorpe, had their eyes now firmly set on the formerly 'pitied' male companion.

On observing this spectacle of these fawning pairs of eyes, Mary could not resist gently teasing her brother about it, but he did not rise to the bait.

They now saw Fitzpatrick. He rarely ventured to the ball, but on learning that Mary intended to be there, had gone to offer his support, if required. Fitzpatrick now saw the couple and smiled. Although he was genuinely pleased to see them, he was also only too glad to have the interruption, as a couple of gentleman, who really should have known better at these occasions, had been tormenting his ear about certain judicial matters. He excused himself from their berating and came over to where Swann and Mary now stood.

'Before I forget,' said Fitzpatrick, 'I have this very evening learnt of some news which I believe will be of most interest to you Mary. The Tilneys have been blessed with a second daughter, whom I believe they mean to name Jane.'

'That is wonderful news, thank you Henry. And the mother, she is well?'

'Yes, I understand Catherine is well.'

'I am glad,' replied Mary. 'The couple actually met in Bath,' Mary now said to her brother. 'What is it now, Henry, five, six years ago?'

'At least that, I would say,' replied Fitzpatrick.

Swann realised Mary's meaning and smiled. 'I do not believe that I shall be so fortunate, even though I can see there are many who would wish it so.'

Before Mary could respond, however, Lockhart appeared beside them.

'Mary, you are here! You did not receive my communication?'

'Yes I did Edmund, but I decided to attend after all. Jack was kind enough to escort me. And now that I am here Edmund, will you kindly ask me for a dance. You do not mind Jack?'

Swann shook his head. 'Of course not, I shall enjoy resuming my conversation with Fitzpatrick.'

Although reluctant, Lockhart conceded and the couple moved off toward the dance floor, just in time for the beginning of the next dance. Lockhart and Mary took their places in the appropriate lines, facing each other, and the music began.

Swann stood with Fitzpatrick and watched the couple.

'What do you know about that gentleman, Lockhart?' asked Swann.

'Not much,' replied Fitzpatrick. 'I am acquainted with him through Kirby, a fellow magistrate. I believe they have mutual interests in London. He does seem to have made quite an impression on your sister. But why do you ask?'

'Precisely because of that impression, Mr Fitzpatrick.'

Fitzpatrick tapped his own pocket. 'Thank you once more for yesterday,' he said. 'It would have caused great inconvenience had you not recovered my bill-purse after it was stolen.'

'You are most welcome,' said Swann. 'It is most ironic though. I saw the very thief emerge from the courthouse, where no doubt he had just been set free from a previous crime, and almost in sight of the building, immediately commit two instances of pickpocketing.'

'There was another victim?'

'He attempted to steal from my person as well, but when on the street I always keep my valuables elsewhere.' At this, Swann tapped his hat to indicate the hiding place.

'I was speaking to Kirby about the incident and told him that we could do with a man like you here. You do not have the inclination to stay on in Bath?'

'I am afraid my place is in London.'

'I hope I do not appear impertinent, but Mary informed me you were adopted by her family, yet you do not share the same surname.'

'It is out of respect for my real father. Has Mary told you the circumstances surrounding the adoption?'

Fitzpatrick shook his head. 'I hope I have not spoken out of turn?'

'Not at all,' replied Swann. 'My father was butler to the Gardiners. He was murdered trying to protect their property in their London residence. In gratitude the family brought me up as their child. I have spent the last number of years searching for my father's killer. His name is Malone, which is why I was asking you about him earlier today.'

Meanwhile, out on the dance floor, Mary and Lockhart circled each other once again, as part of the sequence of figures making up the dance.

'May I ask you a question?' said Mary.

'Certainly Mary, my dearest.'

'Why did you have a change of heart about my coming here?'

'My darling Mary, it was because you put me in a most troublesome quandary. I truly do applaud your action and would have stayed with my original intention of accompanying you, but I did not wish to contend with your brother's possible disapproval. I believe very much in first impressions and I believe from your brother's expression at the funeral that he was not aware of your coming tonight. It might be a matter of pride on my part, but I did not want to prejudice your brother against me.'

'A most diplomatic answer Edmund, I do now understand. May I ask another question of you though?'

'Please, go ahead.'

'Did you return from London on the coach this morning?' This was a question Lockhart had been half expecting since realising the other passenger in the coach had been Mary's brother.

'Why do you ask?'

'Because my brother believes you travelled in the same coach as him from London, but that you continued on to Bristol.'

'Then your brother is obviously mistaken.'

'My brother is most certain it was you on the coach yesterday and it is not like him to be mistaken.'

Mary studied Lockhart with an expression that searched his face, his eyes, and his whole demeanour for the answer she wanted to hear. Lockhart sighed.

'My dear Mary, I do own it then. I did travel in the same carriage as your brother, as I found myself unexpectedly summoned to Bristol, and the Royal Mail coach afforded the quickest option. I cannot disclose to you why I was summoned, but it was awful my dear, I saw you from the coach as you welcomed your brother, yet I could not alight and greet you because I could not risk being seen in Bath at that particular time.'

'Thank you Edmund, although I am sorry I persisted.'

'My dearest Mary, you know I wish I could tell you about my business affairs but I cannot at present.' Mary had not mentioned the two women that Lockhart had been accompanying, so he had chosen not to bring the subject up either. His attention, however, was now taken by the appearance of a gentleman standing at the entrance to the ballroom. 'You have been so patient with me, my love,' he said, 'but I have to beg your indulgence once more. Believing you were not to attend this evening, I had made other arrangements to meet a business associate and that person is now requesting my presence and I fear I cannot ignore him.'

Although disappointed, Mary nodded understanding and once the music had finished, Lockhart escorted her off the dance floor and then went off toward the entrance and the waiting business associate.

CHAPTER FOURTEEN

'Henry, have you seen my brother?' asked Mary, after Lockhart had gone and she had found Fitzpatrick, standing by himself near the entrance.

'We were talking together but a Miss Isabella Thorpe had herself introduced to us. Not long after, however, your brother politely excused himself. I last saw him over there, by the staircase leading downstairs. It looked like he was intending to go down there, although I would not venture as to the why.'

Mary thanked Fitzpatrick and headed over toward the staircase. She smiled. Fitzpatrick seemed puzzled, even perplexed, as to why her brother might have descended a staircase which only led to the servants area. But Mary was not. If there was anywhere her brother might be in a social gathering such as this, it would be downstairs. That seemed to be where he had always found solace, ever since they had been children. She could not understand it as a child, but from this perspective she could see that he felt more comfortable, more at ease perhaps, in the company of those of the same standing as his father had been, than those he had found himself adopted into. She had never talked to him about it, but the amount of times that he had been found in the servant quarters seemed to speak for itself. And no matter how many times he had been gently reprimanded, it had seemingly made no difference.

On reaching the staircase, Mary looked around to make sure she was not being observed and then descended it. The air began to get cooler and by the time she reached the bottom and began to walk along the corridor, the air was decidedly cold and she felt a chill run down her spine. As she continued along, her mind returned to another time and place; a place she called home and a time when she felt alone and went looking for the adopted brother who had proved so elusive.

The five year old Mary made her way tentatively but indomitably along the long basement corridor which ran under the family's country residence. She felt the cold air against her cheeks and goosebumps rose on her legs and arms. The stoned walls were rough to the touch, whenever she placed the palms of her hands against them, in order to stop herself stumbling on the uneven floor. She had never been in this part of the house before. It was a strange new world to her, a world of shadowy shapes, unfamiliar smells and indistinct voices further down the corridor. She was straining to hear those voices and the sound of that one voice she was trying to locate. She felt alone but would not be put off.

Mary had seen Jack enter the building and was determined to find out where he went. She had gained a playmate for the vast gardens and numerous rooms she played alone in before, yet no sooner had she found this companion, he had abandoned her. In the last few months she had made several attempts to find out where he had gone but he had always seemed to get the better of her; but not this time. Not today, of all days. Mary had deliberately pretended to be asleep when Jack passed her room, but as soon as he had gone, had stepped out of bed and gone to her bedroom window. From here she watched as her brother strode across the garden towards a particular building and entered a small doorway that led to what she had been told was the main kitchens and servants' area.

By the time she had reached the building herself, there was no sign of Jack but she instinctively knew where to go. Now she would find out where he went and then perhaps he would stay with her for the rest of her birthday. She pulled her thin clothes tighter around herself and carried on along the corridor until she neared an entrance where the voices seemed to be coming from; one of which she recognised as Jack's. She edged closer and cautiously peeped around the corner. Inside she saw her brother sitting with two servants. He had three cups in front of him on a table and was moving them around each other. As she continued to watch, a voice came from behind her. It was Mrs Hunter.

'Mary. What are you doing here?' her nanny said.

Mary turned toward her but remained mute.

'Is Master Jack down here, as well? He shouldn't be below stairs now he's part of your family. And nor should you. What would your father think of such a thing if he knew you were down here?'

At that moment another voice called her name. 'Mary? Mary!'

She turned her focus back into the kitchen and now saw a present-day Swann sitting at the kitchen table alongside a couple of servants.

'Is everything alright, Mary?' Swann asked.

'I wish to go home now,' replied Mary, 'if you are agreeable.'

Swann said goodbye to the servants and came out into the corridor. There was a look of concern about his face.

'Are you sure you are okay?'

Mary nodded. 'It is merely the cold, I believe.'

Swann took his sister's arm and they walked back along the corridor.

'I thought you might be down here,' she said, as they reached the staircase. 'You always did prefer the company below stairs.'

'It was not that,' smiled Swann. 'Indeed, I was engaged in the most rewarding conversation with Fitzpatrick. It was just that it was interrupted by a seemingly most demanding girl, who had herself introduced to us and then preceded to ask the most personal questions regarding my income and single status. When she asked for a dance, I politely refused and excused myself. I could see she was not to be dissuaded, however, and so felt downstairs was the best place to withdraw. I would have been more direct with her, but she said she was your dear friend.'

'Isabella is a social acquaintance, that is all,' Mary said, a little annoyed.

'So where is our Mr Lockhart?' asked Swann.

'He had a prior engagement, a business associate,' replied Mary.

'Your Mr Lockhart seems to have many such associates,' said Swann.

Back upstairs, they collected their outer garments and then looked around for Fitzpatrick, in order to bid him a good night. They could not see him. Swann did, however, notice Lockhart playing cards in a side room, whilst in a somewhat earnest conversation with a fellow card-player. He said nothing to Mary though and escorted her outside.

As it was still early, the sedan chairmen were gathered in large groups, sharing the latest gossip, moaning about their lot and generally waiting around to be hailed, so they could earn their money. Swann looked over at one large group and saw the pickpocket from the day before conversing with them. Even in the semi-darkness and the crowd of chairmen around him, there was no mistaking the man. Swann saw Mary safely into a sedan chair and after telling her he would see her at home, caught the attention of two night-watchmen. Swann discharged one of them back inside the building to find Fitzpatrick, while he went with the other in the direction of the thief.

By the time Tyler realised what was happening, it was too late. He took a step forward and threw a punch but

Swann ducked and then bundled the other man to the floor. The sedan chairmen were not happy but before they could react, the other night-watchman had appeared with Fitzpatrick and several other men.

'If any man interferes in this matter,' announced Fitzpatrick, 'it will mean their licence.'

The assembled chairmen knew the consequences of Fitzpatrick's threat and so they all stood back as Swann handed Tyler over to Fitzpatrick and his men.

'You'll pay for this,' snarled Tyler at Swann, as the night-watchmen led him off.

Fitzpatrick stepped torward Swann. 'My wallet returned and now the criminal apprehended. Are you sure you will not consider staying on, Swann?'

Swann merely smiled. The two men bowed to each other and then Swann got in the nearest available sedan chair and followed his sister home.

As soon as the melee had ended, one of the chairmen with whom Tyler had been talking to, took off unseen at a running pace towards the Avon Street district. By the time Swann reached Great Pulteney Street, the running chairman had also reached his destination. He entered the Duke of York public house and went straight upstairs to tell to his boss, Wicks, what had happened.

CHAPTER FIFTEEN

After the emotionally draining day and evening Swann and Mary had shared, a resemblance of normality had descended once they returned home from the ball and a contemplative calm now prevailed in the drawing room. Swann reclined in a chair by the windows, reading his book by candlelight. After years of solitude on his island, Robinson Crusoe had seemingly come to terms with his isolation and created an ordered, coherent existence with comfortable surroundings and even domesticated animals. But as Swann read on, a terrifying event shattered this idyllic world. 'It happened one day around noon,' recounted Crusoe. As he was going to his boat, there, on the shore, was a footprint in the sand. The imprint had been made by a naked foot and its presence on the shore struck Crusoe as if hit by a thunderbolt. He looked and listened but could not see or hear anything. Having checked the surrounding area and found nothing more than that solitary print, he had returned to ascertain it had not been his imagination. But there it was still in the sand; a footprint with every part of the foot visible.

Swann laid the book on his lap and contemplated what he had just read. He felt as invaded as Crusoe must have done. This was his island. An island he had not wanted to be stranded upon but having realised there was no other choice, had used the resources available and created an existence which, if not perfect, was at least tolerable. But now, this appearance of a foot print on the shore, representing the presence of another human being and signifying his isolation ended, meant that nothing would ever be the same again. In many ways Swann felt betrayed by its author Defoe, as if through writing this particular scene he had somehow invaded Swann's own seclusion as well, a seclusion he had built up over the past twenty years and which he had taken solace from in the memory of the pages of this particular book.

Swann now became aware of Mary and the piece she played on her pianoforte. After her own return, Mary had chosen to play a selection of pieces by Bach that she felt best reflected her present mood. She had begun with the opening piece from the composer's *Aria with Diverse Variations*, as she had done so the previous day, especially for her brother, but had continued with a selection from the variations themselves. As she reached a particular one, however, it had come to the attention of Swann.

'You play the twenty-fifth slower than I remember it,' he said.

'It is not pleasing to you?'

'No, merely different in its own way,' he replied.

'Yes, I prefer it like this,' said Mary. 'The other way seemed to draw too much attention to its own melancholy. But now it seems to have a more introspective quality about it, as well. Do you not agree, Jack?'

'The tempo is certainly well suited to the piece. I am certain Johann Sebastian would have approved,' said Swann, and they exchanged an affectionate look.

Meanwhile, at the far end of Great Pulteney Street, a carriage travelled slowly along, as its driver looked for a particular house. When he had found the right address he pulled on the reigns and brought the horse to a standstill. He bent down and retrieved something from beneath his seat. He then stood up and steadied himself. The rock left his hand with great force, as he hurled it toward one of the windows. As it reached its target, the driver snapped the reigns again and the horse set off at a gallop down the street.

Inside the drawing room, the window shattered from the rock and a shower of glass fell on to the floor beneath the now bellowing curtains. Swann leapt from the chair and instinctively shielded his sister from any further attack.

'Are you all right?' asked Swann.

Mary nodded her head.

They stayed crouched behind the pianoforte until Swann thought it to be safe. As he stood to investigate, there was a knock on the door of the drawing room.

'Is everything all right, madam? I heard a smashing sound.'

'Come in Emily,' answered Mary.

'A rock has been thrown through the front window,' said Swann to Emily, as she entered. 'Stay here with my sister while I investigate and I do not want either of you going over to the window, is that understood?'

The two women nodded.

'It is for your own safety,' added Swann, as he himself then went over to the smashed window and cautiously peered out from the side of its curtain; the air immediately cool to his face. The street below was empty. He then looked down at the drawing room floor and saw that thankfully the force and trajectory of the rock had been stopped by the curtains and it lay below them amongst the glass. He carefully picked it up and carried it with him as he went downstairs and out through the front door of the house. Whoever had thrown the rock was now long gone. All that remained was its aftermath: the barking of neighbourhood dogs, roused by the disturbance; the servants and domestic staff from nearby houses, who had either voluntarily or else been ordered to venture out into the street to find out what had occurred; and their masters and mistresses who watched covertly from adjacent windows, twitching the curtains back and forth as they waited for reports from their servants as to what lay behind this most disagreeable incident at this most unearthly hour.

After informing the assembled crowd as to exactly what had occurred and telling them they could go back inside as there was nothing more to the matter, Swann then looked down at the rock in his hand. He noticed the piece of paper attached. He untied it and read the contents: *Swann – don't meddle where you don't belong or else.*

CHAPTER SIXTEEN

Bath, Wednesday 19th October, 1803

*I find it incredible to think that it was only yesterday morning
I stepped out of the coach and arrived in Bath and yet the events
which have transpired since then would ordinarily be hard pressed
to occur within a month or an even longer period. No sooner had
I alighted from the coach, than I became involved in a crime which
had seemed to have reached its close earlier this evening, with the
apprehension of its perpetrator outside the Assembly Rooms. Yet
instead this has provoked another incident, namely that of the shattered window, for I must assume it was this felon's apprehension
which is, in some way, connected to this latest occurrence. I will
discuss the matter with Fitzpatrick tomorrow, but in my own mind
I do not assume any other possibility.*

*Whatever reason lay behind this attack though, I believe that I must
now insist on Mary moving to London with me, once my business here
in the city is concluded. Especially with the addition of Lady Harriet's
invitation signalling the potential start of a regular interaction between
them and the most disagreeable presence of Lockhart. I must therefore
use all my persuasive arguments to get her to agree to my decision.*

*With this abrasive intrusion, I feel somewhat like Crusoe on
discovering the footprint. The knowing that there something is out
there to which I am not privy, is not a position I relish. It is not
through fear though, as I am used to danger, but Mary has become
involved and that is something which I would have wished not to*

have occurred. I will not let someone else I care about be hurt in any way again. I remember … but no, I do not wish to disclose in these pages that which should never be recorded. It resides in my memory and that should be enough. I will endeavour simply to send a message back to the instigators of this attack before I leave Bath and allow the matter to rest at that.

I have also been shaken from reading Robinson Crusoe and I have therefore decided to read no more of it. I shall return the volume to the library and there it will stay. I believed the book held a possible release to my solace, however slight, but I see now I was wrong. If anything, it has produced feelings I did not know existed and certainly do not want to experience again.

It is hard to believe what mere words can arouse. But through them, I have come to realise that I find myself seemingly at odds with the world around me. I feel at times like Rousseau's Solitary Walker, walking in a world in which I feel I do not belong, a world which in many ways repulses me, a world which embraces all I loathe and abhor – wealth, greed, and self-aggrandisement – at the cost of the ordinary person.

I ask myself once more, as I have done so on many occasions previously, what drives a person to commit a crime, to murder, to steal, to trick, to leave another human being in a worse state? Morally, I cannot understand it. There must be logic to the world, some natural sense, other than the religious observance which seems to end every such conversation with the words 'it is God's will'. Was it God's will that my father should die, that he should be murdered but the perpetrators walk free, to go about their daily business for all these years, while others, including myself, suffer? For twenty years I have mourned my father and not a day passes when I do not recall a statement he made or a conversation between us or the expression on his face when he regaled to me the memories of the fairs he visited when he was younger. He was the perfect man that I so long to become, yet find I fall short in so many aspects.

*At periods such as this, I cannot help but think Hobbes is right –
that man's nature is intrinsically evil and it is only the rules society
creates that prevents him from killing his fellow man. Left to their own
devices, men would inevitably turn to slaughtering each other, resulting
in everyone's life becoming 'solitary, poor, nasty, brutish and short.' For
did not even Rousseau, who so passionately believed in man's 'primi-
tive state of innocence', eventually come to see his fellow man as agents
of his own discontentment and that all were out to pursue him to his
grave by treacherous means and so leaving him to become, in his own
words, a solitary walker through this world.*

*I do not believe I am as paranoid as Rousseau thought himself to be,
yet I can identify with him in the way he saw the world. We are born
into this world, to fend for ourselves, at the mercies of forces unseen and
at any moment can be swept away into an abyss of grief or despair, swept
by the tidal wave of fate, or incredulity. What would have happened that
evening if those men had gone to the next house and not the Gardiners,
or some divine intervention had called them to tend to other business?
Every scenario that might have occurred on that evening has taken place
within my mind during these past twenty years.*

*As for what I have sacrificed because of it, I cannot even begin to
describe. I have written about this subject in yesterday's entry but it
requires repeating. I have Mary and of that I am thankful. I have
many acquaintances in London, but not friends. As for female com-
panionship of a more romantic nature, of course not, why would I wish
to be with any other female after her. It is not to be. I have long since
chosen my own fate and whether the forces that govern us will allow
this destiny to be carried out I can only wait to see, but mark my words,
as I write them in this very journal, I will do everything in my power
to make sure that it does work out the way I want it.*

*Rousseau comes to mind again. In one of the discourses he wrote
towards the end of his career, he meditated on his life and the state of
mind which had arisen from the varied circumstances of it. Where he
had experienced periods of prosperity, he recounted he had no lasting*

impression or 'agreeable memories', yet by contrast, the times of his life when he experienced hardship, there was an overriding wealth of emotions which seemed to burst forth, which resulted in his existence seemingly more complete and his life more fully lived at these times. Is that why I am perhaps afraid to find Malone, because I believe that there will be nothing left to provoke me, or to stir my soul? Do I somehow find solace in the great wrong which has been done to me? Whatever I may think, I perhaps cannot deny that I only really feel alive when I think of the revenge I wish to take and this sets anger in my heart which warms me.

Now that the funeral is over, I can turn my full attention back to Malone and the criminal aspect of Bath and, if my instincts are correct, I will be crossing paths with them in the very near future.

CHAPTER SEVENTEEN

It was spitting with rain when Swann left the house in Great Pulteney Street the following morning. The makeshift covering over the smashed window had held and it would soon be replaced by a pane of glass that workmen were bringing later that day.

What was on Swann's mind now, however, was who the perpetrator of this broken window had been. Who had sent the warning and disrupted the house the previous evening? He made his way into the centre of town and towards the magistrates' court, where Mary believed Fitzpatrick might be. On arriving at the building, however, he was informed that the magistrate had no session during the morning and would therefore, no doubt, be working from his office in Queen Square. Swann made his way up the High Street and into Milsom Street, reputed to be the most prestigious shopping street in the whole of the South West.

The cross-sweepers were already out in force, clearing pathways through the mounds of droppings from the multitude of livestock driven through the city earlier that morning, on their way to slaughterhouses located near the river. The smell of the manure hung palpably in the air as Swann made his way through the crowd of early morning shoppers, who consisted almost exclusively of young ladies. He turned left into Quiet Street and then Wood Street and into Queen Square, emerging into it by the south-east corner.

Queen Square had been the architect John Wood's first great achievement in Bath and was to have been his inaugural pronouncement of the grand design he envisaged for the city. He had sited it to the north-west of the city's old medieval boundaries, midway between what would later become the upper and lower towns, on land leased to him by its owner, Robert Gay. Excavation work had begun in December 1728 and the first stone was laid the following month at the corner of Wood Street, where Swann now stood. It took seven years to complete the Square and much of his original plan had been changed. Wood had initially envisaged three sides of the Square – the north, east and west – to collectively form a palace forecourt, this splendid view to be appreciated each morning by the architect himself, from the windows of his house within the south range of buildings. While the east side remained basically as he had primarily imagined, the buildings on the west became that of a large mansion.

The magnificently designed north expanse of houses, seven in all, had also remained for the most part intact. Dominating the Square, as it was intended to do, the differing sized buildings nevertheless formed a symmetrical composition which resembled a Palladian palace façade.

In the middle of the Square was a garden and at its centre was an obelisk. The Square stood on sloping land that was going to be levelled but to save money, which at the time had been estimated to be about four thousand pounds, Wood had instead built the houses to the natural contours of the land. The prestige of an address in the Square had been lowered in the preceding years, but even from the brief encounters Swann had already shared with Fitzpatrick, he would not have imagined the magistrate considering even for a moment moving his offices elsewhere. Swann now entered the Square proper, made his way up the east side and then went inside the address he had been given at the Guildhall.

Meanwhile, inside the four-storey building, Fitzpatrick was in discussion with Evans, the local shopkeepers' representative and the man who had attempted to have Tyler prosecuted earlier that week.

'I understand exactly what you are saying, Mr Evans,' said Fitzpatrick, as he sat behind his office desk, 'but I do not know how I can help at the present.'

'That is where you are wrong, Mr Fitzpatrick,' said Evans. 'To start with, you could agree to address our shopkeepers' meeting tonight. As their representative, if you were to attend at my request, it would show credibility on my side and for your own standing would show that the local magistracies are concerned about the problem of rising crime and its affect on trade in the city.'

'I am only too aware of the problems that exist in relation to crime and trade,' replied Fitzpatrick, sounding as sympathetic as he could.

'We are already into the season, Mr Fitzpatrick, and the city should be thriving. Yet visitor numbers are down and those that have come here are under constant threat of violence or being robbed by thieves. And we shopkeepers have not fared much better either; Richardson, the watchmaker, had his entire stock of timepieces stolen from outside his shop only two days ago.'

Fitzpatrick could not restrain himself as he heard this age-old problem again.

'But to be fair, some of this is brought on by yourselves,' he replied. 'You do, for example, leave your wares exposed on the street.'

'But we have to display them there, to encourage trade,' Evans retorted. 'Yet boys so young as not long off their mother's suckling make our life a misery.'

At this moment Swann appeared at Fitzpatrick's office door. An expression of relief could be seen in the magistrate's face.

'Ah, Swann. Come in, please.'

'I hope I am not interrupting,' said Swann.

'Not at all,' replied Fitzpatrick.

Swann entered the office and Fitzpatrick made the intro-ductions. The two men greeted each other cordially.

'Mr Evans is the shopkeepers' representative, Swann.'

'I assume you are kept very busy in your role, Mr Evans.'

'That is correct,' said Evans, appreciative of the insight the other man had shown. 'And if I may enquire, what is your occupation, Mr Swann?'

'Mr Swann is a consulting detective with the Bow Street Runners,' Fitzpatrick interjected.

'That is exactly the type of organisation that we require in Bath,' said Evans' excitedly. 'There are far too many crimi-nals in this city, on both sides of the law. Present company excluded, of course, Mr Fitzpatrick. Why only two days ago, a local magistrate blatantly allowed a known criminal to walk from his court.'

'Well, Mr Evans, you will be pleased to know that at least one criminal is not at liberty this morning,' said Swann, who briefly relayed the details surrounding Tyler's capture and arrest the previous night.

'Tyler. Why, that is the very same felon we speak of,' exclaimed Evans. 'This is indeed heartening news, Mr Swann, is it not so, Mr Fitzpatrick?'

Swann noticed Fitzpatrick looked uncomfortable during the conversation, but for the present decided not to bring attention to it. Fitzpatrick, however, now nodded in response to Evans' question.

'On that good news then, I will leave you gentlemen to discuss your business. But I will see you at the meeting tonight, Mr Fitzpatrick?'

'I will do my very best to attend, Mr Evans, you have my word.'

Evans bowed respectfully and left. Fitzpatrick turned to Swann.

'I do not know what I can do,' he said, somewhat dejectedly. 'The situation in the city becomes increasingly worse every year, but I have no answer. Even if I were to attend the meeting this evening, I do not believe it would make any difference, whatever men like Evans may believe. But enough of my problems, to what do I owe the pleasure of your company at my office this morning, Swann?'

Swann handed the other man the note.

'How did you come by this?' asked Fitzpatrick.

'It was delivered last evening, by a passing carriage, attached to a rock hurled through our window. An unusual method of delivery, you will agree.'

'Was Mary present at the time?' asked Fitzpatrick, concerned.

'Yes,' replied Swann. 'She was a little shaken, but no one was hurt.'

'Do you have any idea who might have done this?' asked Fitzpatrick.

'I was hoping you might be able to shed some light on the matter. Although my instinct tells me it is connected with the man arrested last night, Tyler.'

'If that is the case,' replied Fitzpatrick, 'then it may have been a man called Wicks, a most unpleasant sort.'

'Wicks?' said Swann.

'He is responsible for much of the city's crime, or at least is in charge of those that commit it. Tyler works for him.'

'Well at least that member of his gang is off the streets for the time being,' said Swann.

Fitzpatrick again remained silent.

'Is there something wrong, Fitzpatrick? You seem struck mute at each mention of Tyler's name. He still resides behind bars, does he not?'

'I am afraid that is no longer true. Tyler was freed this morning.'

'And on whose authority was this carried out?'

'My magisterial colleague, Kirby; he recorded a verdict of mistaken identity in regard to the charge of pickpocketing. And Wicks provided an alibi.'

'But it was you that he robbed, Fitzpatrick. Did you not tell Kirby, this?'

'If I am to be honest, Swann, I could not be sure I saw the face of the man who robbed me. It happened so quickly. And I could not tell an untruth under oath.'

'But why was I not called as a witness, or Mary?'

'I don't know. But I was only summoned at the last moment. I thought you had already given evidence.'

'Does this happen a lot?' asked Swann.

'More often than I would desire, let us say.'

'Is Kirby in Wicks' pay?'

'Again, that I do not know, but what will you do about this note?'

'I think I would like to pay this Wicks a visit. Where does he reside?'

'It is said he has interests in a public house called the Duke of York, down in the Avon Street district,' replied Fitzpatrick, 'and I believe he has at least one warehouse across the river. But I would not advise you going there, at least not alone. I can organise some men to go with you, if you desire it.'

'Thank you, but I will go alone. I usually find it is more effective.'

'As you wish,' replied Fitzpatrick.

'If you could provide me with directions as to how to find the public house though, I would be most grateful.'

'I am about to leave for my morning constitutional and I pass nearby the area on the way, if you would care to join me,' offered Fitzpatrick.

'That would be most agreeable,' replied Swann.

CHAPTER EIGHTEEN

The route that Fitzpatrick normally undertook for his morning constitutional was a circular one, taking in several of the architectural landmarks of the upper town. As Fitzpatrick had mentioned to Swann, however, it later passed through the outskirts of the lower town, where the Avon Street district and Wicks' headquarters were located. The two men left Fitzpatrick's office and headed out of Queen Square at its north-east corner into Gay Street, so named for the man on whose land it was built. The rain had eased and the sun was shining, causing the wet pavements to glisten in the morning light.

'The writer Tobias Smollett stayed along here several times,' said Fitzpatrick, having assumed the role of tour guide.

'Although possibly not with the highest regard towards it, I would suggest,' answered Swann. 'You have read his *Humphrey Clinker* I trust?'

'It is scornful of the city, I agree, but I have to confess, much of it is wickedly accurate!' smiled Fitzpatrick. 'I often feel "the noise, tumult and hurry" of this municipality, to quote Smollett, but what I do take umbrage with him over is his comments about our wonderful buildings. I, for one, certainly do not consider they were merely "contrived without judgement or executed without solidity".'

'Perhaps if he had been more successful in the establishment of his medical practice in the city, he might have been less scornful in his writing,' concluded Swann, as they reached the end of Gay Street and entered what was known as the King's Circus. Fitzpatrick stopped to allow Swann to take in the full majesty of the spherical structure in front of them.

'It was designed by the elder John Wood as a residential equivalent to the Coliseum in Rome,' announced Fitzpatrick authoritatively, 'but unfortunately he died not long after laying the foundation stone and so his son completed it.'

'Vespasian's amphitheatre turned outside in,' added a smiling Swann, as he too quoted Smollett.

The two men stood for a moment, taking in the splendour of the vista, with its successive tiers of Roman Doric, Ionic and Corinthian half-columns adorning the facades of the thirty-three houses which comprised the King's Circus. A roadway of cobbles radiated from the centre. The houses were grouped into three separate sections, each divided by an approach, but which was built in such a way that the observer of the whole had the effect of a continuous building.

'Outstanding,' said an impressed Swann. 'I am only sorry not to have visited Bath to have had this pleasure before.'

'It is strange,' said Fitzpatrick. 'I see this view on most days and yet it is only when you are in the presence of someone witnessing it for the first time that you actually realise what good fortune one possesses through living in such an architecturally pleasing city.'

'What a mind to design such beauty,' replied Swann.

'It is more than just beauty,' said Fitzpatrick, with an excited look in his eyes. 'You might find this incredible,' he said, 'but we are standing in the final part of a giant key.'

'What do you mean?' asked Swann.

'Well,' replied Fitzpatrick, 'and do not ask me why Wood decided to design it in this way, but seen from the air, Queen Square, Gay Street and the King's Circus form the shape of a giant key.'

'You know this to be true?' replied Swann.

'Yes. Although I did not believe it when first told about it, I have since seen it with my very own eyes.'

'How did you come by this experience?'

'I was afforded the opportunity of a flight in a balloon last year, not long after Garnerin had made his ascent here. We took off from the actual place as the Frenchman, Sydney Gardens, and once we had risen so far I was able to look down upon the city. It was then that I saw the shape of the key laid out. As I said, I do not know the significance of it, although it certainly was a sight to behold.'

Swann would like to have enlightened his erstwhile companion as to the real significance of the key's design, but it would have to wait until a later time.

The section of houses in the King's Circus to the left, having entered from Gay Street and where Fitzpatrick now guided Swann, had been the first segment to be built, beginning in 1754. And as they made their way round the broad pavement, ringed by tethering posts and mounting steps, the magistrate recalled the most notable person who had lived there. 'William Pitt had this house built especially for him,' said Fitzpatrick, as they passed the specific house.

'I guess he would have witnessed the rest of the circus being erected around him, then,' added Swann, after being told the great statesman had lived there between 1755 and 1765, the latter being the year of the Circus' completion.

Fitzpatrick nodded and pointed out other notable houses. 'Clive of India lived over there,' he said, 'and near there is where Gainsborough stayed.' Fitzpatrick then pointed to a few doors down where, he informed Swann, Kirby had offices.

They turned left into Brock Street, named after the younger Wood's brother-in-law, and headed west. The lined houses, in comparison to what Swann had just witnessed, seemed less decorative or splendid. The most elaborate features being above the doorways and porches of the houses on either side of the street.

'The younger Wood deliberately understated the architecture in this street,' remarked Fitzpatrick, seemingly having read Swann's mind, 'as he wanted his two creations either side of it to be heightened in their dramatic effect.'

'Yes, I did think the architectural expression quite subdued,' said Swann, as they continued along.

Just before they reached the end of Brock Street, Fitzpatrick stopped again.

'We are about to view the Crescent,' said Fitzpatrick, 'and I want you to appreciate it in all its glory.'

If Queen Square and the King's Circus had been the highest manifestation of the elder John Wood's vision, then the Crescent, as it was originally named, was the equivalent of his son's, with many observers believing it to be far greater an expression. It was seen as the summit of Palladian achievement in Bath and one of the most magnificent architectural sights in the whole of Europe. Begun in the year after the Circus had been finished, the thirty houses which comprised this uniformed frontage had taken eight years to build. It was now known as the Royal Crescent but had only acquired this additional 'Royal' moniker after a visit by Prince Frederick, the second son of King George III.

'I am used to architectural wonders,' said Swann, as he stood with the great sweep of Ionic columns, one of the dominant features of the Crescent, in front of him, 'but this literally takes my breath away.'

From its inception it had become the address to have within the city of Bath and had attracted everyone from royalty to artisans since its completion almost thirty years before.

'That is where Richard Sheridan eloped with Elizabeth Linley in 1772,' said Fitzpatrick, recounting one of the most famous scandals of the past century, as they passed number eleven. 'They went from here to France, I believe.'

Swann merely nodded, as his attention was being completely consumed by the architecture in front of him.

Once they began walking along the Crescent's cobbled concourse, Fitzpatrick then expanded on the issues raised earlier in his office by Evans.

'Despite the splendour and magnificence of the architecture, the reality is the city's population has increased almost ten-fold during the last hundred years,' said Fitzpatrick. 'As I am sure you are aware, Swann, with any fashionable society there are always the beggars, pickpockets, thieves and other assorted criminal elements after what they perceive as easy plunder.'

Swann nodded. He did know, only too well.

'But you have law enforcement?'

'We have night-watchmen – the Charleys – as you witnessed last evening, but they are often drunk and are bribed too easily. There are also the thief-takers, but again, not always to be trusted. Sadly, we have nothing comparable to the Bow Street Runners you undertake consulting work for in London.'

'Yes. The more places that instigated runners,' replied Swann, as they turned into Marlborough Buildings and down to the Upper Bristol Road, 'the safer law-abiding people would be going about their business.' On reaching the main road, they turned left and headed back towards the city centre.

'That's why we could do with a man of your calibre here,' said Fitzpatrick.

Before Swann could answer, however, a group of street urchins suddenly raced along the pavement, loudly chanting a rhyme:

Hark, Hark! The dogs do bark.

The beggars are coming to town;

Some on nags, and some in rags,

And some in silken gown.

A cartload of ragged vagrants now trundled past the two men. Their faces black with dirt, their clothes threadbare and torn.

'They are beggars,' said Fitzpatrick to Swann. 'They are transported here from Bristol during the day and then picked up again later.'

As Fitzpatrick finished speaking and if to illustrate his point, the cart stopped further along the road, near the bottom of Charlotte Street. Its occupants jumped out and within a few seconds had scattered towards the centre.

Ten minutes later, Swann and Fitzpatrick reached the end of Monmouth Street, where it intersected with Avon Street.

'This is where I have to leave you, Swann,' said Fitzpatrick. 'Continue all the way down this street and at the end, turn left. I believe you will find the Duke of York public house is nearby. But are you sure you do not wish any of my men to accompany you?'

'No, I will be fine, Fitzpatrick, but thank you again for your concern.'

The two men shook hands and started on their separate ways.

'Swann!' cried Fitzpatrick suddenly.

Swann stopped and turned.

'Be careful of Wicks,' said the magistrate. 'I have heard it said he carries with him a cutlass.'

Swann acknowledged the warning and then continued on down Avon Street, the stark contrast between the grandeur of the upper town he had only recently witnessed and the over-crowded, neglected area he had now entered, becoming only too apparent once more.

CHAPTER NINETEEN

After Swann had left for Fitzpatrick's office, a letter had arrived at the house in Great Pulteney Street. It was addressed to Mary and after Emily had brought it to her, Mary had opened it, set the envelope down on the table, sat down and begun to read the letter.

Thursday 20th October, 1803

My dearest niece

I hope this letter finds you in good spirits after the melancholy of yesterday – perhaps the ball lifted your spirits somewhat.

I am not known for my ability to offer explanations for my actions so please accept this as a once in a lifetime revelation. I have found in life that if one wants to make the most of it and have people respect you, one has to speak their mind and let their actions follow their words in the same way. This is why my manner is forthright and straight to the point. Life is too short to tittle-tattle away endless hours. I may have been a little forward yesterday but please believe me that my heart was in the right place and I only have your well-being in the foremost of my mind.

In regard to my invitation for this evening, which I do most sincerely hope you will be present at, I will send a carriage for you at six o'clock. There will be other passengers being picked up, so if you choose not to come then merely send the coachman on his way. I would be disappointed if you did not attend but would adhere to your wishes. However, all I would say is that I believe the evening, and especially the guest speaker, you would find to be very enlightening and I know that it would change your way of thinking in regard to certain aspects of what constitutes being a member of the female persuasion. With this in mind I have enclosed a relevant pamphlet. It is taken from a longer work, but I believe that it best represents my own thoughts on certain aspects of education and so therefore at some time in the past, I had the excerpt printed as a pamphlet. I suggest that if you can read it before tonight, then both the guest speaker's talk and any conversations arising from it may, in the words of the pamphlet itself, allow the mind to 'be cultivated and its real powers found out.'

As I remarked at the funeral yesterday and will state once again in this correspondence, you have been educated like a man but you are now going to be educated as a woman. This is your first lesson, for want of a better analogy.

Yours

Aunt Harriet

Mary had already made up her mind, on the journey home from the funeral, that she would attend. She took the pamphlet out of the envelope and began to read.

A Theory on the Education of Women

Only within the ranks of the uneducated and the general male population will you find the widely held belief that education is not important to a woman's self-development. Yet, not only is it essential for the full developmental potential of each individual female, it is also vital to the wellbeing of the entire community to which she belongs; education providing as it does, the link between society as a whole and each separate individual.

The way in which this male-dominated nation regards this specific connection, however, highlights the core problem inherent in our society today. The focus on the more factual-based curriculum in our educational system therefore places the emphasis on more measurable assessment elements, in order to ensure successful outcomes rather than highlighting the actual process of learning. This then leads on to the asking of the question as to whether we are not just failing the entire female population through this emphasis, but society itself, through the positive contribution a properly education woman could bring to its development.

This indeed does seem to be the case unfortunately, because instead of creating a social solidarity, in which there is a sense of belonging by all and a feeling that the collective membership of that society is more important than any individual member, the ordinary female sees the education process as no more than turning their gender into 'more suitable companions for their male counterparts.'

Since the time of Plato, his only fault being in that he was born a man, the great philosophers and thinkers of successive societies have turned their attention to education and the three key questions which always need to be addressed: What is education for?; By what process do we learn?; and what should determine the content of education?

For Plato, most specifically in The Republic, he reached the conclusion that education does not appear to be an end in itself, but a tool of social control, which produces the type of people the State requires. Yet herein is the paradox, which successive male governments, despite their schooling in the classics, seem to have constantly missed, and that is Plato wants each ruler of this State to be the type of philosopher who is capable of seeing beyond the passing shadows of sense experience to reality itself. What this means, and for women especially, is that it is not enough for the individual to only learn and accept the values of the society undertaking the teaching, but paradoxically to be able to question and change them at the same time. This, I believe, is achieved through learning the actual process of learning, rather than the subjects which are learned.

In the girls' school that I run in Bath and the teaching that is undertaken there, the students are not working towards a final examination or certification as their sole objective for going through my educational system. What they are learning, or at least what we endeavour to teach, is that it is the process of learning which is more important than the outcome. This way of teaching therefore gives the students the opportunity to think on their own merit and not to become the mere organs of repetitious nonsense. What I hope is gained from my school is the craft of learning, which leads to the individual's expression of that skill throughout the rest of their lives. Through this, they can become manifestations of Plato's Philosopher-King idea, or at least the female representation of it. The more a student can learn this craft and be able to express it, the more authentic they will feel as a woman and subsequently, the stronger any communication will become between members of their own gender or, and this is the real crux of the matter, any conversation they may participate in with men.

One example of this, I believe, is the act of reading of 'worthwhile' books. It has been acknowledged as truth universal by many, including Wollstonecraft, that full employment should always be given to the human mind and that it should be employed from early an age as possible. The most fundamental way in which this can be cultivated is through reading books and periodicals that contain ideas or arguments that help to expand the mind and thoughts of the reader. Through this, the idea of one's own opinion emerging from their reading, rather than the mere form of repetition, soon becomes apparent. For I believe that after a short interaction, it can easily be ascertained as to whether the person one is conversing with has an independent mind or else they are merely the organ of regurgitating the words of others whose works they have only memorised and not instilled or interjected any of their own consideration.

When one truly has an independent mind, therefore, and this can be cultivated largely through reading, as well as conversing with like-minded compatriots, it becomes a resource in itself and the individual is no longer reliant on other's thoughts, beliefs or opinions. When this situation is achieved, then the mind will be thus cultivated and its real powers found out.

It has been 2,300 years since Plato spelled out his ideas on the ideal educational state, but hopefully one day this male government will fulfil his idealism and create an educational system that attends to the actual needs of all its learners, both male and female; and so turning out authentic members of society who not only value what they have learnt but are able to apply it in order to make the society in which they find themselves better.

CHAPTER TWENTY

Before Queen Anne visited at the beginning of the eighteenth century, Bath was firmly entrenched within its medieval walls. There were four gates, one for each of the compass points – north, south, east and west – and these were the only ways in and out of the enclosed city. After Anne's patronage, however, the self-contained conurbation rapidly expanded outwards in all directions: to the east, parades were swiftly built, to be followed later by Great Pulteney Street and the pleasure gardens at Sydney Vauxhall; to the west, the magnificent Squares, Beauford and Queen being the most prominent; and to the north, the crowning architectural triumphs of the King's Circus and the various crescents.

To the south of the city walls, towards the river, was a different matter entirely though. Despite being one of the main routes in and out of Bath, by way of Horse Street and the Old Bridge which spanned the River Avon, both significant architectural developments in their own right, the majority of the southern region had not been built upon. Historically and practically, there was a very good reason for this: the whole area was situated on a flood plain.

Until the onslaught of the property development boom which took hold during the eighteenth century, livestock had grazed on much of the area, with meadows such as Ambury Mead, King's Mead, and the Ham providing an abundant and plentiful supply of flora. These willow-fringed pastures were idyllic in summer, but after the heavy rains of autumn and the melting snows from the surrounding hills in spring, each year saw this terrain flood and disappear under fast-flowing water as the Avon broke its banks, turning them at a stroke into quagmires and rendering it wholly unsuitable land upon which to build any type of residential dwellings.

It had been suggested, during one of the initial outpourings of building work which sprung up elsewhere in the city, that the whole area south of the city walls might be cultivated into a pastoral area, along the lines of Oxford's Christchurch Meadow. This was quickly dismissed, however, within the climate of unbridled greed and expansion that held the city in its tight grip throughout the entire century and it was not long before elegant and fashionable lodging houses were being designed and built with only the flimsiest attempt at flood prevention.

Once the inevitable and regular flooding happened, of course, the fashionable lodging houses swiftly became unacceptable as dwelling-places to the upper and middle class visitors they were intended to attract and as the buildings became almost unliveable to all but the poorest of occupants, the whole area soon became run-down. It was not long before the district became known after the largest street within it, which itself had been named after the river it led down towards. And so it was that the Avon Street district, locally known by many of its inhabitants simply as 'the hate', became synonymous with the most poverty-stricken and desperate section of the population that resided in this most famous of cities.

No sooner had Swann left Fitzpatrick, after their walk around the upper town, and begun walking down Avon Street, on his way to find Wick's headquarters, than he saw Tyler in the distance. The pickpocket was sauntering down the road, stopping briefly at various stalls to converse with the owners. Swann decided to follow Tyler, to gain an insight as to how he spent his days and to try and gauge his standing in the community. In London, Swann had complied a huge dossier on known criminals, their features, characteristics and habits, and instinct took over as he followed the pickpocket into the notorious Avon Street district proper; an area, as he now witnessed, where even though it was still only late morning, prostitutes openly solicited for trade and collapsed drunks, both male and female, already littered the streets. Swann passed the entrance to a yard; from inside the unmistakable sound of copulation reached his ears.

A little further on and Tyler turned down a side alleyway. As Swann crossed to follow, another man, his head down, hurried by in the opposite direction. As their paths crossed, Swann instantly stopped in his tracks, as if physically struck. His bewildered expression showed he was attempting to assimilate something; something, in fact, as he would later realise, he was experiencing now but that belonged to the past, a feeling from another time, another place, another life. After only the briefest of moments, however, Swann turned in the direction the man had been going, but there was no one there. Swann stared transfixed at the empty space where he imagined the man had walked only moments before. He retraced his steps back up to the corner of that particular street and looked in both directions, but the man was nowhere to be seen. Swann turned back and continued on the way he had been going, although Tyler was now out of sight and had also vanished.

Swann carried on his way down the street, taking each step as if in a daze, with his mind reeling, trying to locate in his memory where he had met the person before. It was no good, he had to recover himself and a little further down he sat on the small wall to give some time to think what exactly this was all about. Somewhere deep inside, however, he already knew, but with the shock of the actuality of it being in his presence, it took a little longer for the recognition to ascend the sub-conscious and make itself known in consciousness. The man who had just crossed Swann's path had been the accomplice of Malone on the night Swann's father had been murdered. Although only seeing him for the briefest of moments, Swann had 'seen' the scar with his peripheral vision, the mark of the wound his father had inflicted with the poker.

Swann took a few more moments to recollect the experience fully in his mind. He was now the twelve year old boy, as he replayed the scene where he had left the sanctuary of the kitchen and peered around the door into the hallway. There was his father, struggling with an intruder. Before they fell into the front room, however, Swann was rudely brought back to the present by a tug on his sleeve.

'Looking for a nice time, my love,' a woman whispered, through broken teeth and sore-encrusted lips.

Swann stood up without answering and brushed the woman off.

'No need to be like that, you rich bastard,' she said, then followed him for a short distance, showering a torrent of abuse, until she lost interest and wandered off seeking a more receptive prospect.

Swann rounded the next corner and saw the Duke of York in the distance. Just at that moment, as luck would have it, Tyler crossed the road opposite and entered the public house. As Swann reached the entrance, the door opened. He stepped aside, ready for trouble if Tyler appeared, but it was a drunk who staggered out, vomited against the wall and then collapsed next to it. Ignoring the man, Swann opened the door and went inside.

The interior was dingy and what light there was came through grimy windows at the front and sides. In the half-light Swann surveyed the room and registered the figures of around a half dozen patrons, scattered liberally throughout the place. A couple of rough-looking men were sat in one corner, but he could not see Tyler anywhere. The sight of a well-dressed gentleman in this part of town naturally brought all eyes onto Swann. The landlord stared at him from behind the counter.

'What do you want here?'

'Are you the landlord of this establishment?' asked Swann.

'Who wants to know?'

'I do. I'm looking for a man named Wicks.'

'Don't know anyone by that name.'

'I suppose you haven't heard of a man named Tyler, either.'

'Should I?'

'Well, he has just entered your establishment and has obviously gone elsewhere within it,' said Swann.

The landlord bent down behind the bar and grabbed the metal bar he kept there for using on troublemakers.

'We don't take kindly to folk like you, asking questions,' he said, brandishing the metal bar as he stood up straight. Swann, however, immediately dragged the landlord across the counter and smashed his face against the wood. He did this several times before letting go. When he did so, the landlord fell back behind the bar with a broken and bleeding nose.

'Tell Wicks I do not respond kindly to threats and inform Tyler I am watching him,' said Swann. He then turned and left.

Once Swann had gone outside, however, the two men who had been sitting together in the corner stood up and followed him out.

After leaving the alehouse Swann decided to head for the river and try to locate the warehouse which belonged to Wicks. As he stepped over the prone drunk and negotiated the vomit which had spread out across the street, he became aware of the two men who had followed him out. He did not react though and carried on down the street, to the next corner. Once there, however, he stopped and waited for them to catch up.

A few moments later the two men rounded the corner and were completely taken by surprise. Swann grabbed the more rotund one of the pair and twisted his arm behind his back, as he pushed him against the wall.

'Please sir, we mean no harm,' said the man whose arm was being twisted.

Swann released his arm, but remained alert.

'What do you want following me, then?'

'We know where you can find Wicks.'

The other man, who was watching his companion talk, nodded.

'And why would you want to help me?' enquired Swann.

'It is our business, sir, and if you let us lead you to him we would only ask for a small payment.'

'I see,' said Swann, smiling. 'So who are you?'

'We're thief-takers sir. I am George Cartwright and this is Bridges.'

The other man grunted.

'Does he have a surname?' asked Swann.

'No sir, he's just known as Bridges. He is deaf and dumb, but he understands everything you say from these,' said George, as he pointed to his own lips.

Bridges nodded.

'Okay, George, Bridges. I am Jack Swann. So where might I find this Wicks and yes, there will a small reimbursement for your trouble.'

George smiled. 'Come with us, sir. It is down by the river.'

Swann retained suspicion regarding the pair, and would do so until such time as proved otherwise, but nevertheless he allowed them to accompany him as he headed down towards the riverside. The Old Bridge, which had originally been built in the fourteenth century and was then known as St Lawrence Bridge, due to the minute chapel which resided in the middle of it, was the only route in and out of the city across the river. In 1754, it had been rebuilt by the Corporation on the site of its predecessor, retaining a similar number of arches, namely five, but now extensively decorated by archivolt mouldings and with the addition of a gate enclosed in a stone archway at the far end. The roadway which ran across the structure rose from its respective ends to meet in a sharp break somewhere over the middle arch. On the city side, the bridge led straight into Horse Street, while on the other, the main road led up through an area called Holloway, before it became the Wells Road.

Once across the Old Bridge, however, Swann and his two companions turned right and headed along the riverbank on the farthest side, towards a series of tall, imposing warehouses. The trio reached one particular nondescript building, which looked no different from any of the others, but here George and Bridges stopped. The warehouse was bereft of activity and no one else was around.

'This is Wicks' warehouse,' said George, pointing to the building now in front of them. 'He runs his business dealings from here and the Duke. That's why we were at the pub, we were collecting information.'

'Well, thank you for your help gentleman. I will proceed alone from here,' said Swann. 'If you care to wait nearby though, once I have verified the information you have given me as being the truth, then I shall recompense you, as agreed.'

'We wish to come with you sir, you never know what might happen.'

Bridges nodded in agreement.

'I appreciate the offer, gentlemen,' replied Swann, 'but I would not wish to involve you in my personal affairs. I suggest though, if you want to help in some way further, then wait right here and if I require assistance I will summon you.'

'We will be here waiting then, Mr Swann, if you need us.'

'Good,' said Swann.

He stepped forward and tried a door handle, which he found unlocked,

'Wicks' office is at the back, Mr Swann,' said George.

Swann nodded and then went through the entrance and into the warehouse. There was no one around and Swann deftly crossed the large warehouse floor and climbed up a wooden staircase, towards where he assumed Wick's office would be located, if the pair outside were telling the truth. He reached the top of the stairs and saw a solitary door. He withdrew the pistol from inside his jacket and entered. The only occupant was sitting behind a battered, old wooden desk. On seeing Swann, he went to grab the cutlass propped against the wall.

'Touch that weapon and it will be the last thing you do, Wicks.'

'Who the hell are you,' said Wicks, 'and how do you know my name?'

'My name is Swann and I was the recipient of the message unceremoniously delivered to Pulteney Street last evening. Whether you were the perpetrator of it or not, Wicks, I am sure you know who was behind it and whoever that may be, I have a message for them; I do not take kindly to being threatened and I alone will decide how long I am to stay in Bath. Is that understood?'

Swann edged back towards the open door, the pistol still aimed at Wicks' heart.

'Try to follow me out of your office at your peril,' said Swann.

And then Swann was gone, back down the wooden staircase and across the uneven floor towards the exit. Angry and fuming, Wicks stood up and grabbed the cutlass.

'Tanner! Tyler! Morgan! Get here!' Wicks shouted, as he rushed out to the staircase. At the top of it, however, he stopped and cautiously peered around the corner. The warehouse was empty.

'Tanner! Tyler! Morgan! Where the fuck are you all?'

At the far end of the warehouse a man now came running in, still in the act of tightening up the belt on his trousers.

'What is it, Mr Wicks?'

'Where the hell have you been, Tanner,' demanded Wicks, as he came down the stairs.

'I was out back, boss. Why, what's happened?'

'While you were outside having a shit, I was inside having a pistol aimed at my head. That's what happened!'

'Sorry, Mr Wicks.'

'And where's Morgan and Tyler? I want them here, now!'

'I haven't seen 'em all day, boss.'

'Well, bleedin' go and find them. That Swann is going to pay for this. Nobody walks into my territory and threatens me. Our "friend" from London was here not thirty minutes ago and how do you think that would have looked if this had happened in front of him. No, he won't get away with this. I'm going to send this Swann another message and this time it will be a more permanent one.'

CHAPTER TWENTY-ONE

At the same time Wicks was berating Tanner back in the warehouse, Swann and the two thief-takers had crossed over the Old Bridge and were now heading back into the Avon Street district. George and Bridges had been as good as their word, waiting for Swann outside the warehouse on his return. He subsequently had given the pair the agreed payment and thanked them once again for their assistance. He could do with men like them back in London. Although he had many informers and people in the criminal world working for him, none of them seemed to be trustworthy enough that Swann would want them to be on his side in a fight. These two seemed to be different. As they reached the bottom of Horse Street, they were about to go their separate ways when George spoke.

'Bridges asks if you are here on account of the killings.'

'What killings are those, George?' asked Swann.

'Malone's gang, sir.'

'Malone!' said Swann. In all the tumult of the afternoon he had not thought to ask the pair about *that* name.

'Yes, sir, what we heard is that they were butchered two nights ago, in one of the warehouses over there.' George pointed across the river, to where they had not long been. 'Their bodies were cut up and thrown in the river.'

'And Malone?' asked Swann, with trepidation.

'He was murdered too. They say it was Wicks that did it, ran him through the guts with his cutlass.'

Swann did not respond but stood there, lost within the revelation. For all his thoughts on the matter beforehand, he had not expected it. So Malone was dead. He did not feel satisfied, however, even though his quest was now at an end. But this was now replaced by conflict. The man he had only just gone to see and who had ordered the attack on the house the night before, had been the man who put an end to Malone. And he used the same cutlass Swann had stopped him grabbing in the office. With that weapon Swann's quest had been ended. But Malone was dead, whatever way he had met his end. Justice had been served, even if somewhat ironically by another criminal.

'Are you all right, Mr Swann?' asked George.

'Yes, I am fine, thank you, George. It is just I knew a Malone in London several years ago and I didn't realise he had been here all this time. And now he's dead.'

'What we heard,' said George, 'was he had connections with London but they weren't happy with him. So they ordered Wicks to kill him and take over the city.'

'Yes, that is similar to what I overheard in London,' said Swann. 'Although I did not realise it was to take place so soon. You said the body was thrown in the river.'

'Yes, sir. Malone *and* all his men.'

'That is unfortunate, as I would have liked to at least have verified it was him.'

'Very what, sir?' asked George.

'Verify, George, it means to make sure of something. Did you and Bridges ever see Malone?'

'No, sir, nobody I know ever did.'

'I suppose I cannot return and ask Wicks for a description,' said Swann, wryly.

Bridges then signed to his companion.

'That's right, I forgot,' said George. 'Bridges does know someone who could do it, sir.'

'Could do what, George?' replied Swann.

'Describe to you what Malone looked like, sir. The woman Bridges knows grew up in the same village in Ireland as Malone. Least she says she did.'

'And where is this woman now?'

'She lives close by, in Peter Street, but she won't be there now. She works in one of those factories out on the Bristol Road. We could bring her tonight, if you want, sir?'

'That would be excellent, George.'

Swann could see George now had something on his mind.

'What is it George?'

'Well sir, she might want money to meet you.'

'That won't be a problem, George, and if she provides me with what I require, there will a little extra for the both of you.'

'Thank you,' said George, smiling.

Having read Swann's lips, Bridges smiled too.

'Where do you suggest we rendezvous, George?' asked Swann.

'What sir?'

'Where shall we meet?'

'We are usually found in the Fountain Inn, near the top of Avon Street, sir. It's the largest one in the street.'

'Then I suggest we meet there around seven o'clock this evening, if you think she will have finished her work by then.'

'We shall be there, Mr Swann, but er …'

Swann saw George hesitate again.

'What is it this time, George?'

'Well sir, are you sure about meeting there, sir, at the Fountain?'

'Why do you ask?'

'Well, it's only that it can be dangerous for people dressed like yourself, if you don't mind me saying, especially at night.'

'Thank you for your thoughtfulness, George, but neither of you need concern yourself over my well-being this evening.'

The men parted company and Swann headed up Horse Street, now with the sole intention of going to the nearest bookshop where he could purchase a current and more detailed map of the city than the one which presently hung in the library at the house in Great Pulteney Street. He walked on up the street with a mixture of thoughts and feelings running through his mind. From what he had experienced so far and from what his instinct told him, he believed George and Bridges could be trusted and that they were not attempting to dupe him out of more money by producing a false witness to lie about knowing Malone. And hopefully Swann would be able to ascertain the fact that the man he had been searching for all these years was now dead. Little did he realise, however, exactly what it was he would find out later that evening.

CHAPTER TWENTY-TWO

Theodore Evans turned the key in the door to lock his haberdashery shop, located in Westgate Buildings, and headed towards the city centre. As he walked down the street, the Abbey clock could be heard in the distance striking the hour. It was now seven o'clock in the evening and the shopkeepers' meeting was due to begin at half-past. It was a direct route up Westgate Street and then Cheap Street, before a diagonal left turn would take him across the main High Street to the Guildhall.

The meeting was the one he had invited Fitzpatrick to, earlier in the day. He hoped the magistrate would be there so he could publicly challenge him over the corruption of certain of his colleagues: most particularly that of Kirby. But as much as he would have liked to think the magistrate would appear, he felt it was a lost cause.

Not to worry though, he thought, as he went around the corner into Westgate Street, as he had a speech which was sure to rouse the assembled body of men and perhaps it would incite them enough to march *en masse* to Fitzpatrick's office the next day in a show of solidarity. He had been practising his speech all week and although he wasn't the greatest orator, he felt confident he could deliver it well. He had injected a number of pauses at strategic places, in order to heighten the dramatic effect of several points he wanted to make and had even quoted Shakespeare towards the end. It was the speech from the second scene in the third act of the *Merchant of Venice*, where Shylock laments that if he is pricked, he will bleed and if wronged, he will be justified to seek revenge. By using this particular quote, Evans felt he would make a striking finale and he could almost visualise the cheers and clapping which would hopefully accompany the speech's conclusion. He would then modestly acknowledge the applause and try to get them to agree to march the following day. If he could not have the law on his side, in the shape of Fitzpatrick, then the authority of England's greatest playwright would have to suffice.

He began to recite the speech in his head one more time and when he came to the Shakespearean quote, he outwardly gestured his arms in the manner intended to be used while delivering it for real. The speech would hopefully also inspire his kinsmen to stand up against the likes of Wicks and Tyler. Official channels of justice did not seem to mean anything to criminals like them, as was witnessed not two days previously. Tyler was a troublemaker and perhaps the revenge Evans regaled in his speech would come to fruition against the thief soon. He recited the last line of the Shakespeare quote again. Yes, he would get his revenge on Tyler and it would be swift in coming.

Tyler had left his boss' warehouse office several hours earlier, after having been summoned there by Tanner, who had informed him that Wicks was in a foul mood. Tyler was not happy to be disturbed, as he was upstairs in the Duke of York taking payment in kind from one of the regulars on his round, but you did not keep Wicks waiting. He had gone with Tanner to the warehouse and on his arrival found himself berated by Wicks for not being at the warehouse earlier, when Swann had entered. Tyler wouldn't ordinary let anyone else talk to him like that, and perhaps one day not even Wicks, but he realised from his boss' expression that Wicks had been humiliated by the man who had also recently become a thorn in Tyler's side.

Although angry with his subordinate, Wicks had nevertheless given Tyler two jobs to complete, both of which he now relished. Tyler had then carried out a few other errands before heading for the centre to complete the first of the jobs Wicks had given him.

Meanwhile, Evans was too caught up in his speech and the reciting in his head of various sections of it, that he did not notice a beggar shuffling towards him, coming the opposite way. The old man had his head down and so was knocked against a wall of the nearest building as Evans bumped into him. The shopkeeper immediately went to apologise to the man, but on seeing the state of his clothes, instead gave him an annoyed look and carried on, merely losing only the briefest momentum in carrying on his speech recitation.

Evans now passed the top of Stall Street, near the White Hart Inn, and carried on along Cheap Street, towards the Guildhall. As he did so, he had immediately come into the view of Tyler, who was waiting in the shadows of the White Hart's entrance. Tyler now followed Evans and part by luck and part by design, caught up with his quarry just as the shopkeeper was passing the entrance to a doorway set a little way back off the main street. Tyler took his chance and struck. It was so quick there was no time for any reaction or cry of help from Evans. Within a few seconds the shopkeeper lay dying in the dark, a stab wound to his back, and his bill-purse taken, while his attacker was already on his way past the Abbey and into the darkness once more.

Only in the moment before contact had Evans been aware of someone behind him, as he had been in the middle of his speech's dramatic finale and had not been paying attention.

Ordinarily he would have been more aware and turned earlier, the city could be dangerous at night, but he was too caught up in exacting his revenge in his head. His body had slid down the side of the doorway and ended up in a heap on the dirty floor, on top of the garbage piled there. It would not be until the next morning that his body would be discovered and his missing bill-purse assumed to be the motive behind the killing. Meanwhile, Evans' absence at the shopkeepers' meeting was briefly mentioned in passing but the following item of business was then announced and the speech, which had been practised to near perfection, would never now get the chance to be aired in public.

CHAPTER TWENTY-THREE

By the time Evans had been murdered, the 'old beggar' he had bumped into earlier was already in the Fountain Inn for the pre-arranged meeting with George and Bridges. It had taken Swann around three quarters of an hour to put on the disguise, using items he always carried with him. Tonight it had been a choice between the 'sailor amputee' and the 'old beggar' but he had decided on the latter as he felt it better to have two legs on the ground at all times on this particular occasion.

He had learnt the art of disguise from a troupe of Parisian actors he had spent a summer with when he was younger. 'Any disguise that you assume must be complete from the underclothes upward,' the troupe leader had told him. 'If you are to take on the guise of a peasant, for example, you must make certain there is dirt under the nails.' He had been shown a variety of techniques to achieve this 'completeness' and he used several of them for this disguise, such as walnut oil to darken his face and a globule of wax to create a large blemish on his right cheek.

Swann had begun to don the disguise not long after Mary had gone out for the evening. He had wanted to slip out the back way without Emily seeing him, but just as he had reached the kitchen she had entered. She had screamed at the sight of him. It was a testament to his art that she had been taken in, but Swann then spent the next few minutes comforting her and apologising to her most profusely for his appearance. Once Emily had been suitably calmed, he apologised once more and then made his way out of the back door. He continued his way along the passage at the rear of the buildings and finally emerged at Laura Place. He crossed Pulteney Bridge and followed the route around to the Guildhall, before entering Cheap Street.

As he passed the White Hart Inn he had noticed Tyler loitering outside but there was nothing he could do, as he did not want to break character. He had continued on down into Westgate Street and it was here that he had bumped into Evans. He had not recognised him initially but by the time Swann crossed over Westgate Street and approached Avon Street, he remembered that it was Evans, the leader of the shopkeepers, and the man who had been in Fitzpatrick's office earlier that day. Evans was on his way to the meeting he realised, where he would discover Fitzpatrick's non-attendance. It would not be until the next day though, after Swann heard about Evans' murder, that he realised the true significance of having also seen Tyler within the proximity of the crime scene.

Swann always used disguises when he needed to solicit information without people knowing who he was and also when he first wanted to see if people he was meeting could be trusted. George and Bridges seemed trustworthy but he wanted to make sure. At the same time, they had been right when they advised him that it was probably not wise to go into the Avon Street district in his ordinary clothes. The day time was one thing but he did not want to draw that kind of undue attention at night.

Swann now entered the Fountain Inn, like so many times before in London when he had worn a disguise to enter a den of iniquity. As places went, and considering the area within which it was located, it seemed more welcoming than most. It still had its share of trouble, no doubt, but there was a sense of community and of comradeship that was apparent the moment he entered. The landlord looked a friendly sort. It was alleged that he had killed a man in a street fight years before and not being a violent man, it had affected him greatly. Nevertheless, you still would not want to get on the wrong side of him.

Swann shuffled to the counter and ordered a drink. The pub was only half full at present but the noise gave the impression of its being more busy. George and Bridges sat at a table deep within the pub. There was a woman with them, who Swann assumed was their 'contact'. He handed over the money for the drink and then made his way slowly over towards the table next to them. He sat down and listened to their conversation for a while. When he was satisfied that it did not seem to be a trap, he stood up and shuffled over.

'There's no room here for you,' said George, as Swann went to sit down.

'Now, good sirs,' said Swann, assuming an appropriate downcast accent, 'that be no way to treat an old soldier like me self.'

'That's for a very important gentleman, he'll be here soon.'

'Can I just sit me self down before your gentleman friend arrives, then?'

George started to stand up, angry at this disturbance.

'All right, George,' said Swann, reverting back to his normal voice but in a hushed tone. 'You've done well, but I would prefer you didn't announce my arrival so vocally next time.'

'Mr Swann?' said George, not yet being able to see through the disguise.

Reading George's lips, Bridges now smiled. Swann nodded to him.

'Please Mr Swann, sit down,' said George.

'Thank you George, although I suggest you do not address me by that name this evening.'

'All right sir,'

'Or be that formal. I am an old soldier, remember. If you have to use any name, then call me Jack.'

'Right you are, sir, I mean Mr Swann, no er … Jack.'

'Settle yourself, George, it is alright and we do not want to draw attention to ourselves. This is your friend?'

The woman was in her fifties and her face reflected the life she had lead.

'Yes er … er … Yes. Her name is Rosie.'

'Rosie,' said Swann, quietly, 'has George told you who I am and why I am here?'

She nodded.

'You knew Malone?' he asked.

'Yes,' she replied. 'He's dead now though.'

'That's right, but George said you knew him before, in Ireland?'

'Yeah, I knew all the Malone family there. Nasty pieces of work they were, every last one of them. Good riddance to 'em, I say.'

'And it was the same Malone in Bath?'

'The same Malone as what?' the woman said, puzzled.

'The Malone who was killed here in Bath was the same Malone who you knew in Ireland.'

'Yes,' she replied. 'He came over here 'bout two years 'fore me.'

'So he left Ireland for London and then came here.'

'I don't know nuthin' 'bout London, only when I came to Bath, he was here.'

Swann then got Rosie to describe Malone's features, which matched the image he had held in his memory for the last twenty years.

'Thank you,' said Swann, after she had finished. 'That is all I need to know.'

Swann discreetly took out three coins of varying denomination and distributed them accordingly. Each recipient looked at their coin and thanked Swann. He then addressed George and Bridges.

'Well gentlemen,' whispered Swann. 'May I thank you for all your assistance in this matter today. It has been a pleasure knowing you.'

Bridges smiled and signed to George.

'Bridges says if you are ever in Bath again, sir, he would be more than happy to assist you. The same goes for me.'

'Thank you, George, Bridges.'

Bridges nodded.

As Swann went to stand up, Rosie whispered in George's ear.

'Rosie asked what Malone did that you're so interested in him being dead.'

'I guess it no longer matters anymore to say. Well, Rosie, twenty years ago, Malone murdered my father in London. I have been seeking him ever since, so I could see that justice was served.'

Rosie whispered in George's ear again.

'Rosie is confused,' he then said. 'She says when was twenty years ago?'

'It was 1783,' replied Swann.

After more whispering George spoke again. 'She says if it was 1783 your father was murdered, it couldn't have been Malone what did it. He didn't leave Ireland until 1787.'

CHAPTER TWENTY-FOUR

As promised, Harriet's carriage arrived at six o'clock outside the house in Great Pulteney Street. After Mary entered, the driver had made his way out of Bath and headed to Harriet's manor, located near the market town of Frome, famed for its blue cloth and textile industry. There were three other women in the coach but after exchanging polite greetings, the ninety-minute journey was spent in silence. Although Mary felt some awkwardness in the quietness, there was also a relief at the absence of small talk; that annoying and persistent chatter which was always present at any social engagement in the city and which one felt obliged to reciprocate. Despite the darkness and the severe motion of the carriage at times across the roads, the journey, although conducted in silence, was no less pleasant for it and the absence of scenery to observe was replaced with the anticipation of meeting Harriet once more and the actual lecture itself.

The carriage finally pulled up at Harriet's residence and the four occupants made their way inside. They negotiated their way through the building materials which cluttered up the hallway and were shown into a room where chairs were set out in rows, most of which were already filled. Mary saw her aunt standing at the front of the room with another woman and as soon as Harriet saw her niece, she beckoned her over.

'Mary, I am so pleased you have chosen to attend this evening,' said Harriet. 'Let me introduce you to Catherine Jennings. Catherine is the headmistress of a girl's school in Bath and is our guest speaker for the evening. Catherine, this is my niece, Mary.'

The two women acknowledged each other.

'Is this your first time at one of these meetings?' asked Catherine.

'Yes,' replied Mary, 'but I am thoroughly looking forward to it.'

'Well I hope I live up to your expectations, then,' said Catherine.

'I think it is about time to start,' Harriet now interjected. 'I need to be seated at the front, Mary, but please feel free to sit wherever you wish. I would like to see you afterwards though, before the carriage takes you home.'

Mary nodded and soon found a seat vacant near to her travelling companions. As she took her seat, her aunt addressed the room.

'Welcome to our monthly meeting and I am glad to see so many of you in attendance tonight. It not only reflects the importance of our cause but no doubt the popularity of the speaker we have this evening. Before we begin, however, I wish to apologise for the untidiness around the manor grounds and the hallway. The builders I have employed to undertake essential maintenance and repairs are not only pontificators of the highest degree, but their actions unfortunately fall short of their words and where the building work should have been completed at the end of the summer, we are well into autumn with no sign of completion. But enough talk of my domestic annoyances, we are here tonight to listen to one of the great educators of this, or indeed, any age, a person so enthusiastic about women's education that she began a school of her own to anthropomorphise her own philosophy. The author of several volumes and numerous pamphlets on the subject and the woman who it has been said is "the voice of reason in a multitude of chaos." But now, without any further pontificating on my part, let us welcome to the lectern the one and only Catherine Jennings.'

A loud and appreciative round of applause burst out throughout the room. To Mary, this seemed incongruous for a room full of women, but nevertheless she found it both exhilarating and exciting. She joined in enthusiastically, as did her travelling companions.

'Thank you, thank you all,' said Catherine from where she now stood behind the lectern. 'Firstly, let me thank our host and patron, Lady Montague-Smithson, or Harriet, as she insists we refer to her, for inviting me here to speak this evening. It is indeed a great honour. As Harriet mentioned, I run a school for girls and young women in Bath and it has been open for ten years now. I believe I must be doing a good job because each year some newly-formed, all-male committee tries to find a reason to close us down.'

A ripple of laughter went around the room.

'I want to talk about education tonight,' continued Catherine, 'but specifically women's education. How does it differ from a man's education, and should it matter? And if it does matter, then why?'

Mary felt herself at one with the room and her fellow audience members. There was an anticipation of excitement in the room.

'Since the day Eve convinced Adam to eat of the apple, we women have been portrayed as an evil force within the garden of Eden. But what did that apple contain? As it came from the tree of knowledge we can only surmise it contained that very essence. Therefore, a woman convinced a man to eat from the tree of knowledge and we have been blamed for doing so ever since. Eve should have eaten the apple herself and left men in ignorance.'

This brought another round of laughter within the room, followed by a round of sustained applause.

'Thank you, thank you. But she did convince Adam to eat and we can see only too well what has happened. Man has used that knowledge to ensure that it is *we* who do not have it. He has eaten the apple and kept us in ignorance. At the very best, man feeds us pieces of his apple but with his agenda attached to it. In this way, we believe we are learning to be independently-minded, but what we are really learning is how to behave within his world. And whatever they may say, and whatever words they may use, this *is* the case. In a male-dominated school we learn facts and figures we believe are important if we are to have intelligent conversations with them. But what is this knowledge? It is certainly not for our benefit, it is only for their benefit. So that we may converse with them about subjects that they find interesting but, to be frank, we do not. Yet when we wish to discuss those subjects we find inter-esting, the conversation is either changed or stopped altogether. At my school, however, I believe we have retrieved the apple and are able to eat from it for our own satisfaction. However, what is taught at my school does not come from man's apple, but from our own. This is *our* knowledge. So we must educate ourselves with our knowledge, our history. If you read books on literature you will find it full of men, with only the briefest of any women writers. And yet the writing of women has existed for so long and much of it is full of insight, wit and poetic imagery that would match any man. Daniel Defoe is credited with giving us the novel form, yet Alphra Benn had written at least a dozen of these types of books before him. But this is just one example of how history is rewritten by men for their own purpose. There have been many pioneers of our cause, most recently Mary Wollstonecraft, but she was only the latest. Yet she is being held up as the founder of this movement by men and subsequently ridiculed. Make no mistake, Wollstonecraft's contribution to our cause will be marked in history and not only in our own, but she is not the founder, merely the latest in a line of women who looked around at the world as it is, and then wrote about what they witnessed.'

Catherine continued talking for another hour or so, outlining the way in which her school was run, giving specific examples of the curriculum, and eventually concluding with an invitation for all those in the room to take it upon themselves to re-educate themselves as women and to throw off the burden of knowledge that had been foisted on them by men. On concluding her speech, Catherine then received the most rapturous applause Mary had ever heard.

After the lecture, Catherine remained at the lectern for questions. Mostly they were about women's education but one regarded marriage. It was asked by one of Mary's travelling companions.

'Do you think a woman can remain true to herself if she is married?'

Catherine smiled.

'Yes, if the husband is away on business all the time.'

There was more laughter around the room.

'Seriously, however, I wholeheartedly believe that the responsibility lies solely with the woman herself, to ensure in her own mind the man she plans to marry will not stand in the way of her continuing personal development; whether this is through reading of particular books or the pursuit of suitable creative and artistic activities. If she believes he will, then she only has herself to blame when he does.'

'But what if the woman has to marry, say for money?' The question came from another member of the audience.

'My dear, I hope no one in this room is ever put into that situation. The road of matrimony for financial reasons is surely the road to the spirit's dissolution. I truly believe it is better for a woman to live a financial impoverished existence, rather than a spiritual one.'

Another round applause was forthcoming and this lasted until Harriet stepped forward and said: 'We will have one final question.'

The person sitting next to Mary raised her hand. 'May I ask if you are married? And if so, does your husband have any single male relatives?'

Once the laughter from the room ceased, Catherine answered.

'No, I am not married,' she said, without regret in her tone.

Harriet then brought the evening to a close. There had been several questions Mary wanted to ask, but she did not yet have the courage of her convictions to ask them. Nevertheless, the evening had proved most enlightening and her spirit felt lifted from the trials of the last period of time.

CHAPTER TWENTY-FIVE

Swann stood next to the dining room table in Great Pulteney Street and studied the map spread out across its surface. He had purchased it from a bookseller's shop, located nearby in Argyle Street, earlier in the day and on returning from his evening meeting with George and Bridges at the Fountain Inn, had unfurled it to its full extent, weighting it down at each corner with four vases he had requisitioned from various parts of the house. The map was a detailed one of Bath and from the date on its top-right corner, it could be seen to have been published that very year.

Through the conversation he had not long finished with George and Bridge's contact, Swann had decided not to return to London but remain here, at least for the time being. He had acquired the map of Bath before making this decision, having done so with the intention of studying it purely for his own interest, but he now looked at it with more purpose. Now he had made his decision to stay in the city he wanted to become acquainted with every inch of its layout, especially the Avon Street district. This particular area still lacked comprehensive details in places on the map, the cartographers no doubt not wanting to risk their lives for the sake of completion, but there were enough features and landmarks included to give him the foundation upon which to build his geographical knowledge of the locale.

He had brought the map out immediately on his return from the meeting at The Fountain Inn and was still studying it when Mary returned home from her aunt's gathering. Ordinarily she would have instinctively screamed on entering the dining room to find a 'stranger' there, especially such a rough-looking one as this, but on her arrival, Emily had warned Mary about her brother's disguise, which in his haste to survey the map, he had not taken the trouble to remove.

'Jack, I hope you apologised most profusely to Emily for scaring her earlier. How could you have been so thoughtless?'

Swann mumbled a response but continued surveying the city.

'Jack, Jack! What are you doing? And could you not at least have changed out of those ragged-looking clothes.'

'Look Mary, it was here. I am sure of it,' he said, pointing to a particular place on the map.

'Sure of what, Jack?' she replied.

'Where I saw *him*, it was only for a moment but I am sure he had a scar down his right cheek and when our paths crossed, I felt as if I had been punched in the stomach.'

'What are you talking about? Who punched you?'

'One of the men I have been searching for all these years.'

'Why have you been searching for him? You are not making any sense Jack. I do not understand?'

Swann turned and looked intently at his sister.

'A man I saw on the street in Bath today was the accomplice of the man who murdered my father.'

'How can you be certain it was him?'

'I cannot,' replied Swann. 'But I have always relied on my instinct and it now tells me it is the same man who my father scarred with a poker that night, which is the reason, you will be delighted to hear, I have decided to stay on in Bath, at least for the time being.'

'That is most coincidental,' replied Mary wistfully, 'as I have considered what you proposed on your first day here and I believe it would be appropriate if I moved to London with you.'

'What has changed your mind?' said a surprised Swann. 'Is it Lockhart, has something happened between you two?'

'No. It is merely that Bath perhaps becomes tiresome if one does not partake of its social activities and London offers more opportunities for the expansion of the mind in the arts and other worthwhile subjects. As for Edmund, he can visit me in London, as he is often there on business. I do believe we are also less likely to have our windows smashed there, despite the bleak picture you painted of it.'

'I am thrilled to hear this, my dear sister, though for the time being I hope you understand that I must stay in Bath. I have to at least make an attempt to find the man I saw: I owe it to my father. I have been searching for these men since I was old enough to be able to do so and I will not stop until both of them have either been justly punished through being hanged or else I learn they are both dead.'

On witnessing Swann's determined expression, Mary decided in that moment she would adhere to her brother's wishes and stay with him in Bath for as long as he wanted to be here.

CHAPTER TWENTY-SIX

Later that night, after Swann and his sister had finished their conversation, they retired to their respective bedrooms, but neither of them with the slightest intention of sleeping straight away. Mary, on entering her room, had taken a writing board and placed it upon her lap as she sat up in bed.

She had two pieces of correspondence she wanted to complete. One, she felt, was through obligation, the other through sheer rapture. The former was a reply to a letter of condolence which had been sent from one of her mother's friends. The two women had grown up in Bath, had moved away after marrying and then both had returned to their home city on their husband's retirement. There the similarities ended. While Mrs Austen had given birth to a relatively large family, Mary was her mother's only foray into the act of childbirth.

The Austen family were away from Bath at the present time but on hearing the sad news, Mrs Austen had written post-haste. In the letter she relayed how she felt as if she had to put pen to paper to convey her sadness as to the loss of a dear friend. She also expressed that on the family's return she would dearly like to pay a visit in order to offer her condolences in person and, if Mary was agreeable to it, would bring her daughter, Jane.

Mary thanked Mrs Austen for her thoughtfulness and agreed it would be most welcome for her and Jane to visit after they had returned, whenever that may be.

She finished the first letter and then turned to the second, which she felt a growing excitement to write. She took a new sheet of paper and began.

Thursday 20th October, 1803

Dearest Aunt Harriet

I write this letter to you late at night, still exhilarated following the evening's talk. I never knew anyone of our gender could speak with such elegance, fluidity and clarity of mind and express thoughts that I realise I have had all my life but never dared express them to myself, let alone share them in public.

In regard to our brief conversation after the talk and the mentioning of my brother's proposal I should accompany him back to London, I have news regarding your suggestion I do this and become your 'eyes and ears' there. Jack was still awake on my return and whereas before he was adamant of returning to London as soon as possible, he has now decided to stay on in Bath for the foreseeable future.

The move to London has therefore been postponed for the time being and I shall await your instruction as to how I can best be of assistance to the cause here in Bath.

Your most appreciative niece

Mary Gardiner

Meanwhile, Swann had retired to his bedroom to complete his journal.

Swann sat in the wooden chair, beside the table he had especially brought up to the bedroom from downstairs for the very purpose and opened his journal. He paused for a moment to compose his thoughts, which had been racing all evening and were still doing so, and then began to record the dramatic news he had learnt earlier that evening. The words flowed out of him.

CHAPTER TWENTY-SEVEN

Bath, Thursday 20th October, 1803

It is hard to believe that it was only yesterday that I recorded in this very journal my incredulity at the series of events which had occurred since my arrival in Bath, and yet those of today have surpassed even them.

The Malone I have been searching for all these years is indeed not dead, at least not by the hand of Wicks. The man who was murdered earlier this week is, in fact, Thomas Malone, who I know now from Rosie to have been the twin brother of the man I seek, which is why the description I had of him initially matched that of the other man.

Thomas Malone did, indeed, leave Ireland for England in 1787, apparently having fallen foul of the Rightboys, a secret reformist organisation who sought to bring about certain changes to Irish society through whatever means necessary, to which this particular Malone had refused to join. His brother, Sean, the man I seek, however, had already left Ireland four years earlier. This was 1783, the year my father was murdered, which means Malone had not been long in the country when he committed the crime. Whether Thomas Malone came straight to Bath or initially went to London to join his brother there, I believe, is now irrelevant.

As to the present whereabouts of Sean Malone, I do not know. He could still be in London, although with the connection between the Malone family and Bath established, coupled with the sighting of the Scarred Man, the man I have decided to call Malone's accomplice, I have decided my search must remain in this city until such time as it takes me elsewhere.

I do hear Mary's words echoing in my mind though regarding the Scarred Man. 'Are you sure it was him?' But I know it was. I could not bring forth evidence in a court of law to support my case, but I know it to be true. The only 'evidence' I can go on is my instinct and this tells me it was him. I felt his presence as he passed me on the street, as surely as if it was Malone himself, and the same way I felt at the fair, when I was sixteen, and believed I was in the presence of Malone.

The mixed emotions I have experienced today have left my mind in turmoil. I began the day supposing Malone to be alive, only then to believe midway through that he was, in fact, dead by another's hand. I now realise these latter emotions to have been unfounded, yet nevertheless they have proved to be most revelatory. When I thought my quest at an end, but not through my own labours, I did not feel justice had been served. This has led me to realise that I will not be satisfied unless I administer the final blow to end Malone's life myself, in the way he did to end my father's, and see him die before my own eyes.

My thoughts return to the Scarred Man. If I am sure that it was him, then what is he doing in the city and does he know the whereabouts of the man I seek? I cannot believe it is mere coincidence that he is here and so I feel I will only find out the truth by questioning him to find out what he knows of Malone.

At the same time as continuing the search for Malone, through the Scarred Man, I will attempt to diminish Wicks' criminal activities in the city and also endeavour to discover Lockhart's secret, for I know he has one. Finally, I will do all in my power to protect Mary from what I see as her aunt's dangerous influence.

I aim to visit Fitzpatrick tomorrow and inform him of my decision to stay and take the opportunity to ask him if he can acquire rooms from where I can conduct my investigations, as I do not want a repetition of last evening and the broken window. Given my decision to stay on in the city, I will also attempt to acquire the services of George and Bridges.

I do not know what the coming period has in store for me, but I relish it and will rise to any challenge that may befall me. Meantime, however, it is now time for bed.

CHAPTER TWENTY-EIGHT

The art of deceitfulness came easy to Richard J. Kirby. From a very early age he realised one could literally get away with murder through knowing the 'right' people. He had become a magistrate for his own gain after his arrival in Bath, and it had not taken long to form his 'understanding' with Thomas Malone. He had acquired all the trappings that went with being a successful 'businessman', including an office in the King's Circus, membership of several exclusive men's clubs and all the other perks that came with his connection to Malone. But loyalty, for Kirby, only lasted as long as the situation was agreeable to him, and on learning from an associate in London that Malone's time controlling Bath was coming to an end, he had switched allegiance to the man rumoured to be his successor: Wicks.

Kirby was about to leave for the next court session in the Guildhall when Wicks appeared at the door to his chambers.

'What are you doing here? I told you never to be seen at my chambers.'

'You better watch your attitude, Kirby,' growled Wicks, 'I own this city and I own you, and don't ever forget it.'

Kirby realised it was not the time or place to argue, so he capitulated.

'So to what do I owe this pleasure?'

'I've come to give you some good news. The scheme involving Bristol worked well and our associates in London are pleased. They have given their permission for it to run as often as we think necessary. You can also use your man again.'

'Good,' said Kirby. 'I'll let him know.' He picked up a file and said, 'I heard about Evans.'

'Yes,' replied Wicks, 'he won't be troubling us any more. Have you been given charge of the investigation?'

'No, Fitzpatrick has been but I will convince him I should take over. I assume it was Tyler who killed Evans?'

'It doesn't matter who it was, just make sure the murder remains unsolved.'

'There is bound to be outrage over his death, most likely from the *Chronicle*, as Evans had some standing in the city, but you can count on me,' assured Kirby.

Wicks nodded his approval and his manner relaxed slightly.

'I have a new girl, you'll like her,' said Wicks. 'She's just your type.'

Kirby smiled licentiously. 'I'll pay a visit tonight, then. So when are we to run the scheme again?'

'I'll let you know. But this could be worth a lot of money. Are you sure you can trust your man?'

'Absolutely. Lockhart is also the one meeting that trouble-maker, as you wanted.'

'Does he know the real reason for the meeting?' enquired Wicks.

'No. I merely convinced him it would be a good idea. He is interested in the troublemaker's sister but he mentioned that there has been a misunderstanding between them. I advised him to arrange the meeting to clear it up.'

'What exactly is he going to tell him?' asked Wicks, slightly concerned.

'Nothing approximating the truth, that is for certain,' replied Kirby.

Both men laughed.

'Right, I am due in session in five minutes.'

The two men then left, each in their own way considering how they could get rid of the other once they had outlived their usefulness.

CHAPTER TWENTY-NINE

Swann went out of the main door of the house in Great
Pulteney Street, the house he would now be staying on in
for as long as it took to track down the Scarred Man, and
began his journey to Queen Square. He was on his way
to Fitzpatrick's office to tell the magistrate of his decision
to stay longer in Bath, one he knew Fitzpatrick would be
happy to hear, especially as Swann intended to offer his
services while he was carrying on his own investigation.
The air was fresh and it was a glorious autumn morning as
he passed Argyle Street and then crossed Pulteney Bridge
into the city centre.

At one time, the only way across the river between the
centre and the east side was by the Whitehall Ferry, a boat
service manned by ferrymen who would 'punt' passengers
across the small stretch of water for a fixed fee. Although not to
everyone's taste as a desired mode of transport, it was a much
quicker route to Spring Gardens, the usual destination for
those using the ferry, than crossing the river at the Old Bridge,
south of the city, and coming back around Widcombe to the
pleasure gardens that way.

In the late 1760s, however, the Bath Corporation gave its
permission for the landowner William Pulteney to construct
a bridge. This new structure was to be a key element in the
Pulteney family's plans to develop their land east of the river

and so they commissioned architect Robert Adam, a former Architect Royal, to design it. He based what would become the narrow Palladian structure on the famous Venetian Rialto Bridge, but uniquely added shops on either side. It took several years to build but when it was finally finished in 1775, Pulteney Bridge linked the old centre with the new residential areas being developed on the Bathwick Estate and elsewhere, such as Argyle Street, Laura Place and Great Pulteney Street, along with Sydney Gardens and Sydney Place.

It did not go completely to plan though, as the builder undertaking the work was financially ruined by his involvement and only a couple of years previously, where Swann now stood on the bridge, signs of subsidence had closed it while its western side was reinforced and a wooden bridge temporarily constructed to allow continued access eastwards while this repair work was carried out.

On arriving at Fitzpatrick's office, he found him engaged in conversation with one of his men. As soon as he became aware of Swann's presence, the magistrate dismissed the other man and gestured for Swann to sit down.

'I have this morning been informed of terrible news,' said Fitzpatrick. 'Mr Evans, the shopkeepers' representative and the man you met briefly in this very office yesterday, was murdered last night near the Guildhall.'

'Were there any witnesses?' asked Swann.

'As usual, nobody saw anything. This is the kind of case that could use a man of your quality,' said Fitzpatrick.

'Well,' said Swann, 'you will be pleased to hear that I have decided to stay on in Bath for the time being and therefore offer my assistance in this matter.'

Fitzpatrick's expression turned to one of great relief.

'That is most agreeable news,' said Fitzpatrick, 'and goes a little way towards off-setting the sad news about Mr Evans.'

'Are there any more details surrounding the murder?'

'No,' said Fitzpatrick. 'His body was discovered at first light, so it could have happened any time before that. I have dispatched a man to find out if Mr Evans was at the meeting last night, which unfortunately I could not attend.'

Swann felt it not right to mention anything to Fitzpatrick at the present time, but he was already in possession of certain facts, he believed. Given the presence of Tyler by the White Hart, at the same time Evans was walking up Westgate Street, it could only be assumed that the pickpocket had been waiting to take revenge on Evans over his prosecution a few days earlier. If Evans had indeed failed to appear at the meeting as well, it would seem almost to be beyond doubt that it was Tyler who had murdered the shopkeeper.

'So may I enquire as to your change of heart?' asked Fitzpatrick.

'There are a number of reasons but the main one is that I believe Bath is the best place to continue my investigation to find the man I told you murdered my father.'

'Ah, Malone,' said Fitzpatrick. 'The man you enquired after at the funeral.'

'Yes, the Malone I believed to be him was his brother, his twin in fact. But the connection with the city has been made and there is another man who I believe still to be here that may help me in this search.'

'Very good,' said Fitzpatrick. 'If there is anything I can do to help, please let me know.'

'I would be grateful if you could secure some rooms for me to conduct my business. Near to your offices would be satisfactory, if you could do so.'

'Consider them secured,' said Fitzpatrick. 'In the meanwhile, to celebrate your decision to stay on in Bath, I wish to invite you and Mary for dinner at my house this evening. Shall we say around half past seven?'

'That would be most agreeable,' replied Swann. 'Now, if you will excuse me, I have another matter to attend.'

The two men bowed to each other and Swann left the office. He came back out into Queen Square and headed for the same corner by which he had entered it, the south-east, and then made his way to an appointment off Wood Street.

Earlier that morning Lockhart's business card had arrived at Great Pulteney Street. Accompanying it was a note for Swann that read: *Please meet me at ten forty-five this morning at Gould's coffee-house.*

On entering the establishment, Swann saw that Lockhart was already there. He took the seat offered to him by the other man and sat down. A member of staff came over and took Swann's order.

'Thank you for meeting me here,' said Lockhart. 'I would have ordinarily suggested Molland's, around the corner from here, but I think a more discreet place is required for our somewhat delicate conversation. I believe there has been a misunderstanding between us and my intention now is to clear this matter up. I assume you have been wondering why I was on the same coach as yourself from London the other day and why I did not mention it at the funeral.'

Swann did not respond but showed he was listening to what Lockhart said.

'I did not mention the fact that we travelled together at the funeral, as it was connected to my business and I did not feel it fit for your sister's ears. I believe that men should not discuss business matters with any female he has occasion to be around.'

Swann nodded, as if agreeing this was an acceptable philosophy.

'But to show myself as the reputable person I am,' continued Lockhart, 'I now wish to disclose the circumstances and details surrounding that journey, or at least as many of them as I am able. I had every intention of travelling down from London directly the following day but the journey to Bristol was unexpectedly put upon me at the last moment. I barely had time to catch the coach, as you witnessed, given that I entered the carriage almost at the last possible moment.'

Swann's coffee arrived and after taking the first mouthful, he now spoke.

'And what of the two ladies accompanying you on the journey? What was their purpose in travelling?'

'That, I am afraid, I am not at liberty to disclose. What I can say, however, is that I am very fond of your sister and there was nothing inappropriate in what was being undertaken to undermine that fondness. I wish to protect her as much as you do, which is why I understand you mentioning my presence in the coach with you to her.'

'I fully understand you not wishing to discuss business with Mary and would normally not enquire further into the matter. However, given the nature of your relationship with my sister, I feel I have not been given a satisfactory answer in regard to your business affairs.'

'Please Jack, if I may call you that, I understand your persistence but I cannot disclose any further. Let us say the people I work for demand the utmost secrecy at all times and it would not be prudent for me to go against that demand.'

Swann saw Lockhart's attention focussed on the coffee-house clock.

'Is there a certain time you wish to be aware of, sir?'

'I apologise, but it is nearly eleven o'clock and there is another appointment I am obliged to attend within the next few minutes. I hope this meeting has gone some way in persuading you that my intentions towards Mary are honourable and I am a gentleman of the utmost honesty. I know that you are due to return to London in the next few days, but my hope is that I will have the pleasure of your company once more before you leave Bath.'

'I have decided to stay on longer in Bath and so I am certain of it.'

'Ah, that is news indeed,' said a surprised Lockhart, as he stood. 'Please do excuse me though, I have to leave now.'

Lockhart hurriedly left the establishment as a bemused Swann watched him go. From inside the coffee-house, he saw him turn left towards Milsom Street and then disappear out of sight. Swann finished his drink and vacated the premises himself, completely unaware of the events about to unfold outside.

CHAPTER THIRTY

Swann came out of Goulds' coffee-house and walked back towards Wood Street, the conversation with Lockhart still going around in his mind. The other man had not divulged anything which could be even in the least way construed as 'details' and Swann was still in the dark as to the reason why he had been travelling on the same coach. He mentioned the people he worked for demanded the utmost secrecy. Was he hinting to the fact he was on government business? Swann did not know but he would begin discreet enquiries through his contacts in London. His lawyer acquaintance had some connection with certain government offices, so he would ask him to clandestinely enquire. For now he would not mention anything to Mary about his conversation with Lockhart, or indeed that he had met him.

Swann was on his way to the Avon Street district to continue his investigation in regard to the Scarred Man and Malone. He also wanted to locate George and Bridges to employ their services. This had to be the place to start. No sooner had he turned into Wood Street, however, when he saw them appear further down the street. The pair seemed in great haste as they headed towards him. He now saw them frantically pointing to behind him. In that moment he turned and saw a carriage speeding along Wood Street, heading directly towards where he now stood.

On realising what was going to happen, Swann dived into the doorway of the nearest shop. As he did so, two pistols were simultaneously fired from inside the carriage as it passed by. The bullets embedded themselves harmlessly into the doorway above where Swann landed. The carriage went off into Queen Square, pursued by George, Bridges and, once he was back on his feet, Swann.

With the trio of men in pursuit, the driver whipped the horse hard as it sped along the south side of Queen Square, scattering several pedestrians as it did so. As it neared the south-west corner, the driver showed no intention of slowing down and so the inevitable happened; as he attempted to take the sharp corner, the carriage tipped over, throwing the driver and carriage occupant out onto the street.

As if by predetermined arrangement, both men ran off in different directions; the driver running up towards Charlotte Street, while the assassin sprinted out of the Square and went down Princes Street. Swann shouted to George for him and Bridges to go after the driver, while he gave chase after the other man. The man's build looked vaguely familiar but material wrapped around his face precluded positive identification. On reaching the end of Princes Street, Swann turned left and headed along Monmouth Street, where only the day before he had walked with Fitzpatrick. He could still see the man he was chasing, up ahead. The figure turned right and Swann instinctively knew the man was heading for the Avon Street district.

As much as the man tried to evade Swann, he now doggedly kept on his trail – the study of the map paying off in the way he had intended it to. There were no stallholders in the way this time and he saw the man heading for the riverside. By the time he reached the water's edge, however, it seemed Swann had lost his quarry. There seemed to be no one around. Then a noise perhaps, a sense maybe, made Swann crouch down, just as a shot rang out and hit a wooden post beside him. He now dived for cover behind a stack of boxes waiting to be loaded onto a boat.

Swann was pinned down behind the boxes but in his mind he pictured the map and traced a route which would allow him to come up behind where he believed the would-be assassin was hiding. He readied himself and then ran across the open space and back up Avon Street. He had made it. Either the man had not seen him, or else he had gone. Swann ran along Corn Street and then through a maze of alleyways and passages until he found himself at the bottom end of Horse Street, by the Old Bridge. From here, he could now see the man crouched behind a large bush, obviously still believing Swann to be hiding behind the boxes and waiting for him to appear.

Swann took out his own pistol and aimed it at the man. He fired one shot and hit the man in the arm, causing him to scream loudly as he dropped his weapon. It was an intentional wounding shot on Swann's part, as he wanted to question the man. Swann ran forward and grappled the wounded man to the ground. Although bleeding from the arm, the man managed to stand up and a furious struggle ensued. As they wrestled with each other, their eyes met and Swann's assumption as to the man's identity was now proved correct.

Before he could do anything further, however, another shot rang out. Swann took a step back and saw the blood on his jacket. It took him a moment or two, however, to realise that it belonged to the other man, who had inadvertently shot himself in their struggle. The man, fatally shot through the heart, fell backwards into the river. As Swann looked over the edge into the water, he could see the material covering the man's face had snagged on the branch of a submerged tree trunk. The body stayed there for a few seconds, resisting the strong current, until the material began to unravel, causing the body to turn several times and the man's features to be finally revealed. It was Tyler. His body then turned face down and was swept away towards Bristol.

Swann made his way back out of the Avon Street district with several thoughts running through his head simultaneously. Had he been set up by Lockhart? It seemed too much of a coincidence. For now, however, he decided to say nothing but would watch the man closely and begin his investigation of him. Swann could only assume Wicks was behind this, so he would have to be doubly on his guard from now on. He wanted to protect Mary but he would not be frightened out of the city. He still had a murderer to catch by the name of Malone.

Swann then retraced his steps back up Princes Street to Queen Square, the city already feeling just that little bit safer with Tyler now dead. He emerged once more into Queen Square, where he found George and Bridges waiting there with the captured driver held tightly between them.

CHAPTER THIRTY-ONE

'May I formally welcome you to Bath, Swann,' said Fitzpatrick, as he raised his wine glass for the toast.

'Thank you, Fitzpatrick,' said Swann, as he and Mary did likewise.

After the assassination attempt, Swann had returned home and informed Mary about Fitzpatrick's invitation, but not his meeting with Lockhart or the drama that had unfolded afterwards. They had taken a carriage at the appointed time to Fitzpatrick's house, which was located near the middle of Camden Crescent and the magistrate had personally greeted them at the front door. Fitzpatrick lived with a small number of domestic staff, his wife having died a few years earlier. His decorative style was subdued, though tasteful and Swann made a number of complimentary remarks as they were ushered through the house to the dining room. It was now dark outside but during the day, so Fitzpatrick told his guests, the view from the window included a castle. It was a 'sham' castle, he explained, as only the front façade of it had been built, but nevertheless gave the appearance of a complete castle and what had been Ralph Allen's folly, was now enjoyed by all the residents on this side of the city.

Fitzpatrick had moved into his house in Camden Crescent not long after it had been completed, in the early 1790s, and whereas his office in Queen Square had seen its prestige diminish, that of his residential address had lately risen. None of which mattered in the slightest, however, to Fitzpatrick, as Swann had quickly realised.

'You must be pleased your brother is staying longer in Bath,' said Fitzpatrick, addressing Mary.

'It is most pleasing, although I hope he does not bring his work back to Great Pulteney Street,' she replied. 'I do not think Emily or my nerves could stand it.'

'That is why I have asked Fitzpatrick to secure rooms for my business.'

'Yes, and I have secured some in Gay Street,' said Fitzpatrick. 'No. 40, on the first floor, near the rear of the house. I believe they will prove satisfactory.'

'Thank you,' said Swann. 'I am certain they will.'

'If you believe Tyler to be Evans' murderer,' said Fitzpatrick, after Swan had outlined the morning's events, deliberately not mentioning how the pickpocket and would-be assassin came to be killed, 'then that could be your first case solved in the city, Swann.'

Fitzpatrick again raised his glass.

'Thank you, my friend,' said Swann. 'I could not prove it in court, other than by providing circumstantial evidence, but my instinct tells me it is so.'

'So is there anything else I can do for you during your stay? I can put one of my carriages at your disposal.'

'That would be most appreciated,' said Swann.

'And I can spare a couple of men, whenever you require them.'

'Thank you Fitzpatrick, but I believe I have already dealt with that particular requirement. There are a couple of men I have engaged, who I believe will be more than adequate.'

Fitzpatrick noticed that another bottle of red wine was required.

'If I am not being too forward,' said Swann, 'may I suggest you have served the bottle of wine I brought? I believe you will find it most agreeable.'

'Very well, Swann, I will go by your judgement,' replied Fitzpatrick.

The bottle was brought and each of their glasses filled. Fitzpatrick tasted the wine and his expression became one of elation.

'What is it, Fitzpatrick?' said Swann, knowing only too well the reason for his companion's expression.

'This is the most incredible wine. From my initial impression I would say it is French claret, so almost definitely it derives from the Bordeaux area.' Fitzpatrick tasted it again. 'There is a masculine quality about it, so much so I could only assume it derives from the Médoc region, more specifically from Paulliac perhaps.'

Swann nodded. 'Your taste in good wine is exemplary, Fitzpatrick.'

'If that is the case then,' continued Fitzpatrick, now excited, 'I can only believe what we have here is either from the Lafite or Latour wineries.'

'Your powers of deduction do you credit, Fitzpatrick. What you hold in your glass is indeed from Chateau Lafite, of the '87 vintage.'

'An '87 Lafite, incredible. But where did you come by this?'

'It was given to me by the proprietor of the White Hart Inn, in Stall Street.'

'Pickwick! But his taste in wine is infamously inept, he is renowned for it.'

'Evidently, as this is how I came by this bottle. I was in his establishment this afternoon when I chanced to overhear him in conversation with a wine seller. Pickwick was about to purchase two dozen cases of, well being diplomatic, wine that was being completely misrepresented by the other man. I merely informed Pickwick of this situation while the merchant was otherwise disposed. And in his gratitude he offered me any bottle from his cellar. I can only assume the Lafite had been laid down there by one of his predecessors who knew about wine. I did attempt to compensate him for it, as I felt my paltry advice was not worth such a prized wine, but he insisted.'

'Well, his loss is our gain,' declared Fitzpatrick, taking another sip. 'Your brother certainly has a way about him, Mary, would you not agree?'

'I would most adamantly agree with you, Henry.'

'Then let us all drink a toast with this wonderful wine to Swann's way.'

They raised their glasses and after clinking them together, toasted in unison: 'Swann's way.'

VOLUME II
SWANN AND THE FUTURE PAST

PROLOGUE

The snow was falling in flurries as the flat-bed wagon careered up Cavendish Road, in the upper part of the city, and headed for the junction of Sion Hill. On reaching the intersection, it turned right and continued to climb again towards Lansdown Crescent. Once there, the driver instigated the whip and urged the solitary horse on even faster. As they raced across the level but white-shrouded cobblestones the ends of the scarf that masked the driver's features billowed out behind him into the cold night.

At the far end of the crescent another carriage came into view; its occupants, two elderly sisters, being driven home from their regular weekly excursion to the dress ball at the New Rooms. Their numerous ailments precluded participation in dancing there, so to compensate they fully immersed themselves in the latest gossip, both the receiving and distribution of, and tonight had been no different. Inside the carriage they were in the process of briefly revisiting the evening's highlights, which would be more substantially explored over a late-night sherry or two on their return to Somerset Place, the small enclave off the main crescent.

Within moments the two vehicles found themselves in direct collision on the crescent's curving concourse. It rapidly became apparent that the driver of the wagon had no intention of slowing down or changing direction and so it was left to the sisters' driver to veer off at the last moment. As he did so, the wheels of the carriage skidded across the slippery surface and onto a steep slope, causing it to tip over and trap the elderly ladies inside.

With the overturned carriage left in its wake, the wagon negotiated the sharp corner into Upper Lansdown Mews and its single track alleyway. It sped off once more up the steep incline, this time narrowly missing a couple engaged in carnal relations within the shadows. The girl of the town stood up from her kneeling position, from where she had been servicing her well-heeled gentleman client, and they both angrily gestured at the wagon as it hurtled off away from them.

The abrupt manoeuvre around the tight bend, however, had dislodged a loose covering in the back of the wagon and as its driver continued his reckless journey upwards, the top half of a gagged and tied girl now lay exposed behind him, her eyes wide in terror as she continued to be tossed around the flat wooden boards.

The girl had not recognised her assailant when he grabbed her, as it had been dark when she had left her place of employment and the man had come at her from behind. Even when she was being tied up and bundled into the wagon, a scarf covered his features. There was something familiar about him though. She had no idea what it is was, what he wanted, or where she was being taken to; only that she was cold, frightened and wanted to be any other place but here.

As the full moon became enveloped in a blanket of cloud and the lights of the city diminished far away into the background, the wagon finally ascended the summit of Lansdown Hill. Here, it turned into a small lane and traversed the virgin snow-covered ground to the end of it.

Ahead lay the woods.

CHAPTER THIRTY-TWO

The White Hart was its usual hive of early morning activity, reflecting its place as one of the main coaching inns in Bath. Jack Swann sat drinking a black coffee at what had now become his regular table. A copy of *The Times* lay spread out in front of him. At present his attention was being divided three ways: reading the obituary section; watching passengers as they boarded various coaches outside; and finally, and perhaps of most personal interest, eavesdropping on the nearby conversation between the proprietor of the establishment and a wine merchant.

'So Mr Pickwick, to clarify your order, you will take two cases of the Spanish *Vino de La Tierra*, at thirty shillings each, and three cases of *Vino de mesa* at twenty-five shillings each.'

Pickwick nodded.

'You are certain you will not take any hock? The price is only fifteen shillings per case.'

'My clientele here at the inn do not care for German wine.'

'Not even at this price?' asked the wine merchant. 'I secured them at auction recently. They are unlabelled but the paperwork is all in order.'

'I am certain,' replied Pickwick, but as he spoke he looked over the other man's left shoulder to where Swann was now shaking his head.

'Will you excuse me one moment,' said Pickwick to the merchant. The man nodded. 'I shall use your back room,' he said.

As soon as the merchant had left, Pickwick came over to Swann.

'How am I doing, Mr Swann? I believe I was making a good deal but you do not seem to agree.'

'It is not a bad deal, Mr Pickwick, but you are also passing up the opportunity of a most agreeable transaction.'

Pickwick looked puzzled.

'The hock, Mr Pickwick.'

'The hock?' repeated Pickwick, disbelievingly.

Swann nodded.

'But my clientele do not … '

'Whatever the paperwork may say,' said Swann, 'I would suggest you buy as many cases as the merchant holds.'

Pickwick looked hesitant. Swann smiled.

'To put your mind at ease, I will stake half of what you purchase and if your clientele do not take to it, I shall acquire the remainder from you at no loss.'

It seemed too good a deal to be true and the proprietor's expression showed his scepticism.

'You have my word,' said Swann. 'Besides, how did your clientele receive the case of Portuguese Madeira you purchased last week?'

It was now the turn of Pickwick to smile. As he did so, Swann gestured to him the return of the wine merchant.

'And the Spanish wines?' Pickwick asked.

'That is your choice,' replied Swann discreetly, 'but he is overcharging you by at least three shillings on each case.'

Pickwick nodded his thanks and went back to where the merchant waited.

'I have had a change of heart,' said Pickwick, loud enough for Swann to hear. 'How many cases of hock do you have for sale?'

'I have six cases,' replied the merchant.

This number caused Pickwick to hesitate and he instinctively turned to Swann, who nodded his approval. For a moment the merchant eyed up the proprietor suspiciously but any doubt was dispelled by Pickwick's next sentence.

'I wish to purchase all the half dozen at fifteen shillings per case …'

The merchant could not believe his luck, as he had only paid five shillings a case for them.

'… but I will rescind my Spanish order,' added Pickwick.

The wine merchant looked confused.

'I do not understand,' he said.

'Well, perhaps if they were a little cheaper …' replied Pickwick, now with a new-found confidence, '… say by five shillings a case.'

The wine merchant realised he had been caught inflating the prices but had no intention of admitting it.

'I am an honest man,' he said, 'and even at the price I am offering them to you I will almost be losing money.'

'Then, I am perhaps having second thoughts about the hock as well.'

In the time since Pickwick mentioned the reduced price of the Spanish wines, the merchant had used it wisely, re-calculating his outlay and income. Even at a five-shilling reduction, he concluded, the transaction would still give him a very agreeable profit overall. And he would finally be rid of the cheap hock.

'Three shillings off each case is the best I can do,' said the merchant, offering up the opening salvo of what he antici-pated to be a short bout of bartering.

'A deal!' declared Pickwick, and before the merchant could say any more, the proprietor had taken his hand and shaken it to seal the transaction.

'I will start to unload the cases around the back,' said the bemused merchant, knowing something had just happened to which he was not privy.

The merchant left to begin unloading and Pickwick came over to Swann.

'How did I do in conducting my business?' asked Pickwick.

'Like a professional wine-buyer,' replied Swann. 'That was inspired to ask for a five-shilling reduction.'

Pickwick smiled at this compliment of his financial acumen.

'I am once more indebted to you, Mr Swann,' he said. 'Is there anything I can do for you?'

'Yes,' replied Swann, taking out his bill-purse to pay for his half of the recent purchase. 'You can organise delivery of the three cases I have just bought. Two cases are to be taken to my address in Great Pulteney Street and the remaining one is to go to the magistrate, Mr Fitzpatrick, at this address.'

'Certainly, Mr Swann,' said Pickwick, taking the card from Swann.

'And what is the wine, really?'

'It is best you do not know,' said Swann, 'but I would advise that you charge your top price for a glass and if there is any protest, let them taste it first. I guarantee you will receive no complaints then.'

'I am obliged to you, Mr Swann, and I bid you a good day.'

Swann nodded.

Pickwick turned and walked off, rubbing his hands at this most recent and agreeable transaction.

Swann returned to reading *The Times* buoyed by the knowledge of the wine he had just purchased. It was always a good way to begin the day, although today's purchase was especially satisfying. He had settled into a routine of sorts since coming to Bath, having now been here more than a month. He would leave the house he shared with his sister in Great Pulteney Street around eight o'clock in the morning, undertaking a contemplative-paced stroll to the White Hart, where he observed the comings and goings of various people, read the papers and, like this morning, occasionally participate in Pickwick's wine dealings. He would stay there until the Royal Mail coach passed by outside, around half past nine, on its way to The Three Tuns Inn down the street. He would then leave the White Hart to see who had arrived on the coach and collect any post from London. There were a couple of outstanding investigations which had been put on hold since his departure to Bath, but a lawyer acquaintance kept him updated on any developments through regular correspondence.

Although Fitzpatrick had procured rooms for Swann on the first floor at No.40 Gay Street, where he could receive potential clients or interview witnesses, he found it more conducive, at least during the earlier part of the day, to be out in the city. And it was here, at The White Hart, where the most vital information could be gleaned, either through overheard conversations or chance remarks, the reading of local newspapers, or else the observation of people going about their daily business. And as for the comings and goings of the criminal fraternity, he had secured the services of George and Bridges, who had become his eyes and ears inside the Avon Street district, the most notorious area within the city.

As he took a mouthful of coffee, Swann's thoughts returned to the overheard conversation he had chanced on in a London public house several weeks before; the one which had prompted him to Bath in the first place. Although the Malone it concerned was not the one Swann had sought all these years, but his twin brother, the connection between the family and the city had been established. And, along with the possible sighting by Swann, after his arrival, of *the* Malone's accomplice on that murderous night, he had decided any further quest for his father's killer, at least for the time being, should be conducted within this particular metropolis.

He had just finished reading the final obituary in *The Times* when George and Bridges entered. Their shabby clothes and bare feet were, as always, in marked contrast to the majority of the well-dressed clientele that frequented the coaching inn, either as guests staying in the rooms above or else as passing travellers using it as a welcome break before continuing on their journey. The two men headed over towards Swann and as they did so, he folded the newspaper. He smiled as he noticed George's black eye.

'The husband of a lady friend arrive home early again, George?' asked Swann.

'No, Mr Swann, I got this from one of Wicks' men.'

Swann's amused expression vanished and he said, 'I'm sorry to hear that, George. How did it happen?'

'It was on account a couple of them didn't take kindly to us asking about your Scarred Man, Mr Swann.'

'Then forgive my teasing of you George and I apologise if I have caused you both to become embroiled in an affray.'

'It was nuthin' we couldn't handle, sir.'

George's companion began to sign.

'Bridges says you should see Wicks' men, though,' said George.

'I would not have expected otherwise,' replied Swann, with a wry smile.

On reading Swann's lips, Bridges grinned and covertly revealed the knuckleduster hidden in his coat pocket.

'I wonder why they were so aggrieved!' said Swann. 'But were you able to ascertain anything nevertheless?'

'Nuthin' sir. But if I may beg your pardon, Mr Swann, if we had more to go on … men with scars in that part of town is two a penny.'

Bridges nodded in agreement as he watched George speak.

'I know gentlemen, but unfortunately any further description I could supply may be too long ago to be of any use in the present.'

'All right, Mr Swann, we shall keep askin' with what we have: a Scarred Man with a possible connection to London.'

'Thank you,' said Swann.

Bridges tugged at his companion's sleeve and signed again.

'He asks if you have any other jobs for us today, Mr Swann,' said George.

'Yes, I do,' replied Swann. 'How does an outing to Bristol sound?'

Both men's faces instantly lit up.

'Bridges has never been to Bristol before, Mr Swann.'

'But *you* know the city, George?'

George nodded. 'I've been there once, sir.'

'Good,' said Swann. 'I want you to follow a certain gentle-man while he is there. And you'll be pleased to know that for this undertaking I have something more instructive than a verbal description.' Swann produced a small sketchbook and opened it at the pre-marked page containing a drawing of a man's head and shoulders. It was of Edmund Lockhart, his sister's suitor. 'You do not need to know the man's identity, but I believe he will be on this morning's Royal Mail coach. I want you to board the coach when it stops outside The Three Tuns and then report back to me this man's movements while he is in Bristol. But I do not want him to realise he is being followed.'

'We'll be like shadows, sir, as always,' said George.

'Very good,' replied Swann, as he put the sketchbook back in his jacket pocket and took out a small brown envelope, which he handed to George. 'The coach tickets are inside and there is enough money to adequately cover your vitals.'

'Thank you, sir,' said George.

'You are welcome, George.' Swann then put his hand in a dif-ferent pocket and produced a handful of loose coins. 'And this is a little extra for a few mugs of ale. Consider it as payment for the trouble you both encountered last evening on my behalf.'

Bridges and George both grinned widely.

'Thank you again, Mr Swann,' said George.

As George went to take the coins, however, Swann closed his fingers around them. 'You can each have one mug of ale with your food,' said Swann, 'but the rest is to be consumed *after* you have accomplished what I have asked. Is that understood?'

As the two men nodded, Swann opened his fist to let them collect the coins.

'I know you will not let me down,' said Swann, with a discerning expression. 'The Royal Mail coach returns to Bath, on its way back to London from Bristol, at half past eight this evening, so I suggest we meet at the Fountain Inn around nine o'clock. Enjoy your day, gentlemen.'

George and Bridges bowed respectfully and headed excitedly towards the exit, as if two children had just been let loose in a confectionary shop. As they went outside to the street, a magistrates' clerk rushed by them and entered the inn. He glanced around anxiously but on seeing Swann headed directly over to him.

'Mr Swann,' said the clerk. 'Mr Fitzpatrick supposed I would likely find you in this establishment at this hour.'

'Then he knows my routine well. But what is your urgency, sir?

'There has been an occurrence elsewhere in the city and Mr Fitzpatrick would value your opinion on the matter. His carriage awaits you outside, if you do not mind.'

Swann took the last mouthful of his coffee and stood up. 'Then let us depart immediately,' he said.

CHAPTER THIRTY-THREE

Mary stood in the middle of her drawing room in Great Pulteney Street perplexed. She had searched everywhere in the room – as well as having looked for it in her bedroom – or at least everywhere that she thought it might be. It was unlike her to misplace anything, but especially the small sketchbook, given she had been drawing the previous evening. She was certain her memory was not faulty in recollecting that she had put it away in the bottom drawer of her dresser, but even if that had been the case, it no longer resided there this morning. She had questioned Emily about its possible whereabouts, but to no avail. She would ask Jack on his return.

After her brother had decided to stay on in Bath, the days had naturally fallen, or so it felt to Mary, into a most agreeable and mutually beneficial routine. They would each rise around seven o'clock and while Jack went for morning coffee in town and to collect any post off the Royal Mail coach, she would busy herself with her ablutions. On Jack's return around ten o'clock, they would sit down to breakfast together and discuss any relevant matters of the day. Her brother had not returned for breakfast this morning, although this was not an unusual occurrence, so Mary had eaten alone.

She was now getting ready for Mr Luchini's arrival at eleven o'clock. Since the death of her mother, Mary had spent more time at home and a weekly art lesson being one of the activities she pursued. Mary had made her stand against the current conventions, she believed, by attending the ball whilst in mourning, but then had withdrawn from Bath's social life on, she felt, her own terms. And so consequently now only attended intimate dinner parties and private gatherings, or else immersed herself in long walks to the city's outlaying villages, such as Weston and Swainswick, when the weather was conducive and Edmund was free of business commitments; both of which seemed to have become rare of late.

The absence of these walks did not perturb Mary too much, however, as on her aunt's insistence she had recently begun a concentrated programme of reading. This consisted of several volumes borrowed from Harriet's own library and all of which had been written by women. Up until this point in her life, the subject of women's writing, or at least writing by women *for* women, had seemed too contentious for her to become involved in and she had always viewed that type of writing with trepidation. Her parents, although not outwardly condemning writing by such women as Mary Wollstonecraft or Hannah More, the latter having actually been a close neighbour at number seventy-six Great Pulteney Street until the previous year, had nevertheless not encouraged discussion of it either; despite her mother's appetite for gothic novels written by women. And whether by chance or design, her father's library contained only one book by a woman writer; Burney's *Evelina*, which Mary had retrieved the day of her mother's funeral.

The first major revelation on undertaking this course of reading, along with the lecture she had attended the previous month and also through discussions with her aunt, had been the realisation of the voluminous amount of books that actually existed whose contents could be described as radical and the number of women who had written them; going as far back as a century and a half before the present day.

For Mary, and she believed this to be true for many of her gender, any thinking about their status in society or indeed questioning women's position in life, had begun with Mary Wollstonecraft. When *A Vindication of the Rights of Woman* had first been published a decade or so ago, it immediately became notorious and brought vilification upon its author. Mary had yet to read the book, but what she did know about the contents, which had been received second or even third or fourth hand, was that the authoress' main idea – equality of women to men – was deemed far too dangerous for polite society. At least this was the belief held by many of the male members of her social world – and perhaps this included her brother as well – and, so she had heard on several occasions, any association with it would only lead to misfortune. The malice towards her namesake while alive continued in the present, six years after her death, and one particular venomous piece of prose she remembered reading recently advocated that her life and works should be read with disgust by every female who has any pretensions to delicacy, with detestation by everyone attached to the interests of religion and morality, and with indignation by anyone who might feel any regard for the unhappy woman, whose frailties should have been buried in oblivion. And yet, as Mary had now come to recognise, this tradition of 'dangerous writing' and vilification towards its creators stretched back further than she could ever have imagined.

'Now that you are truly an independent woman, you must learn to think like one,' Harriet had told her, as they stood together next to a bookcase containing what her aunt termed 'the collection'. 'And the first thing you need to do is begin a systematic and chronological reading of the writers I have assembled here.' Many of the volumes in the collection were either long out of print copies, or else privately published, but nevertheless they *existed*. Women it seemed, at least since the time of Shakespeare, had taken the time to reflect on the situations they had found themselves in, as part of the female race, and then had the courage to set those thoughts down on paper for publication.

The first writer Harriet recommended, as she pulled out several volumes of her work, was a woman with the unusual sounding name of Alphra Benn. Although born to neither position nor fortune, Benn had lived the most extraordinary of lives, during which she had travelled extensively, including to the West Indies, become a spy for Charles II, the reigning monarch, and had been an early advocator of the abolishment of slavery; the latter most forcefully promoted through her writing, Harriet explained, which she turned to in order to make money when she found herself imprisoned for the debts incurred during the King's service but which the monarch, either indifferently or deliberately, chose not to reimburse. So successful was Benn that she had become the first English woman to earn her living by the pen and her prodigious output, as Mary could see for herself, took up almost an entire shelf and included several plays, at least a dozen works of fiction, and many collections of poetry and translations.

'And yet, if you read any history of English literature,' exclaimed Harriet, angrily, 'it is as if she had never existed.'

Despite the immense success her work achieved during her lifetime, Benn was constantly ridiculed, belittled and verbally abused by male 'critics', who not only excluded her from their literary circles of power, but accused her of putting her name to works which had, they claimed, actually been written by her male lover. The final and most enduring insult though came after death, with her burial in Westminster Abbey. This was not in poets corner, however, as her achievements might suggest, but under the floor of a doorway, said Harriet, through which 'countless generations of feet would slowly erase her name, her reputation, and even her existence from the annals of literary history.'

If Benn had been one of, if not *the*, first woman writer to speak on behalf of her gender and question the imbalanced roles women and men occupied, then the writer of the volume Mary most recently finished reading carried this argument even further. *A Serious Proposal to the Ladies for the Advancement of their True and General Interest*, which had been originally published, Mary had noted, a century before Wollstonecraft's *Vindication*, made its central argument in a satirical but thoroughly entertaining manner. If men were seen to be superior and women silly, the authoress wrote, then it was because men had used their power to arrange society so as to reflect and continue this notion, thus allowing them to retain authority. But what was more incredible was that in many ways, women were blamed for these 'social arrangements' men devised. 'Women are from their very infancy debarred from those advantages,' the writer had argued, 'with the want of which they are afterwards reproached, and nursed up in those vices which will hereafter be upbraided to them.' It was a problem of education, it had been concluded. Men educated themselves, limited it to their female counterparts and then put the blame wholly on them because they were not educated! And what was more, it seemed, was that men preferred it this way. It reminded Mary what the speaker Catherine Jennings had so adamantly said the previous month about the Garden of Eden and the apple of knowledge. *'So partial are men to expect bricks where they afford no straw,'* Mary also now recalled reading somewhere recently. This *was* 'dangerous' writing indeed, yet at the same time she also experienced a strange sensation of realisation. If the talk at her aunt's house a few weeks earlier had been a spark to it, then the reading she had undertaken since had given rise to the full expression of viewing things in a totally different way for the first time in her life. And it was also after reading this particular book that she had begun to realise what her aunt had meant at the funeral of Mary's mother, when she remarked Mary had been educated like a man and it was now time for her to be educated like a woman. With the books she had already read and the ones Harriet had promised to continue sending to her, she now felt well on the way to attaining a 'proper' education.

Emily now entered the drawing room and announced Mr Luchini's arrival.

CHAPTER THIRTY-FOUR

Fitzpatrick's carriage turned into the narrow lane, at the top of Lansdown Hill, and its driver pulled on the reigns to bring the solitary horse to a halt alongside the morgue wagon. Swann stepped out and with the precise instructions of the magistrate's clerk echoing in his ear, followed a single track into the woods to where Fitzpatrick would be waiting for him. Behind him, the carriage now turned and began its journey back down to the city, returning the clerk to the desk in the Guildhall from where he had been summoned, not an hour beforehand, to find Swann and bring him to this location.

Swann deliberately walked on the track's edge as he made his way along, so as not to contribute to the number of footprints already visible in the snow-covered footway. There had been a heavy snow storm the previous evening and while the snow had all but melted in the centre by the morning, it remained here on the higher ground. At one particular spot, where the track opened out slightly, the various pairs of prints could be more clearly distinguished between one another and so Swann stopped. He brought out a different pocketbook to the one which contained Lockhart's portrait and made swift, but nevertheless accurate, sketches of each pair of boot prints, before continuing on his way through the woods. He reached a fork in the footpath but up ahead, on the right-hand side, now saw Fitzpatrick knelt down on the white ground beside a tree. As Swann approached, the magistrate stood up straight and dabbed his mouth with a handkerchief. A pale-faced Fitzpatrick then turned and saw Swann.

'Ah, Swann. Thank you for responding so promptly to my request. As you can guess, this is a most unpleasant business. The poor creature is through here.'

The men walked together in single file for a few yards, with Fitzpatrick in front, before coming out into a small clearing where two of Fitzpatrick's men stood guard. Behind them, Swann now saw, was a girl of about seventeen. She hung naked from the trees, suspended there by a number of ropes.

'I thought you would wish to view the body before we brought it down.'

'Yes, thank you Fitzpatrick,' replied Swann. 'What time was the girl found?'

'About six o'clock this morning. A gamekeeper on his rounds discovered her.'

Swann stepped forward and lifted up the girl's matted brown hair to reveal a bruised neck.

'From those markings around the neck,' remarked Fitzpatrick, as he watched Swann examine the girl, 'I would say she was strangled. Would you not agree?'

Swann did not reply.

'But what is your opinion as to these?' added Fitzpatrick, as he pointed to a couple of marks in close proximity on the right side of the girl's neck. 'You don't think these may suggest the murderer was a vampi …'

'Fitzpatrick, you surprise me,' said Swann. 'Do you really believe this girl will fly off like a bat when night falls?'

'Sorry Swann. But what do *you* think made them?'

Swann leant forward and inspected the twin marks more closely. 'These were inflicted by a type of sharp instrument, not human teeth.'

'But why, if she was strangled?' asked Fitzpatrick

'I do not know yet,' Swann now took a step back and stood beside Fitzpatrick, 'but I have seen enough for my requirements. I appreciate the fact you waited for me, but we need to give this unfortunate child some dignity now.'

Fitzpatrick nodded and gestured for his men to begin untying the body.

'Do we know her identity?' asked Swann.

'No,' replied Fitzpatrick. 'Her clothes were discovered nearby though and on them was what might be ink from a printer's press. On my return to my office, I will dispatch an officer to visit all the printing establishments in the city.'

Swann nodded his approval.

'I have to return to the magistrates' court now, as a sordid case of blackmail requires my presence,' said Fitzpatrick.

Swann was already elsewhere in his mind, however, scanning the scene and trying to reconstruct the sequence of events in his head.

'Swann?'

'What? Oh, yes. I will call on you later at your office, Fitzpatrick. I wish to stay here for the present time.'

'Very good. I will instruct my carriage to return for you?'

'That will not be necessary.'

'But how will you return to town without transport?'

'A constitutional walk,' replied Swann. 'It will allow time for contemplation, especially as the weather now seems to be set fair.'

'Then I shall await your visit later,' said Fitzpatrick. He gestured to his men to pick up the makeshift stretcher with the girl's covered corpse upon it and then strode off back through the woods towards his carriage.

The two men picked up the stretcher and began to follow the magistrate.

'Wait!' ordered Swann.

The men did as they were told.

'Show me the bottom of your boots.'

The stretcher-bearers exchanged a puzzled expression but nevertheless both lifted their boots as ordered.

'Thank you,' said Swann. 'You may go.'

By the time the men were out of sight, Swann had brought his pocketbook out and opened it at the page containing the footprint sketches. Beside two of them he wrote the word *F-men*, short for Fitzpatrick's men. Against another sketch he marked *F*; this was Fitzpatrick's boots, the pattern of which he observed as the magistrate knelt by the tree, having just been sick. This left two pairs, of which at least one, he assumed, to be that of the murderer.

Swann turned back towards the large tree from which the girl had been hanging and brought his mind to a place where he could begin to piece together what had occurred here and, in this way, begin the process of finding the perpetrator of this most heinous crime.

CHAPTER THIRTY-FIVE

After leaving Swann at the White Hart, George and Bridges had twenty-five minutes to wait before the Royal Mail coach was due at The Three Tuns. After a brief exchange of gestures between the two men, it became apparent that their opinion as to how to spend this time was divided. George was all for going to the Gallon Pot in Kingsmead Square for a few glasses of ale and to reacquaint himself with a couple of women he knew would be there at this time. Bridges, on the other hand, wanted to stay close to their departure point and suggested The Three Tuns, or at least the steps nearby, so as to be there when the coach arrived and make sure the man they had to follow was on it. Following another, slightly longer exchange of gesturing, which at one point became heated, they reached a compromise.

The building which housed The Bear was, in its early years, one of the biggest in Bath and this had gone a long way to securing the establishment's status as the foremost inn in the city. Its heyday had long since passed though, and for as far back as anyone could now remember, the site had been under constant threat of demolition. This being due not only to the questionable character of the present-day hostelry, but also because it had of late become a serious impediment to those visitors wishing to travel from the developments in the north of the city to the amenities in the centre.

For George, visiting The Bear meant a chance to meet the renowned, if slightly disreputable, barmaid who worked there, while at the same time Bridges would be afforded the opportunity to see the Royal Mail coach as it came along Cheap Street, so allowing them enough time to be able to board it. They entered the gloomy, subdued atmosphere which prevailed throughout The Bear and ordered a jug of ale between the two of them. George quickly engaged the barmaid in lewd conversation and, in his own mind at least, had immediately established a most promising rapport. Bridges took his glass of beer to one of the front windows to keep watch, but no sooner had he sat down than his thoughts swiftly turned to their journey ahead and the anticipation of leaving the city of his birth for the very first time.

As is often the way in such establishments, the marking of time can become disassociated with that of the outside world and whereas one might swear that only five minutes had passed, the reality is sometimes four-fold, and so the sudden appearance outside the window of a coach with its distinctive black and maroon panelling, red wheels and the Royal insignia emblazoned upon its door caught the daydreaming Bridges totally by surprise. Downing the remainders of their drinks the two men then consequently dashed outside. Ordinarily George would have been more reluctant to leave, especially as he had struck up such a promising conversation with the barmaid, but even he knew that if they did not board the coach they might not get any more work from Mr Swann.

By the time George and Bridges reached The Three Tuns, the post had been exchanged and the guard was announcing the last call for boarding: 'Gentlemen, take your places.' As the two companions climbed up on to the roof of the coach, Bridges handed over the tickets. There was a moment of suspicion on the guard's part, as the incongruity between the tickets and their owners' attire registered in his vigilant mind, but with the driver about to set the horses off and everything seemingly in order with the paperwork, he could do nothing other than console himself with the fact that the pair were not travelling inside the coach, with the more affluent passengers.

As the coach jolted and jarred its way through the streets of the city George and Bridges secured themselves the best they could and then exchanged a glance that expressed their pleasure at finding themselves riding on *the* Royal Mail coach and suggesting that 'this was the only way to live'. This unfor-gettable experience was made even more gratifying through seeing the disbelieving expressions on the faces of people they knew, as the two men hurtled passed them, waving from on top of the most prestigious carriage of its day.

The coach crossed over the River Avon by means of the Old Bridge and then continued along its south bank for some way, passing through the village of Twerton, and then out on to the open road to begin its journey proper.

Although for Bridges it was his first time out of the city boundaries, with the cool wind whipping through their hair and the autumn sun warming the skins of their faces, feet and hands, both men realised this to be one of the highlights of their lives and they were determined to enjoy every last moment of it. For the next hour or so it would take to cover the dozen miles to Bristol, they were kings of the road. Other travellers had to pull over to the side of the road at the sound of the coach's horn and with its constant ten miles an hour the coach maintained, other vehicles quickly disappeared into the distance. With the expansive fields and surrounding snow-capped hillsides stretching far out in front of them, along with the ale coursing through their veins, they felt invincible and the misery of their existence back in the Avon Street district was temporarily forgotten.

Halfway into the journey they passed Keynsham, 'a little dirty town' according to one traveller, somewhat derogatorily, beyond which lay a great mansion and stables, the latter housed in the most fantastic building the pair had ever seen.

The coach descended into the valley of the Avon, before climbing another hill as it continued on its journey. The river became visible only intermittently as they reached the outlying village of Brislington, which lay two miles south-east of their destination, but everywhere could be seen the veins of the coal mines which scarred the landscape. The valley now opened out once more, as the coach came down into an area known as Arno's Vale and carried on beside the river again, to begin the final stretch of road before reaching Bristol.

From their superior position on the roof of the coach, the exhilarated George and Bridges could now see the city of Bristol ahead. An ominous cloud of thick black smoke hung over many parts of the city, expelled from numerous furnaces and factories that belched out its waste day and night. Its acrid smell reached the companions' lungs while the vista became one of foreboding and 'impenetrable obscurity'; the crisp white landscapes of earlier now turned a dark, doom-laden grey. But they were men not easily perturbed and even if they were not certain of what lay ahead, they were determined to enjoy the experience once in the city.

The only consideration to dampen their elated mood though, was the question which had followed them all the way from Bath but only now, on seeing the city, became conscious in their minds. The question as to whether the man they had been asked to follow was a passenger beneath them. In their haste to board the coach, they had not been able to check who was inside and so would only find out once they reached Bristol.

CHAPTER THIRTY-SIX

Swann stood alone in the silence of the clearing and began to apply the System – his method of inquiry using 'givens' and 'assumptions' – to the events of the previous evening. Although Fitzpatrick had left the body as it had been found for Swann to examine, any other potential evidence from the scene had been mostly obliterated, unintentionally of course, by the magistrate and his men. From the observations Swann had made both here in the clearing and along the track, however, added to the information he had overheard at the White Hart Inn earlier, before the clerk had arrived, what he believed to be a fairly accurate reconstruction had begun to emerge in his mind.

Given that there had been a heavy snowfall the evening before, it could be assumed that any footprints along the track must have been made after the snow had ceased. The snowstorm had begun about half past eight and stopped around two hours later. Therefore, if one of the unaccounted sets of footprints belonged to the murderer, the crime he perpetrated had taken place after half past ten last night and before six o'clock this morning, the time when the girl's body had been discovered. Given the news he had heard at the White Hart Inn earlier, however, Swann felt confident in assuming it was nearer the former time of half past ten.

The Bridewell sisters' accident that had left them trapped but, as it transpired, merely shaken and unhurt in their overturned carriage the previous evening, had been the talk of the early morning conversations at Pickwick's establishment. To what degree the details had been exaggerated Swann did not know, but what seemed certain was that their carriage had been in a near collision with a manically-driven wagon which, after failing to stop, had headed off towards the Lansdown area. Common sense suggested this was more than pure coincidence, especially as Swann had observed a third set of wheel markings – different to both Fitzpatrick's carriage and the morgue wagon – at the entrance to the woods, where he now made his way back to from the clearing. And so given that fact, it could be safely assumed that the driver of the wagon was the murderer.

The snow at the lane's end, where there was just enough space for a vehicle to turn, had been reduced to slush by Fitzpatrick's carriage and the morgue wagon, as they manoeuvred around for their return journeys. Nevertheless, Swann had been able to discern a third distinct set of wheels and from this he could imagine the wagon stopping and the killer jumping down onto the virgin, snow-covered ground. Given also that it was a solitary figure which had been spotted driving erratically the night before, it could be assumed that he committed the crime alone. The girl was perhaps in the back, tied up under some kind of covering. As Swann stood at the end of the lane, he stilled his mind and imagined himself in the mind of the driver.

The wagon had no doubt arrived in the lane not long after eleven o'clock, given the time of its near-collision at Lansdown Crescent. After jumping down from his seat, the driver had dragged the petrified girl from the wagon and hoisted her up onto his shoulder, as if a carcass of meat. He then made his way along the snow-covered track which led into the woods. The assumption that the killer was male was due to the size of the footprints left in the snow. A little way into the track he was briefly pulled back, as part of his victim's dress became caught on a branch of the tree and torn off, the small piece of fabric still hanging there the following morning when Swann had spotted it. It could be assumed the murderer was a little under six feet tall, perhaps five feet ten inches, given the height of the over-reaching branch where the material had snagged and the depth of the footprints in the snow, which Swann measured using a torn-off branch.

When making his observations on the track earlier, Swann had squatted down on his haunches and surveyed the various prints on the ground. When he had satisfied himself of certain facts he stood and carefully followed the half dozen trails belonging to Fitzpatrick and his two men, along with the two remaining sets and his own as well, back to the clearing. He could account for four of the half-dozen but the two other sets of footprints he could not. Swann assumed that at least one of them belonged to the murderer and this was the one with its prints deepest in the snow. The stretcher-bearers had obviously carried the girl back along the track, but these led in the other direction, while the final remaining set seemed also to have been carrying something, given the depth of its own prints, but they did not seem deep enough to suggest it was a human load.

After the branch had momentarily pulled him back, and with Swann back in the murderer's mind, he had continued on his way, through the woods and into the clearing. Here he set the girl back down onto her feet; a single, naked footprint in the clearing the only remaining evidence that this had happened. The murderer then untied the dirty rag which had muffled the girl's screams throughout her terrifying journey and discarded it onto the snow, within a clump of trees, from where Swann had retrieved it. A knife glinted momentarily in the moonlight and with several clean strokes the remainder of the girl's dress was cut and fell off her to the ground, leaving her body naked and shivering as she faced her abductor. The girl was turned around and shown the ropes that awaited her. Her eyes no doubt filled with absolute terror and her bladder control lost, as her abductor attempted to push her forward. The girl had perhaps attempted to resist at this point, but had simply not been strong enough. At exactly what time during this evil episode the girl had been murdered, Swann did not know, but he only hoped for her sake it had been swift and her suffering short.

Given the macabre nature and location of the murder scene, it seemed more than probable that it had been chosen and arranged earlier; leading Swann to assume the perpetrator visited the clearing at least once before carrying out the crime. This showed the killing had been premeditated, with the woods and this isolated spot in particular, selected specifically. Given that the scene had been so deliberately 'staged', and perhaps not only in order to terrorise the girl, Swann felt, it could be assumed that the location held significance or importance. Again though, Swann did not know what that might be at present. What he did know, however, was that the killer had been unskilled in his work and Swann believed this to be his first victim. No sailor would claim the knots that had bound the girl to the trees and no surgeon the knife wounds that peppered her body. Had the girl been part of a sacrificial rite? The scene seemed to have been put together quickly; too quickly in fact, to indicate the girl had actually been a victim of a genuine ritual. It therefore seemed to Swann to be the work of a person who wanted to *show* the scene rather than use it for a specific purpose. If this was the case, then what did the murderer want to show? And why was this particular girl chosen? Could any girl have carried out the same role, only this one was known to the murderer?

Swann picked up the branch again, the one he had used back at the track, and more out of a meditative practice rather than for further investigation, began to place it vertically within each of the footprints that still remained intact within the clearing. He left the naked footprint untouched but measured the footprints surrounding it; this was the spot where the murderer had brought the girl down, as one pair of footprints was etched less deep in the snow than the previous set immediately before. Swann squatted down beside them in contemplation.

Whatever Fitzpatrick may have thought, this killer was definitely of the human species. Swann then shook his head momentarily at the remembrance. He could understand that kind of superstitious nonsense in perhaps the uneducated circles that George and Bridges circulated, and possibly even from educated women who read too many gothic novels, the genre of writing that had become popular during the last few years, but Swann had been surprised to learn that Fitzpatrick might also believe it. This was perhaps it though; the scene was reminiscent of those found in the pages of that type of book. He wondered if there was actually significance to it, but before he could think further, a noise came from behind.

'She's gone then, poor lass,' said a voice.

Swann turned to see a man standing there.

'It was you that chanced upon her?' Swann asked, observing the recognisable clothes of a gamekeeper.

'A terrible sight to come across first thing in the morning,' the man replied.

'Indeed, at any time I would suggest,' said Swann. 'Did you remove or touch anything?'

'I am an honest man and a Christian one, Mr, er …'

'Swann. I am sure that is the case, sir, and I did not wish to imply otherwise. But I needed to ask. What can you tell me about the scene as you discovered it?'

'There is not much to tell, sir. I was shooting over in the woods to the east – it is the best time to catch rabbits you know, early in the morning – and I was making my way back to begin delivering them, when I came across this unholy sight.'

'May I enquire as to where you deliver?' asked Swann.

'I would rather not say, sir.'

'You were hunting illegally, then?'

'No sir, this is my trade and I am allowed to pursue it honestly, it is just …'

'Just what?' said Swann.

The gamekeeper remained silent.

'May I remind you an innocent girl has been murdered here. Now what are you not telling me?' demanded Swann.

'Well sir,' the gamekeeper now spoke, 'one of my customers is a very private man and he does not like his business known by anyone, even the fact he gets rabbits from me.'

'Would I be correct in believing that you were on your way there when you found her?'

'That is right, sir.'

'Very well, I will not pry into your business further. It is the facts at this scene which are important and not who you were delivering rabbits to.'

'Thank you, sir. Will that be all?' asked the gamekeeper.

'Yes, thank you,' said Swann. 'Although is that your cottage over on the hill, in case I require any further information?'

'Yes sir, it is.'

'Thank you,' said Swann, once more.

As soon as the gamekeeper had gone, Swann crouched down and looked at the freshly-made footprints. They were analogous to one of the unidentified sets but only less deep. A few moments later Swann stood and marked the fifth sketch in his pocketbook with a *GK*, eliminating the gamekeeper as a suspect: the earlier, deeper footprints, he now realised, created through the carrying of his rabbits.

And then, beside the one remaining set of footprints Swann had yet to identify, he wrote the letter *M* for murderer.

CHAPTER THIRTY-SEVEN

'No, no Miss Gardiner. Your stroke is still too heavy. A delicate touch is required, a *delicate* touch.'

'But Mr Luchini, perhaps I have no feeling for it?'

'And yet it is on your insistence that we are painting land-scapes. It is on *your* insistence.'

For a few moments the elderly Italian art teacher and his pupil remained in silence, as they contemplated the half-completed landscape on the easel in front of them, before Mr Luchini felt compelled to expand the point.

'The more delicate the touch,' he explained, 'the more an observer will be taken in to the scene you have created. Your aim should always be to transport the person viewing your painting into the very landscape itself. With this view of Bath, for example, the intention is that you want someone in London looking at it to feel transported to the city, as if they are here.' He stroked the graying hairs of his untidy goatee beard and continued. 'That is why painting exists, to carry people elsewhere. But you do not feel it within you, do you Miss Gardiner? You try to do two things at one time and therefore become, how you say, confused.'

'What do you mean, Mr Luchini?' asked Mary.

'You attempt to paint what you believe the observer wants to see, while at the same time being drawn to wanting to paint what *you* see. Do you see?'

'I am afraid I do not, Mr Luchini,' replied Mary truthfully.

'You are afraid of your gift, Miss Gardiner. You are scared to express yourself fully as a painter, or at least as a landscape artist. And because of this, you move the brush too heavily on the canvas. The brush should caress the canvas, like this.'

Mr Luchini took the brush from the easel and softly brought it across the canvas, then made another stroke next to it, only heavier.

'Do you see the difference?' asked Mr Luchini.

'I think so,' replied Mary.

They stared at the two splurges of paint on the canvas with Mr Luchini glad to have been able to illustrate his point, while Mary, despite what she had said, still unable to see the difference between the two strokes. As they continued to stand transfixed in their silence, they heard someone enter through the main door of the house and a few seconds later Swann appeared at the entrance to the room.

'Jack, you were not expected at this hour,' said Mary.

'I have returned only briefly to consult a particular volume,' he replied.

Mary made the introductions and the two men acknowledged each other.

'I look forward to seeing your work at the gallery tomorrow, Mr Luchini,' said Swann. 'Mary was most insistent that I should attend but I do not require any coercion to view an exhibition by the finest Italian painter of landscapes at present in England.'

'That is too kind of you, sir, too kind,' replied Mr Luchini.

'So, what do you think of my landscape, Jack?'

'You wish me to be honest, Mary?'

'I would wish nothing else.'

'Then I would have to say that your strokes are too heavy.'

Mary sighed in frustration.

'Ah, it is like there is an echo, Mr Swann, an echo. Your sister's ability resides in the painting of faces, not trees and grasses.'

'I believe you are right, Mr Luchini,' said Swann.

'The portrait work in her sketchbook is excellent, most excellent,' continued Luchini, 'most life-like and many of them drawn from memory, I believe. Have you seen these portraits, Mr Swann?' the Italian art teacher enquired.

'My sister has yet to grant me that pleasure, Mr Luchini.'

'And I am no longer able,' interjected Mary, 'as the sketch-book is now lost.'

'Lost?' said Mr Luchini, 'Oh, the tragedy, the tragedy.'

'Indeed it is Mr Luchini. I was not able to locate it before your arrival this morning and I fear I shall not be able to do so after you have left.'

Swann turned to his sister. 'I am certain it is not lost Mary, merely misplaced and will be found before the day is out. But now, I must continue on my way. It was a pleasure to meet you Mr Luchini.'

'The pleasure is entirely mine, Mr Swann, entirely mine.'

As Swann left the room he covertly patted his jacket pocket to make sure the sketchbook still resided within it. He then went to his sister's room and after he had replaced her sketch-book in the bottom drawer of the dresser from where he had earlier taken it, continued upstairs to the library.

CHAPTER THIRTY-EIGHT

Lockhart sat silently as he gazed out of the window. Things had not proceeded according to plan this morning but then that seemed to have been the way lately. It had been a somewhat turbulent year overall, although he had come through it largely unscathed, as he usually did. And this time, of course, was the additional bonus that at last his abilities and skills had been recognised for what they were and he was being handsomely rewarded for them.

Although he spent time in London, as he had done so the previous day, his visits were always brief and the place he now called home was Bath. In all his previous travels he had not spent any length of time in the city and that had been one of the reasons they had chosen it as his new base. Making the acquaintance of Kirby in London, earlier in the year, had been the turning point to his change of fortune, or so he believed, as he was certain that the series of fortuitous events which transpired since then had been in some way connected with that meeting.

Lockhart had, at one time, held notions of becoming a Member of Parliament, relishing the exemption from arrest the position carried with it, but he no longer needed that kind of protection; he belonged to a world which provided him with all he required. And yet he still did not feel completely safe, the letter he had received the day before, at the London hotel he used when staying in the capital, had seen to that. He would deal with it of course, as he always did, employing his quick wits and steely nerves that he had put to such good use during the preceding years.

And then there was Mary, sweet dear Mary. He had taken a shine to her the very first time he had seen her and although knowing he should not, given the implied stipulations inherent of his current role, could not help conversing with her and not long after, instigating a relationship. He had been introduced to her by Kirby, through his magisterial colleague Fitzpatrick, at a social event in Bath, not long after he had arrived there. Mary had made an immediate impression on Lockhart. There was something independently spirited about her he liked, although what was more attractive to him was that she also seemed to possess a naivety of heart. The relationship had been progressing most agreeably until her mother had died and Mary's brother had arrived in Bath for the funeral.

There had been the initial complications, such as having travelled down on the same coach from London as Swann, and being indirectly involved in the assassination attempt on the man's life after meeting him in the coffee-house (although later finding out he had been more directly involved than he realised), but once again it seemed as if everything had worked out to his advantage, as Swann had seemingly relinquished any interest in him.

In many ways it would have suited Lockhart for the attempt to kill Swann to have been successful, but as he had subsequently found out from Kirby, it had been fortunate it had not. After the attempt, word had come down from London that Swann was to be left alone. He did not know why but he knew that you did not argue with orders from London.

He now smiled to himself as he thought of the sum of money he was going to receive later that day. Normally it would have gone to settle debts, but he no longer had any; they had been 'underwritten' as soon as he had begun working for *them*. Given the events of the last few days, however, he had no choice, he felt, than to move things along more quickly and so would spend it on a special gift, one that would bring him closer to all that he had ever wanted to achieve.

CHAPTER THIRTY-NINE

Thirty minutes after arriving at the house in Great Pulteney Street, Swann was again on the street and heading towards the city centre. It had been a fruitful search, as he had found what he was looking for in the volumes he consulted. He let the information percolate in his mind as he crossed over Pulteney Bridge and made his way up Bridge Street.

Swann was on his way to Fitzpatrick's office in Queen Square, but he wanted to avoid what he knew would be the late morning hustle and bustle of Milsom Street, so he chose a more circumvent route through the city. After reaching the top of Bridge Street, Swann crossed into Upper Borough Walls and at the end of it, made his way into Beauford Square, before turning right up into Princes Street. As he walked up to Queen Square, he remembered the attempt on his life the previous month, which had subsequently involved him chasing the would-be assassin, Tyler, down this particular street and on through the Avon Street district to the river; where in a final confrontation the pickpocket had been killed. Swann had been on his guard for further attempts on his life since, but so far no other incidents had occurred.

Swann came out into Queen Square by its south-west corner, next to number thirteen, with a 'lodgings available' notice in one of its windows. From there, he headed along the south side of the Square, towards Wood Street, and then up the east side to where Fitzpatrick's office was situated, around two-thirds of the way up. On reaching the building Swann went inside. He ascended the two flights of stairs and proceeded along the short corridor towards the magistrate's office, located at the front of the first floor. As the door was closed, he knocked on it and waited.

'Enter,' said Fitzpatrick.

Swann did so and found another gentleman with the magistrate.

'I apologise Fitzpatrick,' said Swann. 'I did not realise you had company.'

'No, come in Swann, you are most welcome,' replied Fitzpatrick, seemingly grateful for the interruption. 'This is Mr Tozer. Mr Tozer, this is Mr Swann.'

The two men nodded to each other cordially.

'Mr Swann is an associate of mine who is kindly offering his assistance in this dreadful business. And Swann, Mr Tozer is a publisher and both the victim's employer and guardian.'

'Then please accept my sympathies on both counts,' said Swann.

'Thank you,' replied Tozer. 'Lizzy is the daughter of my wife's sister, who passed away this year. She came to live with us about three months ago and also worked at my publishing company.'

'That is why she had ink on her clothing,' interjected Fitzpatrick.

'I cannot believe anyone would do this to her,' said Tozer.

'Please rest assured, Mr Tozer, that we shall do everything in our powers to apprehend the perpetrator of this terrible crime,' said Swann.

'This may be the easiest case you have ever been involved in Swann,' said Fitzpatrick. 'Mr Tozer believes he may have already identified the killer.'

Swann raised an eyebrow at this disclosure but said nothing.

'Please show my associate the manuscript, Mr Tozer.'

The publisher took out a loosely bound sheaf of papers from a brown sachet.

'This is the latest book from a writer that Mr Tozer's company publishes,' said Fitzpatrick, almost unable to keep in his excitement. 'Mr Tozer, please hand it to my associate.'

Tozer did as he was told. Swann looked at the handwritten title page. It read: *Blood for the Vampyre's Thirst* by Henry Gregor-Smith.

'Before you arrived here Swann, Mr Tozer informed me that there is a murder within the manuscript identical to that of his neice.'

Swann looked at Fitzpatrick and then at Tozer.

'I do not wish to pour scorn on your theory, and certainly not at this cheerless time, Mr Tozer,' said Swann, 'but surely this fact means only that the murderer is among those persons educated enough to be able to read.'

'But that is exactly the point, Swann,' said Fitzpatrick. 'Tell him Mr Tozer.'

'The manuscript has yet to be published.'

'That is right, Swann,' added Fitzpatrick, 'and Mr Tozer, please inform my associate where this Gregor-Smith resides.' Despite the tragic nature of the case, the magistrate's tone of voice could not conceal the exhilaration he felt at being able to reveal these facts.

'His residence is a grotesque building adjacent to Lansdown Woods,' said Tozer.

'This is more than coincidence, Swann,' Fitzpatrick exclaimed.

'Geographical proximity of a person's dwellings to a crime scene has never been any implication of guilt, Fitzpatrick.' Swann then addressed the publisher. 'Apart from yourself, who has access to this manuscript Mr Tozer?'

'Only the senior typesetter, Johnson,' replied Tozer.

'What about the editor of the book?'

'Being a relatively small publishing firm I undertake all the editorial work myself.'

'Would your niece have had access to the manuscript?'

'No. She may have seen one or two of the proofs but would not know what they said, as she could not read.'

'And when and where was the last time you saw your niece?'

'I left the office early yesterday afternoon but I had requested her to work late in order to get ready for a print-run today.'

'Did Mr Johnson work late yesterday evening, also?' asked Swann.

'I do not know; as I said, I left early.'

'But surely you would know which of your employees were working late, Mr Tozer?'

'Not all the time, as it depends on what work they are undertaking. What importance is it who was working late though, Mr Swann? I hope you are not suggesting that …'

'I am not suggesting anything, Mr Tozer. I am simply trying to establish who the last person to see your niece was, as they may possess valuable information regarding her murder. Do you know of any reason why your niece might have been killed?'

'No. She was a quiet girl, a good girl.'

'And where are your premises?'

'The company is located on the Bristol Road.'

Swann nodded at this piece of information. 'That makes sense.'

'What is it, Swann?' asked Fitzpatrick. 'Do you have some information?'

'There was an incident last night involving a carriage and a flat-bed wagon,' replied Swann. 'The direction from which the wagon traveled suggests it might well have originated from the Bristol Road. Mr Tozer, I suggest we hasten to your premises and discuss the matter of murder with this Mr Johnson.'

'He did not arrive for work this morning,' said Fitzpatrick, almost unable to contain himself at the amount of circumstantial facts that were openly displaying themselves, despite what Swann thought.

'Is this correct?' Swann asked Tozer.

Tozer nodded. 'He did speak of feeling unwell yesterday, but I cannot believe him to be the murderer. He was fond of Lizzy.'

'Nonetheless,' Swann said, 'I would still wish to visit this Mr Johnson, if only to eliminate him as a suspect in my own mind. If you would be so good as to write his address down, Mr Tozer.'

Although visibly reluctant, the publisher did as he was asked and handed the paper to Swann.

'Thank you,' said Swann. 'It is imperative to consider all possibilities if we wish to bring your niece's killer to justice.'

Swann held up the manuscript.

'And may I take possession of this for a while, Mr Tozer?'

'Well, I, er …'

'Rest assured the utmost care will be taken with it,' assured Swann.

Tozer nodded and then picked up his overcoat from the back of the chair on which he had been sitting.

'Gentlemen, if you will now excuse me,' Tozer said. 'I have to return to my business.'

'Thank you for coming in Mr Tozer,' said Fitzpatrick. 'You will be informed of any developments and once again, we are sorry to hear of your loss.'

As Tozer reached the door, however, Swann called him back.

'For my information, Mr Tozer, is Mr Johnson shorter or taller than yourself?'

'He is about the same height,' replied Tozer, somewhat puzzled.

'Thank you,' said Swann, 'that is all.'

Once Tozer had left the office Swann turned to Fitzpatrick.

'You will send a man to this address?' he asked, handing his companion the piece of paper Tozer had written on.

'Of course,' replied the magistrate, 'but why did you ask about the height?'

'I have calculated the murderer to be around five feet ten inches tall, which is around the same height as Mr Tozer, I believe. Therefore, as Johnson is the …'

'… same height, he is our man,' interjected Fitzpatrick.

'Again Fitzpatrick, as with geographical location, similarly physical attributes alone does not attest to one's guiltiness. But there is certainly something not right here,' continued Swann. 'I sense Mr Tozer to be protecting his typesetter, but for what purpose I do not know.'

'Well, I will bring this Johnson fellow to this office for your questioning later Swann, as I presume you wish to visit Mr Gregor-Smith first.'

Swann nodded and looked at the manuscript again.

Blood for the Vampyre's Thirst, a most anticipated read,' he said.

'I did not realise gothic novels were an area of interest to you, Swann?'

'The workings of a mind that devises such plots fascinate me, although I must confess I do derive certain pleasure from reading Gregor-Smith's books. I had no idea, however, that he resided in Bath.'

'If he is the writer I believe he is, he is a most reclusive and strange man. They say he sleeps in a coffin, employs disfigured servants and, according to a recent newspaper report, once served rabbit's blood to his guests instead of wine.'

'Fitzpatrick, really!' replied Swann. 'I feel that may be in the same fantastical realms as your earlier belief as to the killer being a vampire. Besides, whatever circumstances one chooses to live their life, why would the writer kill the girl?'

'To allow him to write his book more realistically,' replied the magistrate.

'The manuscript was already at the publishers when the girl was murdered.'

'Oh yes, I forgot that. So Johnson, the typesetter, *is* our man. Yes, it all makes sense,' continued Fitzpatrick. 'He knew the girl, he had read the manuscript and then, to crown it all, he does not turn up for work the day after the murder.'

Swann smiled at his companion's impetuousness. 'I grant you the odds do not seem to be in Mr Johnson's favour but I have to contemplate the facts properly before I can make any judgment. And I will know more once I have talked to Mr Gregor-Smith.'

CHAPTER FORTY

If Bath was the fashionable face of the South West, then Bristol was its heart; a busy sea port built up over the centuries from its location on the Severn estuary and which at certain times in its illustrious history, had been second only to London in terms of maritime importance. This is not to say it did not have areas of splendid architecture or pleasurable streets to rival its more illustrious and glamorous neighbour – Clifton being perhaps the most principal example – but above all it was a working city and most of the leisure activities available were pursued and conducted by those wealthy individuals passing through; either coming from or going to London. And although some of the acquired tastes of these affluent travellers were sometimes hard to satisfy away from the capital itself, there were always enterprising individuals who could cater for them.

Throughout the ages numerous kinds of cargo, including human, had passed through Bristol's docks and made its way either into the interior of the country, or else been exported to the foreign shores of the wider world. As the most traversable route between Bristol and London passed through Bath, a connection between the three cities was inevitable. There were many similarities that the triumvirate shared and one such aspect was a thriving market in prostitution. While each metropolis had its own districts and areas where ordinary inhabitants could indulge themselves, there was also a handful of more up-market establishments which provided for the well-heeled clientele that wished to be discreet in their liaisons and not run the risk of blackmail, while still within stylish surroundings. The Windsor Hotel, situated a little way out of Bristol's city centre, however, was not one of these establishments. A sign near its main entrance announced it had been built less than five years previously and yet within even that short space of time, it had fallen into disrepair and had acquired a reputation of being a sordid place where various kinds of business could be conducted without attracting attention to oneself but in less salubrious environs than the up-market ones.

Across the street from the Windsor Hotel, George and Bridges now kept watch on the building from their vantage point. Bridges was attempting to sign to George, but he pretended that he did not see his companion. He tried again but it was obvious George was deliberately avoiding eye contact, as if he knew what was going to be signed but did not want to acknowledge it. Bridges was equally determined, however, and tugged at George's sleeve.

'I know he's been in there a long time,' said George, somewhat annoyed, 'but we can't go in, he may see us, and you know what Mr Swann said.'

Bridges continued to sign between the pauses in George's replies, with their 'conversation' ending up somewhat heated.

'Why would he go out the back way if he don't know he's being followed … yes, I know we don't even know if it's him, but he was the only passenger on their own, so what else could we do … alright you don't have to keep on, I know we should've been outside the Three Tuns in Bath, like you said, rather than having a drink … hey, don't take that tone, the trouble with you is …'

Before George could finish his sentence though, Bridges nudged him forcefully and gestured to the hotel entrance. A gentleman with two well-dressed women, one on each arm, appeared at the doorway. The gentleman was bearded.

'Do you think it's him?' asked George.

Bridges signed.

'Yeah, I do too,' agreed George. 'He's got a similar build as the man we saw go in, but I know he certainly didn't have any women with him though!'

On arriving in Bristol the Royal Mail coach had made its way to the heart of the city centre and the final destination on its outward journey: the Bush Tavern. The famous coaching inn stood across from the main Post Office and the Corn Exchange, the latter having been the sole contribution towards the city's urban landscape by its close neighbour's most famous architect: namely John Wood of Bath.

When the coach stopped at the Bush Tavern, four passengers had alighted from inside; three gentlemen and a lady. The lady accompanied two of the gentlemen, while the remaining male had made off towards Baldwin Street. For a moment George and Bridges considered whether one of them should follow the group, while the other pursue the solitary gentleman, but they quickly decided it would not be practical, especially given Bridges did not know the city, so they stuck together and quickly hastened after the lone man. They had trailed him for about fifteen minutes through the streets of Bristol, until they had reached The Windsor Hotel and the man had gone inside.

Bridges now intently watched the lips of one of the women as she spoke to the bearded man. He then signed to his companion.

'So his name is Mottram, eh?' replied George, as the small group opposite now began to move off. 'That has to be the man Mr Swann wants us to follow. I say we go after them.'

Bridges nodded and the two thief-takers followed at a distance as the trio in front of them made their way down the street and around the corner. As soon as George and Bridges turned the corner, they were confronted with the sight of the gentleman in the act of hailing a carriage and in a few moments one had arrived and they were being driven away.

'What do we do now?' cried George, panicking.

Bridges, however, had already hailed another carriage and even before it had stopped the two men had bundled themselves in. The driver was suspicious of them, however, especially when George said they wanted to follow the carriage in front, but as soon as George had showed some of the money Swann had given them, the driver took off after the other carriage.

Although George recognised a few landmarks from his previous visit, as they continued on their way out of the city centre his recollections became vaguer, so much so that when their carriage came to a halt, George had to ask the driver what area of Bristol they were in. George paid the fare and both he and Bridges then got out. A little way ahead, the carriage carrying Mottram and the women had stopped outside an up-market looking establishment called The Beaufort Hotel. The passengers alighted from the carriage and entered the main door.

George and Bridges rushed over to the building. On reaching it, they peered through one of the hotel's large windows at the scene inside. The man they knew as Mottram and the two women sat in the foyer, on an elongated leather couch. From elsewhere in the hotel, a well dressed, rotund man approached the party. Mottram stood and they shook hands. From outside the window, George and his companion thought they saw a small packet pass between the two men, but they could not be sure. The women then stood and the quartet looked as if they were about to go in to the depths of the hotel. At the last moment, however, Mottram veered off from them and headed toward the main door. Outside, George and Bridges realised this fact too late and as Mottram came out onto the street, they were caught beside the window. Their unsuspecting quarry, however, walked right past them and headed in the direction of a sign which pointed towards the city centre.

'That was close,' breathed George.

Bridges signed in agreement, thought about it, and then signed once more.

'You're right,' said George, laughing. 'If he don't know we're following him, why were we worried. But yeah, we'll wait a little 'fore we start after him again.'

They waited until Mottram turned the corner at the end of the street and then hurried after him. As they rounded the corner, ahead they saw the man enter a jewellery shop. Ten minutes later he came out and then made his way back to the first hotel, the Windsor, with George and Bridges behind him all the way. Once there, Mottram went inside again.

George and Bridges were not quite sure what they had witnessed through their following of this man, but hopefully Mr Swann would be happy with the information. It was George's turn now to tug on Bridges' sleeve and for the other man to ignore it. Eventually though Bridges looked at George.

'We can watch what's going on from inside the hotel, we've done our job.'

Bridges signed.

'I know about being seen at the other place, but he didn't even look at us when he walked by. And we can find some-where in the hotel out of the way. Better to be inside with a glass of ale than out in the cold,' said George, the morning warmth of the sun having now been replaced by a decidedly colder afternoon.

Bridges agreed and they crossed the street towards the hotel entrance.

CHAPTER FORTY-ONE

Under the watchful eyes of a solitary stone gargoyle above the main entrance, the carriage with Swann inside arrived at Gregor-Smith's residence. He stepped out and addressed Fitzpatrick's driver.

'Wait for me,' said Swann.

The driver nodded as Swann turned and strode to the large wooden door. The imposing castle-like gothic building rose up far above him. He pulled a cord that hung by the entrance and a loud bell clanged inside. Swann then heard footsteps approach and a moment later the door opened and an oriental servant appeared.

'I am here to see Mr Gregor-Smith.'

'My master cannot be disturbed at this time.'

'This matter is of too great an urgency to wait,' replied Swann. 'I must insist.'

'My master has very strict instructions about visitors. I am sorry.'

From elsewhere within the building a disembodied voice called out. 'What is happening down there Sung-Lee?'

'A gentleman asks to see you but I have told him you are not to be disturbed.'

'Very good, Sung-Lee.'

'Please give this card to your master,' said Swann, 'and inform him it is of the utmost importance.'

The servant was reluctant but nevertheless took Swann's card and asked him to stay where he was. He then closed the door. A few minutes later the door re-opened and a somewhat puzzled looking Sung-Lee invited Swann inside. He followed the heavily limping servant into a huge living room where the extensive walls were decorated with numerous erotic frescos and large oriental rugs covered the floor. The servant then pointed to a stone staircase, which spiraled upwards.

'My master is at the top of the tower,' he said.

Swann went over to the staircase and began to climb the narrow stairs, which ascended in a clockwise direction. At intervals were small slit windows through which Swann could see further and further as he rose, until finally he was able to observe in the far distance the city of Bristol. At the top of the staircase was an archway, which led through to a turret room.

Gregor-Smith's writing room was small, made more so by the elaborate gothic decorations adorning the walls and floor and the large stone sarcophagus which occupied its centre. Inside reclined a gentleman dressed in a burgundy dressing gown. An opium pipe lay on a small table beside him and a writing tray rested on the man's midriff. As Swann entered, the writer raised his gaze towards him.

'Mr Swann, please do come in. I have been looking forward to meeting you.'

'You know me, sir?'

'The newspaper reports on your various exploits, since your arrival in the city, have whetted my appetite, although I do realise this is not a social visit.'

'Then you are aware of the reason for my being here?'

'Yes. When the gamekeeper delivered the meat for this evening's supper, news of the poor child in the woods accompanied it. Indeed, it was my own carriage which allowed the man to so promptly share the news with the authorities. And along with that newspaper coverage of your presence, I presumed I could expect a visit from you in the not so distant future.'

'I am intrigued. Exactly how did you arrive at this presumption?'

The writer took a toke from his pipe and then answered.

'To start with there is the close proximity of my residence to the actual murder scene. Apart from the association with the gamekeeper, either my good self or one of my servants may have seen or heard something. More than that, however, is the description of the scene itself, for did not the perpetrator replicate one of the murders from my most recent outpouring – the very manuscript of which you hold in your right hand. As this particular volume has yet to reach the unsuspecting public, the number of possible suspects is reduced dramatically. I would suggest that it only leaves myself, the publisher and perhaps an employee or two at his publishing firm as the guilty party. Forgive me if I have been remiss of anything.'

'No, that is an incredibly precise piece of deduction,' said Swann.

The writer held up his left hand in a gesture of modesty.

'Please, Mr Swann, it does not warrant your praise. I am a writer of fictional stories and so I am used to constructing plots, although from those recent reports of your exploits, this is much less than your own achievements. And given that I delivered the manuscript to my publisher last week, I would suggest that only a handful of people would have had access to it, or the time to read it, and added to this the fact I do not discuss my work with anyone else, it is therefore limited to those who I have mentioned.'

Gregor-Smith took another toke and inhaled deeply. This time he offered it to Swann, who politely refused.

'Besides,' Gregor-Smith continued, 'my being a suspect is similar to the plot of my first novel. A writer is accused of a murder copied from a story he has created. But tell me, Mr Swann, do you believe it is the writer in this case?'

'I consider all possibilities before making any judgements,' replied Swann.

'Surely you must have an intuitive feeling though,' the writer urged.

'I allow the facts as they reveal themselves to guide me,' said Swann. 'All else is conjecture and so the very antithesis of my mode of investigation.'

As Swann finished speaking he scanned a shelf located within an alcove of the turret room. The shelf contained numerous editions and volumes of the writers' own books. By the side, on a small table, however, was a manuscript. The title 'Susan' was handwritten on the front cover.

'I am familiar with your work,' said Swann, 'yet I do not believe I have read the volume you mentioned. It is this manuscript?'

'No, that was written by someone else, an aspiring local authoress. A mutual acquaintance asked if I would read it and pass comment on it. I dislike engaging in critical analysis of another writer's work, especially an unpublished one. All they really wish is to hear how it is the best writing you have ever read. If you start to point out any faults with it, however, they jump to its defence and quote a line or two from the work that supposedly addresses your criticism. Having said that though, this particular lady's writing is acceptable; the subject, a gothic parody, is timely; the locations are fitting and, if she continues to write, I would suggest she has a promising literary future ahead of her. I have yet to tell her this, however, and for all I know the manuscript may have already secured a publisher. As for *my* first novel, you have not heard of it for the simple reason that it was never published. After being rejected by several publishers, I burnt the manuscript in a fit of frustration.'

'Before the flames consumed it, what fate befell the story's writer?'

'He was found guilty and executed.'

'And was justice served?' asked Swann.

The faint trace of a smile appeared on Gregor-Smith's face. 'Only in so much as the manuscript deserved to be destroyed. The character of the writer required much more depth, the story was in need of proper structure and still being a tyro back then, the prose was far too putrid and purple.'

As Gregor-Smith finished talking, a small figure entered the room. It had the form of a child but was, in fact, as Swann now realised, a female dwarf. She carried with her a tray on which stood a glass of green liquid. Swann watched her as she went silently to the sarcophagus and put the tray down beside the opium pipe. She turned to leave, but kept her eyes averted from Swann and her face lowered.

'Martha, wait,' said Gregor-Smith. 'Has the amulet been located yet?'

The girl shook her head. As she did so, Swann noticed her face was disfigured.

'Ask Sung-Lee to search the grounds again.'

She nodded and then left the room.

'I do not know which I desire more,' said the writer, after the servant had left. 'The return of the amulet, which was a gift from a dear friend, or the potion it contains.' He took a sip from the glass and raised it toward Swann. 'I have this absinthe imported from France, covertly of course, it is the finest … '

'I do not wish to appear rude, sir,' said Swann, 'but my time is limited.'

'Yes, I apologise, I have digressed,' said Gregor-Smith. 'Mr Swann, I am thorough in my research but I only commit murder in my imagination. Contrary to the image portrayed in certain periodicals and newspapers, I promote life and compassion – as you have just witnessed with Martha.'

'May I enquire the origin of her disfigurement?' asked Swann.

'It was caused through the nightly torture endured from an Albanian brothel keeper, as entertainment for his clients. I "liberated" her somewhat surreptitiously when I passed through the country during my last Grand Tour. Mankind has a sickness, Mr Swann. We consider ourselves human, yet too many show by their nature to be otherwise.'

'You are right, sir. A man cannot hide from his true nature,' said Swann, 'as it will always expose him for what he is, eventually.'

'And what have you learnt so far about my true nature, Mr Swann. Although without wishing to slight your method of investigation, the questions you have asked are yet to be probing.'

'There is plenty to be ascertained without the need of words,' replied Swann. 'Answers can often be revealed without the necessity of asking questions.'

'And what have I revealed without words?'

'You advocate life and compassion but are drawn to death and horror,' said Swann. 'Yet, I do not believe you act the latter out in the real world, but only here, where you immerse yourself in their twin imagery; be it the stone casket which you write within, or the stories you create there.'

'You are right, Mr Swann. I have been fascinated by death for the whole of my life. I was a sickly child from the very day I was born, but became much worse at the age of four, after my father's death. I spent a year confined to my bed, with no doctor able to diagnose what was wrong with me. My mother, god bless her soul, read to me every day, although the only books in our house belonged to my late father's collection of macabre stories, which he himself had written, so I grew up listening to all manner of horrors. When I was well enough again, I used to visit the graveyard where he was buried and read his own stories back to him.' Gregor-Smith paused and took another sip of Absinthe. 'They have a separate section you know, for suicides. So I would spend my days reading grisly stories to my dead father, surrounded by the graves of people who, for one reason or another, found the will to live gone and had taken their own lives. It was only later though, that I would come to wonder what drives these people to take their own lives and subsequently devoted much of my writing to the subject of death.'

'And was there anything specific which made you interested in vampire lore?' enquired Swann, momentarily distracted by a painting hanging on one of the turret room walls.

'I presume it is the possession of someone else,' replied Gregor-Smith, 'the survival of one through the death of another. When I was younger I often wished my father had been a vampire, so he could have survived, but then I thought, why wish a person to continue an existence they wanted to end in the first place. But do we not all live in the shadow of the shroud of death in our own ways, if only we knew it. Do you believe in vampires, Mr Swann, and are you asking about my interest as you think one was responsible for the girl's death?'

'The answer to your questions is no on both counts, sir. This was definitely the work of a mortal man, although perhaps one attempting to make it look supernatural in order to create something that it is not. For that fact alone though, I believe there is a good possibility you are in some way being set up for the murder.'

'But who would do such a thing, Mr Swann? I am no doubt disliked by certain people but I am certain not to the extent that they would do something like this.'

Swann did not respond, his attention now completely taken by the painting on the wall. It was a portrait of an aged and decrepit-looking man. The subject had more than a passing resemblance to the writer but an older version, as it gazed corpse-like down into the room.

'I am cursed to write this material through my life circum-stances,' continued Gregor-Smith, 'but what does it say about those people who are fascinated by it merely for pleasure? I am not disagreeable to the financial situation, of course, as the money affords me the lifestyle I wish and the ability to lead a private life, away from the prying eyes of the public and press. What I find comical, or at least I would if it was not so damningly intrusive, is the press reaction to my work. They ridicule and even abuse me for my work within the pages of their newspapers and yet I am one of the best-selling authors of the genre. And they write such scandalous lies. Take a recent example. The gamekeeper that discovered the girl's body was stopped recently and questioned about me. Although he did not reveal anything, he was carrying rabbits with him and the next week there was an "exclusive" article regarding my use of rabbits for sacrificial purposes, when the only thing they were used for was Martha's stew. They also intercept my post, which is a complete breech of privacy, you would agree Mr Swann? Mr Swann?'

Swann's attention was still completely taken by the painting on the wall.

'Mr Swann!'

'I am sorry,' replied Swann. 'I was just looking at this portrait of your father, or is it an earlier ancestor?'

'That is not my father, nor indeed any ancestor Mr Swann. It is *my* portrait.'

Swann stared at the painting in genuine confusion. 'But this man looks older than you by at least thirty or forty years.'

'The artist who painted it had the ability to alter a person's features to portray them at any stage in their past or future. I chose mine to be a constant reminder of life's ephemeral nature and inevitability of my own death and deterioration.'

'This artist,' enquired Swann, 'does he live in the city?'

'I do not know. It was some while ago now, when I still held my gatherings. He came as the guest of someone else, if I remember correctly.'

Swann did not answer, as he was once more mesmerised by the portrait.

'Mr Swann?' said the writer, a little louder.

'What, oh yes, of course,' replied Swann, realising his distraction. 'I do not wish to keep you any longer from your work, sir. You have been most helpful.'

The two men bid farewell to each other and Swann left. Once outside the main entrance, Swann entered Fitzpatrick's waiting carriage and the driver flicked the reign. As the carriage turned and drove away, Swann gazed back at the building and at one of the windows saw the disfigured servant staring down at him.

CHAPTER FORTY-TWO

'So, no word of Johnson?' asked Swann, as he stood inside Fitzpatrick's office.

'I am afraid not,' replied the magistrate. 'One of my men called at the address of the lodgings Mr Tozer supplied but the landlady said she heard him go out early this morning, as if in a great haste, and he has not been back since.'

'If I was convinced of Gregor-Smith's innocence before this news, I am certain of it now,' said Swann. 'I believe it is time we paid a visit to Tozer's firm. Will you accompany me, Fitzpatrick?'

The magistrate nodded and within a few minutes they were on their way along the Bristol Road towards the premises of Tozer Publishing. Fitzpatrick brought out a journal he had with him and handed it to Swann.

'I think you might want to read this. It is my book in which I write up the cases I preside over. I believe you might find the notes from the blackmail case this morning revealing. A rather odd affair but there is a matter of interest to you.'

'All aspects of blackmail interest me,' replied Swann, as he began to read.

'As you can see,' said Fitzpatrick, unable to wait until Swann had finished reading it, 'during the proceedings the name of Mary's suitor was mentioned.'

At that moment Swann also read the name and spoke it out loud: 'Lockhart! What was his connection?'

'He was one of a group of men the defendant provided as an alibi.'

'Was he present in court?' asked Swann, surprised.

'No, he sent a sworn oath that the defendant was with him and several others at the time he was accused of being somewhere else regarding the blackmailing.'

'So unless Lockhart was committing perjury, there was no mention of wrongdoing on his part, then?'

'No, but I thought you would wish to be informed, because of your previous enquiries regarding him and, of course, Mary, and possible reports in the press.'

'Thank you,' said Swann. 'I appreciate your consideration.'

The magistrate acknowledged his companion's gratitude and then asked, 'So how was your meeting with the writer and why do you not believe him to be the murderer?'

'It went well, he is a very intriguing man,' replied Swann. 'As for him being the murderer though, I think it seems highly implausible. Why would someone commit a crime that they had already written about? It does not make sense and seems far too easy a solution to me.'

The carriage now reached its destination and the two occupants alighted and entered the large nondescript building. Inside, they found Tozer in his office and knocked on his door.

'Ah, gentlemen,' said Tozer. 'I must say, that was quick. I assume that you have come to tell me you have arrested Gregor-Smith?'

'No, sir, we have not,' replied Swann. 'We are here to talk to your workers.'

Tozer was not pleased at this statement. 'I do not understand why you need to question them,' he said. 'It will only upset them and we are very busy.'

'Mr Tozer,' said Fitzpatrick, 'it is not a task we undertake with any relish.'

Swann could not contain his growing frustration. 'Sir,' he said, stepping forward, 'your reluctance, if continued in this manner, might give rise to the misconstrued assumption you are in some way attempting to protect a man suspected of murdering not only a member of your workforce but a relation.'

Tozer stood up from behind his desk, as if he had just been challenged to a duel. 'That is gross slander, sir. How dare you!'

Fitzpatrick stepped forward to ease the situation. 'Mr Tozer, please,' he said, in the calmest but most authoritative voice that he could muster. 'My associate is merely trying to bring to your attention a possible consequence of your refusal.'

Tozer realised he had no choice but to comply and his body language showed this. 'You can use the typesetting area,' he said.

'Thank you, Mr Tozer,' answered Fitzpatrick. 'We will endeavor to intrude as little as possible on both your time and that of your staff.'

After the relevant room had been promptly organised, Swann and Fitzpatrick began their questioning. The first few workers all seemed to reiterate the same thing: that the victim was a quiet girl who kept her own company, while Johnson did much the same. No one could account for the typesetter's absence, all were shocked at what had happened the previous evening, but not one of them could think of any reason why their co-worker would have committed such an act.

A young lad of around seventeen now came in and after being instructed to do so, sat down on the makeshift seating.

'And what is your name?' asked Fitzpatrick.

'Richards, sir,' replied the lad. 'William Richards.'

'And what is your job here?' asked Swann.

'I prepare the ink for printing, sir.'

Swann sensed that the boy was tenser than the others had been.

'If you tell the truth in this room you will have nothing to fear, William,' said Swann. 'Now, in your own words, when did you last see Mr Johnson?'

'It was yesterday afternoon, sir.'

'Was that here, on these premises?'

William nodded.

'And how was Mr Johnson behaving?'

'Sir?' asked the young lad, looking puzzled.

'What was his manner?' expanded Swann. 'Did he seem anxious, excited?'

At this, the lad looked out to where Tozer stood watching the proceedings.

'Do not worry about your employer, William,' said Swann, looking behind him for a moment. 'If there is a problem after we leave, come to Mr Fitzpatrick's office to inform us.'

The magistrate nodded. Swann's instinct now took over as he asked the next question.

'What is your relationship to Mr Johnson, William?'

The lad did not answer. Swann gestured for him to do so.

'Remember what we said, the truth will not harm you William.'

'He is my uncle, sir, my mother's brother.'

Swann nodded at this revelation. 'You must realise William,' he continued, 'that if a crime has been committed and your uncle is the perpetrator, he must be brought to justice. Alternatively, if he is innocent then his name must be cleared so the real murderer can be brought to justice. Do you understand?'

William showed he did and then said, 'Well sir, he did seem nervous.'

'Why do you think he would have been nervous, William?'

'I don't know sir, but it was like he was thinking about something else, as if there was something distracting him.'

'Do you know what that could have been?'

'No, sir.'

'And how was your uncle's relationship with Mr Tozer's niece, Lizzy?'

'Sir?'

'Did they get on together?'

'For most of the time they did, sir.'

'And what about the times they did not?' interjected Fitzpatrick, a little too hastily for Swann's liking, although he did not show it.

'Well sir, Miss Lizzy was er … she could be …' William glanced briefly outside at Tozer again.

'Go on,' urged Swann.

'Well, sir, she could be quite simple-minded and used to get things wrong. At times, that is.'

'And your uncle became frustrated by this?' asked Swann.

'Yes, sir.'

'Did your uncle ever show this frustration to her?'

'Yes, sometimes he had cross words with her.'

Swann paused momentarily before asking the next question.

'Did your uncle ever physically threaten Lizzy?'

'Oh no, sir, least not that I was aware.'

'Are you sure?' said Fitzpatrick, thinking the lad had answered too quickly.

'Er, well, er … I suppose he might have, sir, under his breath like, but as I said, if he did, I never heard it.'

'And how long has your uncle worked here?' Swann now asked.

'Since Mr Tozer started the company,' replied the young lad.

'How long have *you* worked here, William? 'Fitzpatrick asked.

'I came here last January, sir. It was my uncle who got me this position.'

Swann was about to ask his final question but Tozer now rushed in.

'Gentlemen, please,' Tozer exclaimed. 'I have a business to run.'

'We have just finished Mr Tozer,' said Fitzpatrick. 'Thank you, William.'

As William returned back to his bench, Tozer 'escorted' Swann and Fitzpatrick out of the building to their waiting carriage. Once inside, they began their short return journey to the centre.

Fitzpatrick was the first to speak. 'What do you make of this business?'

'I think William is an honest lad but was not able to tell us everything he knew and I still believe Tozer is protecting Johnson,' said Swann emphatically. 'The murderer definitely works within that building.'

'What leads you to believe that conclusion?' asked Fitzpatrick.

'The main reason is that I noticed a footprint within a dried pool of ink, near a small printing press. I did not get a chance to examine it properly but I believe it was made by the murderer.'

'So it *is* Johnson,' declared Fitzpatrick.

'Quite possibly, although at the same time I cannot overlook the fact Gregor-Smith delivered the manuscript there last week. It is quite a conundrum.'

'How do you mean, Swann?' enquired the magistrate.

'If you were a publisher, Fitzpatrick,' replied Swann, 'who would you rather lose from your business, a writer or a typesetter?'

'An interesting question for thought,' said Fitzpatrick, putting his hand to his chin as he pondered it.

'Fitzpatrick!' exclaimed Swann. 'You should not have to even think about it, the writer *is* your business.'

Swann reclined in his seat and smiled. He was beginning to get a sense of the case but needed to know a few additional details before he could spring his trap and capture the murderer.

CHAPTER FORTY-THREE

The old beggar made his way up the dimly lit Avon Street, unnoticed and undisturbed. It was obvious he had no money so there was no attempt to either induce him into a backstreet liaison by the various women plying their trade or by any other of the reprehensible characters loitering around with the intention of robbery. On reaching the entrance to the Fountain Inn, at the top of the street, the beggar entered, exactly on time for his rendezvous with George and Bridges.

The public house was crowded with various salubrious characters and the atmosphere was already awash with revelry and merriment. As Swann entered, a trio of musicians had just that moment finished one song and begun another. Several customers, including George, called out for Seth, the landlord, to take the lead in singing the first verse. For a moment he was reluctant, but then after a little more encouragement started to sing:

> Ye tipplers all as you pass by,
> Come in and drink when you are dry,
> Come spend my lads your money brisk,
> And pop your nose in a jug of this.

Everyone inside the pub, except Swann, now joined in:

Ye tipplers all, if you've half a crown,
You're welcome all for to sit down,
Come in, sit down, think not amiss,
To pop your nose in a jug of this.

Bridges recognised Swann through the beggar disguise and signed 'hello' to him. Swann nodded his greeting back. Once he had secured a drink, he made his way through the crowd to the table where Bridges and George sat. A drunken customer staggered to his feet, nearly bumping into Swann, and demanded to sing the next verse of the song. Allowed to do so, he began:

Oh now I'm old and can scarcely crawl,
I've a long grey beard and a head that's bald,
Crown my desire fulfill my bliss.

As the drunken man sang the next line of *'A pretty girl and a jug of this'*, one of the Fountain's barmaids walked past. The drunkard grabbed at her breasts but she moved out of the way and then clouted him hard, much to the amusement of everyone else in the public bar.

As Swann reached Bridges' and George's table, the latter, still caught up in the atmosphere and so oblivious to Swann's presence, stood and began to raucously sing the next verse:

Oh, when I'm in my grave and dead,
And all my sorrows are past and fled,
Transform me then into a fish,
And let me swim in a jug of this.

George then flopped back down into his seat and as he did so, recognised Swann.

'Mr Swann, sir,' he slurred.

'George, remember where we are and call me Jack.'

'Right you are, Jack sir.'

Swann realised George was a little bit the worse for drink.

'Is there somewhere else more quiet where we can talk?' Swann asked as loud he felt appropriate without drawing attention.

Bridges read Swann's lips and gestured next door, to the snug. As they stood, George whispered in the ear of a woman sitting next to him, who nodded and blew him a kiss. Swann then followed George and Bridges through to the snug, as the rest of the pub clientele carried on singing. Although still noisy in the snug, it was quiet enough for them to converse and although he slurred the odd word, George now relayed to Swann the events of their outing to Bristol, to the point where they had been waiting outside the jewellers.

'And you say he was using the name Mottram?' Swann asked.

'That is what Bridges lip-read one of the women calling him,' replied George.

'And after he left the jewellers, you followed him back to the Windsor Hotel?'

'Yes,' said George, 'and then we waited outside that place until he left to get the coach back to Bath.'

'But he did not have his beard when he left this hotel again?' queried Swann.

'That's right,' George replied.

'And you waited *outside* the Windsor Hotel after trailing him back there?'

George nodded and then exchanged a guilty glance, unseen by Swann, with Bridges.

'That is a shame, George,' said Swann. 'As it was a rather cold afternoon, you could have both spent the last part of the afternoon inside the hotel.'

George looked at Bridges again. Swann smiled.

'And you are certain this Mottram you followed was the same man I showed you the sketch of this morning?' pressed Swann.

The hesitation in their response was enough.

'George?' said Swann. 'Tell me the truth.'

George looked at his companion, who nodded.

'The truth is we are not sure, Mr Swann. We only just caught the coach in time and had no chance to look inside. The only time we were given the chance of a good look at him it was when he had the beard, but we are both sure it was the same man.'

Having read George's lips, Bridges nodded in agreement.

'Okay,' said Swann, realising there was nothing more he could do. 'You have done well.'

A look of relief spread across George and Bridges' faces.

'Thank you, Mr er … Jack,' said George.

Swann's attention, however, was now taken by a portrait hanging on the snug wall. It bore a resemblance to the landlord of the Fountain, Seth, but much older.

'That portrait, who is it?' asked Swann.

'That's Seth, the landlord,' laughed George, 'when he gets to be old.'

'Do you know the artist who painted it?'

'Yes, it was us that found him. He can paint people as they'll be in the future.'

Bridges signed to George and the two men laughed.

'Bridges reminded me that Seth was not best pleased at receiving it. A few of us regulars gave it to him as a bit of fun for his birthday. He didn't like it at first but he's got used to it now.'

'I cannot imagine Seth sitting to be painted,' replied Swann.

'No, we brought the painter in a couple of times, secret like, so he could sketch Seth without him knowing. It's funny to think in twenty years time he will look like that.'

They all looked at the portrait and Swann became lost in his thoughts.

'Are you okay Mr Swann?' whispered George.

'Yes, I'm fine George. How long ago was this painted?'

George glanced at Bridges who held up two fingers.

'It was two birthdays ago.'

'And do you know where this artist lives, George?'

'If he is still there, then it is down near …'

Before George could finish, however, Bridges abruptly stopped him.

'Hey, what is it?' said George.

Bridges signed something only his companion could see. George then covered his mouth as he relayed it to Swann.

'Bridges says there is a man near the door reading our lips.'

Swann turned and looked. At that moment, the man moved and bumped into another patron. There was a brief exchange of words and the lip-reader punched the other man hard. He then quickly left the inn.

George stood to go after him but Swann stopped him.

'Don't worry George. Do you know who that was?'

'That was Irish John,' replied George. 'He works for Wicks.'

Bridges nodded his agreement, but Swann's attention was now fully on the portrait of Seth's older self, one that was twenty years in the future.

CHAPTER FORTY-FOUR

Bath, Tuesday 29th November, 1803
A most absorbing day in many ways but a tragic one nonetheless and once again I find myself with many more questions than answers. Why was the girl murdered in such a grotesque manner? Is it simply part of an attempt to frame an innocent man or is there something more sinister at work? I am certain clarity will be attained once Johnson the typesetter is located, although the behaviour of Tozer, the publisher, I find somewhat strange. On one hand he appears to be trying to protect his worker and yet on the other, he seems content to allow the blame and subsequent repercussions to fall upon his most profitable and successful author. There is definitely more to this matter which needs to be explored.

If one positive aspect has emerged from this sad situation, it has been the opportunity to converse with Gregor-Smith. I have been an admirer of his work for some time and to finally meet with him in person did not disappoint, especially as the sarcophagus in which he reclined was, of course, the preferred method of creative inspiration by John Donne, a favourite metaphysical poet of mine.

It was also at Gregor-Smith's residence where I chanced upon the portrait artist's work for the first time and what had been no more than a vague notion on my return has since taken a firmer hold on visiting the Fountain Inn and observing Seth's aged portrait there. I therefore intend to seek out the artist tomorrow and commission him to produce a portrait of Malone's accomplice, the Scarred Man, as he would appear today, twenty years on. I have reached this decision, as it has struck me that if the artist can take a person as they appear today and paint them as they will be in the future, then surely would he not be able to create a portrait of someone as they are today, using as guidance a description from the past. If this is possible, and I can see no reason why not, then I remember the features of his face in my memory clearly enough that I know I can describe them to the artist as accurately as if the man was sitting in the studio himself. And then, once I have the image, I can show it to George and Bridges, as I did with Mary's sketch of Lockhart, so they will have a more accurate likeness than a twenty-year-old remembrance.

With this mention of Lockhart, he now takes over my thoughts completely. What is one to make of him? He has appeared from nowhere, as if pulled from a magician's hat. My enquiries in London have so far yielded very little, other than a tenuous association with Kirby, the name of the hotel where he stays overnight, and a business address which does not exist. And then there is also the question as to what Lockhart undertakes when he travels on to Bristol after each visit to the capital. At least today I have found out certain details about these activities, even if I do not understand how they fit into the larger picture: the use of an alias, in this case Mottram; a disguise; the visit to the jeweller; and the escorting of the two women to, and then the leaving them at, an up-market hotel.

I am also still convinced as to Lockhart's involvement in the attempt on my life last month. Although he has claimed to be horrified at the thought of what might have happened, because of our meeting, I cannot see it as coincidence that Tyler was at that particular spot at that specific time if not pre-arranged. For the time being though, I hope I have lulled Lockhart into a false sense of security which, if successful, will allow me the time to investigate him further. And finally, there is the association with Fitzpatrick's blackmailing case which, although not directly implicated, I believe conceals something bigger behind it. What this is though, I can only hope time will disclose and reveal the truth behind Edmund Lockhart.

CHAPTER FORTY-FIVE

Although the hour was early, the lower part of the town was already full of life. An assortment of heavily loaded wagons and carts trundled their way up Horse Street, having entered the city from the south, over the Old Bridge, while the cries of numerous stallholders and market traders hawking their wares could be heard from all around the area. Women of the town, even at this time of the morning, openly plied their trade, while the rest of the ragged population of scavengers, pickpockets, tradesmen and labourers all rubbed together as they went about their business amidst the squalid and filthy surroundings.

After Swann had consumed his usual morning coffee and briefly scanned *The Times*, he left the White Hart and headed down Stall Street to where it merged with Horse Street. Once here, he followed the route straight to the river. As he walked along the thoroughfare, minus disguise, he was eyed up suspiciously by a few of the inhabitants and singled out as a possible mark by others. However, he reached the far end untouched and turned right into Broad Quay, which ran adjacent to the river and had been designed to become the very heart of Bath's docklands. Yet despite the grand nature of its conception, the grey quayside had become a lackluster area of little maritime bustle, resulting in the deterioration of the vicinity to its present-day ramshackle state, with the few houses that lined the waterside in various stages of dilapidation and ruin.

The stench was palpable and Swann had to cover his nose and mouth with a handkerchief. There were numerous slaughterhouses, breweries and industrial factories nearby and each pumped their waste directly into the river, where it mixed with domestic effluent and other refuse to produce the nausea-inducing pollution. He could see rats roaming freely along the alleys and passageways, while grimy, sodden washing hung in rows with the vain hope of attracting whatever fragments of sun prevailed within this dismal corner. And everywhere, from the rancid brown puddles of stagnant water to the tide marks on the walls, there was evidence of the regular flooding which took place, due to its close proximity to the river. At one point, Swann noticed, as he continued his way alongside the houses, the highest flood mark reached just below the level of the first floors.

From the address given to him by George and Bridges the previous day, along with details of the map he had memorised since staying on in Bath, it did not take Swann much time to locate the specific building he was looking for. Now all he could hope was that the artist still resided there. The city was known for having a transient populace, which moved on to wherever the work – or at least better prospects – took them. Fitzpatrick had mentioned the city's building trade, where men would be laid off during the winter when construction ceased. But then Bath had been a seasonal place for a long time, where the city's workforce and criminals adapted accordingly. The artist, if he maintained a studio here, might be less transient though. Swann knew of several painters whose studios were their sanctuaries and once they had found a place they felt they could work in, there was little that would cause them to give it up. This was what Swann was hoping for, that even in such a transient location as Bath and in such a dilapidated and slum area as Broad Quay, the artist had found stability.

Swann stepped inside the building and walked across the sodden floor, strewn with discarded rubbish, to the stairwell. Visibility was limited and the smell of decayed wood and rotten food permeated throughout the entire hallway.

As he reached the bottom of the stairs, a voice shouted from behind.

'I told you what would happen if you came back here!'

Swann turned just in time to prevent a thick wooden stick striking him on the head. He grappled with the middle-aged woman in whose tight grip the weapon was held, but managed to wrestle it from her. As they pulled apart, the squat, mean-looking woman fell on her backside.

'I think you may have mistaken me for someone else, madam,' said Swann.

'Are you the bailiff?'

'No, madam, and I certainly have no interest in any of your possessions. I am looking for a man who I believe resides at this address.'

'There are several men living here, the building has six floors.'

'This man is an artist by trade.'

'Yeah, we have one of those. He's at the top. I hope you're buying something, he owes me three months' rent.'

'Quite possibly,' said Swann, as he helped the woman up and returned the wooden stick to her.

She grabbed it, went back into her room and slammed the door shut.

Swann climbed the several flights to the top of the dwelling. A freezing blast of air came through a smashed window as he walked over to the solitary door on that floor. He knocked on what was left of the disintegrating brown wood.

'Hello?' Swann called out.

There was no answer. He tapped again and tried the handle. It was unlocked. The sparsely furnished main room had been turned into a makeshift studio. In the middle, standing behind a large canvas, was the artist. From his appearance Swann estimated his age to be slightly older than his own. The majority of his ginger hair had been lost, however, and what remained called to mind that of a monk. The dirty-white smock he wore was bespattered by paint seemingly from his entire palette and this was repeated around the floor where he stood. In front of him was his subject matter, two naked pubescent girls posed in an overtly sexual position and stretched out upon a fifthly, decrepit chaise longue. From their glazed expressions, Swann concluded they were under the influence of drugs.

'Excuse me,' said Swann, to attract the artist's attention. For whatever reason, the man did not respond.

Swann tried again.

'Whoever you are, I'm busy,' said the artist sharply.

'I only require a small amount of your time,' replied Swann.

The artist carried on painting. Swann moved forward and touched the man on the shoulder.

'Excuse me, sir, but ...'

The artist turned abruptly.

'Didn't you hear me, I'm working! Now sod off!'

Before the artist knew what was happening though, Swann took his right arm and brought it up behind his back. The man dropped his brush and cried out.

'Aaaargh! You're hurting me.'

'Obviously you did not hear me properly. I said I only require your attention for a short while.'

'Don't break my arm, it's the one I use to paint,' pleaded the artist.

'Then you will listen to what I have to say?'

The artist nodded and Swann let go. The artist staggered forward, indignant at his treatment but brought to order.

'Is there somewhere we can talk privately?' asked Swann.

'This is it,' replied the artist, rubbing his arm where it had been twisted.

Swann looked across at the two naked girls. The artist understood.

'Lose yourselves for a while, will you,' ordered the man.

'Where are we meant to go?' said one of the girls.

'Figure it out between you,' he replied indifferently.

The girls grabbed the dark green throw which covered the chaise longue and huddled together as they wrapped themselves in the material before going out, unhappy at their treatment.

'So what do you want that is so important to nearly break my arm?' the artist said, after the girls had gone.

'I have recently seen two examples of your work,' said Swann.

'Ah, you're one of those. Like 'em young, do you?'

'No, you misunderstand me. I meant, your other work, the portraits where you age the sitter.'

'Oh yeah, they're mine.'

'Well, I wish to commission you to complete one for me.'

'I don't do that kind of painting anymore.'

'You will be well paid for it.'

'The work I do now pays well enough,' said the artist and gestured to where the girls had been posing.

'You will also be performing a great service in bringing a criminal to justice,' Swann added.

'Look mister, for a start I'm not a performing monkey and unless you didn't hear me properly, I don't paint *those* kind of portraits anymore.'

Swann abruptly grabbed the artist by the throat.

'Unless you didn't hear *me* properly, let me explain more fully. This isn't one of your morbid curiosities or practical jokes,' said Swann angrily. 'I want this portrait completed for a specific and personal reason and you *will* do this for me. Otherwise I'll make sure you're not able to paint anything for a living again.'

The two men's gazes met as the artist looked straight into Swann's eyes.

'Alright, I'll do it,' gasped the flush-cheeked artist, his windpipe squeezed by Swann's right hand. At this Swann released his grip and the artist staggered back a step or two, dropped to his knees and then coughed violently several times.

'Don't blame me if you aren't happy at what you become though,' spluttered the artist from his subservient position, after he had recovered slightly.

It took a moment for Swann to realise what the artist had meant but then he said, 'It is not a portrait of myself I seek, but of a man I knew twenty years ago. I wish to know what his appearance would be like today.'

'And you have an image of him from that time?'

'No, but I can give you a description of him.'

'Then I'm sorry, I can't do it.'

Swann went to grab the artist again but the man raised his hands submissively.

'No really, I can only paint from what I see,' he clarified, 'not what I hear. It is the truth.'

Swann stepped back and listened as the artist continued to speak.

'I need something visual to work from. Do you not have anything with his image on it as he was then, a portrait, a drawing?'

Swann shook his head but thought for a moment.

'If I could supply you with a sketch of this man as he looked twenty years ago, but drawn from memory, would that be enough for you?'

The other man nodded.

'I don't care how it is done,' the artist said, 'I just need something tangible to focus my attention. The more accurate your sketch is though the more accurate my portrait will be.'

'Then you agree to it?' clarified Swann.

'Yes, but I'll name my price, as the process takes a lot out of me.'

'Then we have a contract, sir,' said Swann. 'I will aim to bring you the sketch later today. Will you be here?'

'I am always here. I never go anywhere,' replied the artist.

Swann left and went back downstairs. The girls were huddled on the staircase, their bodies still covered by the threadbare dark green material, but what Swann had momentarily witnessed in the studio caused him to stop beside them. Their pubertal breasts were not yet fully developed but other than that, nothing else betrayed their tender years. Their scrawny bodies were pock-riddled and undernourished, while their eyes held the wretchedness of having to live out their god-forsaken existences here. He placed a handful of coins beside them.

'Use these to buy something to eat,' he said, softly. Whether they would, he could only hope, but he had made the gesture. As he reached the bottom of the stairs, he heard the artist shouting to the girls to go back up to his studio.

Swann left the building with a melancholic air and headed back towards Great Pulteney Street. There was not a moment to lose.

CHAPTER FORTY-SIX

By the time Swann had returned to the house following his visit to the artist, he was in a slightly better frame of mind than when he had left the studio, as during the walk back he had convinced himself that Mary would be willing to undertake the task he was to ask of her. He certainly possessed the utmost confidence in being able to recall every detail of the Scarred Man from all those years before, he thought, as he entered the house, but whether his sister could transpose those would be another matter. He did not know whether she had drawn Lockhart's portrait from memory, but it was definitely accurate, that much was true. So hopefully she would also be able to sketch the portrait he required.

On being asked, Mary had initially been reluctant to carry out her brother's request, but after seeing how much it meant to him, she had relented and agreed to at least try and sketch a portrait of the man, whose features had been locked in his memory for all this time. Swann had closed his eyes as he began to recall the man's face, but in doing so, his mind had been transported back once more to the events of that fatal night.

The boy stared at the third upturned cup and the empty space beneath it. He could not believe it, he *would* not believe it. The pea had not been under the first cup, his pick of the three, even though he had observed the small, shrivelled-up object being put under the inverted wooden cup and, with all the concentration he could muster, had then watched as his father shuffled it around the other two cups on the table. It had not been under the second cup either, which he had lifted once his father had left the kitchen to greet the master. This had left the final cup, the remaining one under which the pea must be located. And yet, as he could now see, even if he did not believe it, there was also nothing beneath that one.

In that moment, however, he suddenly realised what had happened. The pea had never been under *any* of the cups! His father had somehow managed to retain it before commencing the game. It was an illusion. There was no way one could guess correctly. As for the boy's part in his own deception, he had been too busy focusing on the cup his father had made a show of putting the pea under that he obviously did not see him slip it into his pocket.

The sound of the smashing vase in the hallway crashed into his thoughts and the next moment he found himself watching as his father struggled with the man he now knew as the Scarred Man. He caught a brief glimpse of his features sideways on, but it was only when the two men were on the floor in the front room that he had got a sustained look at his face, the details of which remained in his memory to this day.

'Was it like this, Jack?' asked Mary. 'Jack? Jack!'

'Sorry Mary, my mind was elsewhere,' replied Swann as he opened his eyes. Back in the present he now viewed the sketch on the small easel in front of him.

'Is it a good likeness?' asked Mary.

Swann did not answer as he was utterly entranced by the image in front of him. Mary turned to her brother.

'Jack?'

'That is him,' he said. 'That is the man I saw that murderous night.'

Mary gazed at her brother empathetically and stroked his arm. 'Oh, Jack,' she said quietly. 'Perhaps I should not have done this for you after all.'

'No Mary, thank you. You can not begin to imagine what you have given me.' Swann stared at the sketch again. His sister's ability to produce what had been inside Swann all these years was a true gift. If the artist was able to visualise the future, then Mary had been able to reconstruct the past and in doing so bring it alive for him. It was as if the man was in the room now and had been sitting for the portrait which his sister had sketched. Every time he looked at the likeness a shiver went down his spine. Mary had more than done her job, now it was up to the artist to do his.

'Jack, I have to express what is on my mind,' Mary said, gently but firmly. 'What if the artist is a charlatan, if he has no gift and is only deceiving you?'

'You did not see the other two portraits,' replied Swann.

'Yes, but they are of men as the artist believes they will become in the future and so they cannot be authenticated for years to come.'

Swann looked at his sister intently. 'I am sure of this,' he said. Somewhere deep inside of him he knew he had to seize this opportunity and had nothing to fear except disappointment. 'I have no choice, Mary,' he added. 'Besides, as the portrait will be of a man as he is today, the artist's authenticity can therefore be substantiated swiftly.'

Swann stood up.

'I had better deliver this sketch to the artist,' he said. 'The quicker he receives it, the earlier he can begin his process. Thank you once again, my dear sister.'

Swann took the drawing and prepared to leave. As he opened the main door of the house, however, he recognised one of Fitzpatrick's men standing on the front step, in the act of raising his hand to knock on the door.

'Oh, Mr Swann, there you are. I hope it does not trouble you to be disturbed at home, sir, but I have already visited the White Hart Inn, as well as your rooms in Gay Street, in order to find you.'

'Not at all,' said Swann. 'I assume Fitzpatrick requires my assistance again?'

'I do not know, sir. I only know he has asked me to inform you that there has been another murder earlier today and they have since arrested a man.'

'Ah, so they have located Johnson the typesetter?' enquired Swann.

'Once more, I do not know sir, but I am sure that Mr Fitzpatrick will enlighten you as to the full details of this matter if you care to come with me now.'

CHAPTER FORTY-SEVEN

'You have arrested the wrong man, Fitzpatrick!' cried Swann, as he stood in the magistrate's office. 'Gregor-Smith did not commit this murder or any other, I would stake my reputation on it.'

'As I have mentioned to you, Swann, Kirby was the arresting magistrate. My hands are tied in regard to this matter,' insisted Fitzpatrick, 'but regardless, I thought you should hear the news from myself, before you heard it from anyone else.'

Swann realised he could not pursue this line of action, as he knew his associate was right. Fitzpatrick was unable to be involved in the case. He would therefore visit Kirby later, to secure Gregor-Smith's release, once he had visited the crime scene to gather evidence.

'So outside which church was the reverend murdered?' asked Swann.

'How did you know the victim was a clergyman?'

'It is the next killing in Gregor-Smith's manuscript. The clergyman is guarding the freshly dug grave of the first victim, the girl, in order to protect her from the vampire, who he believes inflicted the wound and may return to claim her soul. So what marks were on the second victim's body, Fitzpatrick?'

'I do not know. Kirby ordered the body taken elsewhere, as he does not want the press to find out yet, and I have not been privy to its present whereabouts.'

'So over which parish did the reverend administer?'

Fitzpatrick did not respond.

'Were you not privy to that information either, Fitzpatrick?'

The magistrate looked slightly embarrassed.

'What is it?' enquired Swann.

'Well, Kirby has said that he does not want you interfering any further in this case and is holding me responsible for ensuring that you do not. I would prefer not to have any confrontation with him, Swann.'

'I understand, my friend, and do not worry, as far as Kirby is concerned, you will be seen to have upheld your responsibility. I would wish to look at the latest murder scene, however, before it becomes too disturbed.'

The magistrate remained silent.

'Fitzpatrick please, you must tell me if you know where it is. An innocent man is being falsely accused of two murders. If he is found guilty, and I am certain Kirby will do everything in his power to make sure that he is, Gregor-Smith will hang for these crimes.'

'But what makes you so convinced the writer is innocent?' asked Fitzpatrick.

'There are three reasons and the first is the murderer's height. As I mentioned in your office yesterday, the man who killed Tozer's niece – and he worked alone – was around five feet ten inches tall. Gregor-Smith is only five feet four inches and so is too short to be the perpetrator.'

'If I am honest, Swann, I still do not quite understand how you arrived at such a precise piece of information,' sighed Fitzpatrick.

'It was a relatively simple technique to implement and consisted of measuring the distance between the height of the branch which snagged the girl's dress as she was carried along the track and the depth of the murderer's footprints within the snow on the ground.'

'Your deductions never cease to astound me, Swann,' said Fitzpatrick.

'It is purely the ability to observe, to see what is in the clear sight of one's vision. The second reason I believe Gregor-Smith's innocence is from the cuts on the girl's body, which suggested the murderer to be right-handed. When I observed Gregor-Smith drinking at his residence, he used his left hand.'

'And your third reason?' asked Fitzpatrick.

Swann hesitated momentarily. 'It has yet to be ascertained, but I believe when Gregor-Smith's footwear is checked his prints will not match any of those at the first murder scene.'

'You did not check his boots when you questioned him?' enquired Fitzpatrick.

'I intended to do so at the end of my visit with him, but I am somewhat ashamed to admit I became distracted. And of course, there is also the fact that I assume Johnson is yet to return to his lodgings?'

Fitzpatrick's nod confirmed this to be true.

'I cannot help but believe we are somehow being deceived,' Swann now said.

'What do you mean?'

'It is similar to the old pea and cups game. Do you know it, Fitzpatrick?'

'I think I have witnessed it being played,' said the magistrate, trying to conceal his embarrassment at losing each of the four times he had participated in it.

'In the game, a person is given the opportunity to bet on one of the cups, under which a pea has supposedly been placed, so giving a one in three chance to win.'

Fitzpatrick nodded his understanding.

'But the pea is actually never under *any* of the cups,' continued Swann. 'The person has no chance of ever winning. It is an illusion, as the owner of the game palms the pea before shuffling the cups. So therefore anyone gullible enough to bet on it is always bound to lose his money.'

'Palming?' enquired Fitzpatrick.

'Yes, it is where a confidence trickster retains something in his palm, out of sight of anyone watching, until he is able to secure it away in a pocket.'

'Why are we not able to see it?' asked an annoyed Fitzpatrick, as he realised what had happened each time he had partaken of the game.

'It is called distraction and is the foundation upon which all conmen ply their trade. The person being duped is told to concentrate on one thing, in this case the cups, while the performer is actually doing something else, in this particular situation, pocketing the pea.'

'Where did you learn all this, Swann?'

Swann paused for a moment before he replied. 'My father had an interest in it.' He then said, 'As I mentioned though, I cannot help but think we are perhaps ourselves in a similar game now.'

'In what way do you mean?' asked Fitzpatrick.

'Well, we have three possible suspects and yet it could easily be none of them. Maybe we are being shown something other than what we should actually be concentrating on. I have not yet been able to fathom what exactly that is, but I am certain someone is trying to deceive us into thinking Gregor-Smith to be the murderer. They are weaving a story that they want us to believe as the truth and obviously Kirby has done just so, since he has arrested Gregor-Smith.'

Swann now looked at Fitzpatrick and said determinedly, 'It is time to set an innocent man free, so I will ask you once more about the whereabouts of the murder scene.'

∞

Thirty minutes later Swann entered the graveyard where the second murder had occurred. He had secured the location from Fitzpatrick and made his way there. This had also enabled Swann to visit the artist, as it was on the way to the crime scene, to give him the sketch drawn by Mary. From their brief interaction, the artist had said the sketch would suffice to allow him to undertake the process and assured Swann the portrait would be completed by the following afternoon. From the artist's studio in Broad Quay, Swann had crossed the Old Bridge and headed to the outlying parish where the deceased reverend had presided over.

Swann now stood just inside the main entrance of the graveyard and observed the scene. The area was deserted and he was alone. It was obvious that Kirby did not feel a further need to search for potential clues as he had not left anyone to guard the evidence. As Swann usually did at the start of any investigation at a crime scene, he brought out his small pocketbook and sketched various elements. His drawing was not as accomplished as that of Mary, or otherwise he may have attempted to draw the portrait of the Scarred Man himself, but nevertheless it was competent enough to make a truthful record of what he saw in front of him. He outlined the border of the church and cemetery, filling in the rest of the details as he methodically made his way across the path leading from the gates to the entrance of the building.

If the murder had been carried out as outlined in Gregor-Smith's tome, then the reverend was attacked near the main door. As Swann had earlier explained to Fitzpatrick, the second victim is watching over the grave of the first, in the book, to prevent the claiming of her soul by this most unnatural of beings, but the man is caught unaware from behind and his soul ends up in the same place as that of the girl he has been trying to protect.

However, the murder in the book had taken place at night, while from the little information Swann had been able to glean from Fitzpatrick, while in his office, it seemed this one had occurred during the day. Not that he needed to convince Fitzpatrick about this fact, he hoped, but given the murder had happened during daylight hours, it could be assumed the murderer was not an actual vampire, as he had been in Gregor-Smith's writing.

Swann was now completely convinced the author was being set up. There was still no sighting of Johnson, who perhaps was hiding somewhere in the city, and emerging only to undertake the next killing, but if that was the case, then the killings should at least stop, as Gregor-Smith had been arrested and so possibly the murderer's intention had been fulfilled.

Although much of the immediate area surrounding where the body must have lain was disturbed and any possible evidence therein destroyed, either through deliberate or unintentional action on the part of Kirby and his men, after careful observation, Swann discovered a footprint slightly beyond the back wall of the graveyard. He consulted his pocketbook and the sketches from the scene of the first murder. The footprint matched the last remaining set, next to which Swann had written the letter *M*. Not that Swann required any evidence to prove it in his own mind, but nevertheless here was proof that the same person had most likely carried out both of the murders. He quickly sketched his latest footprint.

Swann finished his investigation and prepared to leave the sanctified grounds. The afternoon sky had begun to turn dark, with a bank of cloud making its way from Bristol that looked as if it held rain. Hopefully, having come out without an umbrella, he would make it back to Great Pulteney Street before any downpour. Despite this, however, he turned and walked away in the opposite direction: he was not yet ready to return to the city.

CHAPTER FORTY-EIGHT

A few minutes after Swann had crossed the Old Bridge on his way out to the parish church to conduct his investigation, Wicks and Irish John had come across in the other direction. They had left Wicks' warehouse on the far side of the river and were making their way into the Avon Street district, their destination was the Fountain Inn. Wicks wanted to know what was going on. It had begun a few days before, with a couple of nosey thief-takers asking questions in the Duke of York about a particular person Wicks did not appreciate any questions being asked about. The pair was no doubt in the pay of that troublemaker Swann and Wicks was anxious to find out what he wanted.

There were many things about Swann that Wicks did not understand. Why, for example, after the failed attempt on the man's life, had the order been sent down from London to leave him unharmed? Wicks had not been happy about this to start with, but did not want to disrupt his newly-formed relationship with *them*. Besides, Swann had not been interfering in his money-making schemes since staying on in Bath, so Wicks was content to go along with this set-up for a while. He would have his revenge one day though, he told himself, and pay the man back for the death of Tyler.

Despite the restraint on an outright killing of the man, it did not stop Wicks from having Swann followed and since the night the thief-takers had been asking their questions, his men had taken it in turns to do just that. The previous evening Irish John had trailed Swann from his house in Great Pulteney Street, even though he had left by the rear entrance of the property and was in disguise, to the Fountain Inn, where he had met the two thief-takers. Wicks knew them both. They were irritants but small time. He could easily have them killed but they might prove useful in the future, as he might be able to use them for his own purposes, such as giving them false information so as to distract Swann from the truth regarding the man he was asking questions about. Wicks always held sway by the phrase 'better the devil you know'. At the Fountain Inn, Swann and the thief-takers had discussed Mottram, or Lockhart, to use his other name and from what Irish John had learnt, he had carelessly allowed himself to be followed to Bristol and to be watched as he carried out his part in the scheme. Thankfully though, it seemed as if they were in the dark regarding its overall purpose.

Wicks was beginning to have doubts about Lockhart, especially given the fact he had almost messed up in London as well. He had been supposed to catch an earlier stagecoach the day before, along with the two women, but missed it and caught the Royal Mail coach instead. This had cost Wicks a lot of money, or would have if he had not recovered the ticket fare from someone else. What to do about Lockhart could wait until another day though, as the reason for their visit to the Fountain Inn was the other subject of Swann's discussion with the thief-takers; that of a portrait which hung on the wall in the inn.

The landlord, Seth, was serving behind the bar of the snug when Wicks and Irish John entered the inn. His face dropped on seeing them. He knew them on sight and also the fact they were certainly not here to savour his ales or pass the time in idle conversation. Nevertheless, he quickly composed himself before they noticed.

'A rare pleasure to see you in here, Mr Wicks,' said Seth.

Wicks walked over to where the aged portrait of Seth hung on the wall.

'So, is this your grandfather, then?' he asked.

'No, Mr Wicks, it is how I will look in the future,' replied Seth.

Wicks stared at the decrepit and wrinkled face in the portrait.

'I can't see any difference from how you look now, if you ask me,' said Wicks sarcastically. 'Where did you get this done?'

'I don't know, Mr Wicks. Some of the regulars gave it to me.'

'That's not the answer I want to hear now is it?'

'They found a painter who does them. He lived down by the river, I think, but I don't know any more than that. It's the truth, Mr Wicks.'

Wicks came to the bar and brought his face only inches away from Seth's.

'I know it's the truth, because I know you know what will happen if it isn't.'

Wicks then gestured to Irish John, who stepped forward and took the portrait off the wall.

'I'll bring it back when I've finished with it,' said Wicks.

'Of course, Mr Wicks; you keep it for as long as you want.'

After the two men had left, Seth and the patrons who were seated in the snug remained silent for a while, until the first mumblings began once more and the atmosphere returned to as normal as one could get after a visit from Wicks.

CHAPTER FORTY-NINE

Swann stood upon the summit of Beechen Cliff, on the southern slopes of Bath, and looked over the panoramic view of the city that was afforded from this spot. From here, he watched as the dark rain cloud that had been heading from Bristol passed the city on its northern side, leaving the centre dry as it headed off in the direction of Chippenham and then on, perhaps, to London.

He had left the church grounds, on concluding his investigations, and then made his way across a series of fields before striding up the steep incline of this hill to its pinnacle. Mary had mentioned a little while before about the view which could be obtained from this particular vantage point and its being worthy of the climb which preceded it, and as he now gazed out over the city he saw she was right. There was a sense of omnipotence surrounding this vista, with its opportunity to comprehend the city from above and so perceive it in all its completeness. Down there, at this moment, Wicks was no doubt going about his criminal activities, while Gregor-Smith languished in jail for a crime he had not committed. The Scarred Man roamed the streets a free man, although the artist was hopefully in the process of capturing his present-day likeness. Mary was also down there somewhere, going about her daily business, as was Fitzpatrick, Lockhart and all the other people Swann knew in Bath. From this elevated position

he now saw the Royal Crescent and Avon Street simultaneously and through doing so pondered, for a few moments, on
their respective inhabitants as they lived out their contrasting
existences. If there was anywhere in the city to gain such an
overall perspective, this was it.

Kirby would not be back in his office until five o'clock,
according to Fitzpatrick, which was in just over two hours
time, and so Swann looked eastward towards the rural landscapes which bordered the city on that particular side and
decided he would undertake a walk across the area, creating a
route in his mind which would leave him by Great Pulteney
Street at its close. There was nothing more to be done at
present in regard to Gregor-Smith and so an afternoon walk,
with its potential for contemplation, seemed the most pro-
ductive way to spend this time.

Leaving the slopes of Beechen Cliff behind him, Swann
walked down into the valley known as Lyncombe Vale.
The area fell within the parish of Widcombe, which lay just
outside the city centre and was situated in a narrow and
secluded basin. Meandering across the moss-covered valley
floor was a brook, which was enclosed on one side by a
wooded incline, whilst open ground lay to the other. Swann
navigated his way along an ill-defined track through the trees
which mirrored the line of the fast-flowing water. The brook
was swollen with the run-off from the snow that had fallen
earlier in the week, having now melted and found its way
down here from the hills, bringing with it various loose sticks
and vegetation. It was late autumn and the scene throughout
the vale reflected this time of year; birdsong was sporadic and
only a spattering of leaves remained on the branches, rendering the summer canopy all but gone and the valley exposed
to the grey-laden, mid-afternoon sky. The uneven trail under
Swann's boots became slippery in places as he made his way

over the layer of mulch that comprised the shed leaves which had begun their inevitable decay into the soil to enrich next year's growth; such was the cyclical nature of things.

Swann now came to a raised narrow footpath which bounded the small stream on one side. As he walked alongside the water, a robin appeared and for many yards seemingly led the way, flitting from branch to branch, here to there, all the while accompanying Swann as he made his way to the end of Lyncombe Vale. Once there, Swann emerged out onto an elongated roadway, situated in an area synonymous with one of the three renowned 'creators' of eighteenth-century Bath, who, along with John Wood the elder and Richard 'Beau' Nash, had left his indelible and permanent mark on the city. This was Ralph Allen and he had been the subject of a book Fitzpatrick had recently lent Swann.

Ralph Allen was born in Cornwall, according to the magistrate's book, *Ralph Allen: His Life and Legacy*, but arrived in the city that he would later become so closely associated with in 1710, at the age of seventeen. He promptly secured the position of Bath's deputy postmaster and two years later became the youngest postmaster in the country. Through his audacious developments of the postal service while in the role, including the establishment of 'cross posts' – a network of postal routes that ran between the more provincial towns – along with certain fortuitous events which furthered his standing, he began to amass the beginnings of a fortune that allowed him to take full advantage of the burgeoning expansion planned for Bath from the early 1720s onwards. In anticipation of the vast stocks of building materials that would be required, he purchased land at Combe Down and began to quarry the oolite limestone found there, although this sedimentary rock, which stonemasons had found could be sawn or 'squared up' in any direction, would become more famously known around the world as 'Bath Stone'. In order to transport this malleable freestone material from his mines to the riverside wharf he especially constructed at Widcombe, Allen designed the ingenious tramway, an extended, steep roadway that used nature's gravity to its advantage. Two thirds of the way down, it passed the spot where Swann stood, although it had ceased to be in operation since Allen's death in 1764. As he looked up the deserted thoroughfare, however, he could visualise what the scene must have looked like in its heyday, from an artist's impression he had seen reproduced in Fitzpatrick's book. Heavily laden, cast-iron wheeled trucks, each one containing between three to four tons of the stone which would provide the buildings of Bath its distinctive warm, honey-coloured appearance, would hurtle down the steep gradient on oak rails night and day, using gravity to propel them from the top and the skill and courage of brake-men at the bottom. Once unloaded, horse-power would then return the trucks back up the incline to begin the process once more.

Allen became a rich man through his quarrying and as his wealth and standing in the city increased inordinately, he decided to have built a residential seat that would at once reflect his achievements and stand as a permanent monument to the qualities of the material it was built with. In 1737, work commenced on the enormous mansion Swann now observed high on a shallow curve of a hillside, to the east of where he stood, and which contained magnificent views of the valley below and the centre of Bath beyond. Given the name of Prior Park, in respect of the Benedictine Priory that had originally existed on the land, it took twenty years to fully realise Allen's vision but once completed, was described as 'a noble seat which sees all Bath and which was built for all the world to see.'

Swann walked down the remainder of the old railed route to its lower end and turned right. After passing the site of Allen's wharf, he continued along towards the Widcombe turnpike and once through its gates, found the land opened out in front of him. The road here was well maintained and it did not take Swann long to cover the distance between Widcombe and Bathwick. As he did so, however, he observed ongoing construction work to his right. This was the building of a canal that was to connect Bath with Reading. Ultimately it would join the River Avon at Widcombe as planned, but the scheme had been severely delayed, Swann understood, due to technical and legal difficulties and it was predicted to take several more years before its completion. At present, he could see the work had now reached just beyond an area known as Sydney Wharf.

Ahead was the beginning of the Bathwick estate, where the pleasure gardens of Sydney Vauxhall could be seen in the distance; the contrast between the current expanse of land and the more built up areas of the estate being all too marked. The Bathwick estate lay adjacent to the Pulteney one, on which Great Pulteney Street had been built, and as Swann made his way to where it started, he passed the gardens on his right.

Sydney Gardens was opened in 1795 and during its eight-year existence had already witnessed several momentous events, such as the inaugural Gala held in 1796, which had attracted more than four thousand visitors, a visit by the Prince of Wales the same year, and a Royal birthday celebration for the King himself, three years after that, which had, according to Mary who frequented the gardens often and had attended all these events herself, included a firework display 'to exceed all expectations'. More recently, the previous year in fact, there had also been the ascent from its grounds by the balloonist Garnerin, which Fitzpatrick had witnessed.

As Swann reached the start of Great Pulteney Street he looked across the road to a line of terraced houses opposite, which comprised Sydney Place. In one of them, he believed, lived the Austens. He had not met them yet, but they were friends of the family, Mary had told him, and he would surely do so soon. They had been away in Lyme Regis, he understood, but were due back at any time. In fact, as he maintained his gaze across the street, he saw a young woman enter the fourth house along and wondered if this was one of the two daughters Mary had mentioned, but he then continued on his way down Great Pulteney Street, refreshed from his walk and ready to confront Kirby over Gregor-Smith.

CHAPTER FIFTY

Swann stopped briefly at the house in Great Pulteney Street, to confirm the arrangements for the art exhibition that evening with Mary, before continuing into town in order to visit Kirby in his office located in the King's Circus. The route Swann took through the city went by Queen Square and Gay Street, as he wanted to stop at his rooms in the latter, which ran off the former from its north-east corner. Swann entered the premises at No.40 Gay Street and went up to the first floor, where his rooms were located towards the rear. He went inside and consulted the giant map on the wall. He wrote down the details of the murder on a piece of paper and attached it to the wall, beside the map. He then fashioned a line from the paper to the spot on the map, to show its precise location. It had been a most eventful day and the walk through Lyncombe had done much to lift his spirits. He checked the time and saw it was a little after five. If Fitzpatrick was correct, his magisterial colleague should be in his office now.

Swann left his Gay Street rooms and headed up towards the King's Circus, to where Kirby's business premises were situated. He was in no mood for anything other than the immediate release of Gregor-Smith by Kirby. On reaching the top of Gay Street he turned right, towards the section which contained Kirby's office. He found the relevant numbered property and was about to knock on the main door when it was opened. Swann allowed an elderly gentleman to leave and then entered. The building sounded empty from his echoed footsteps, as he climbed the stairs, and it took a little while to find where Kirby was situated, but eventually he saw an open door and the magistrate sitting behind a desk. He knocked and an already unhappy Kirby looked up. He had been told by Wicks earlier in the day that Lockhart had been followed to Bristol on Swann's orders, as well as the matter regarding the Royal Mail coach ticket; the latter for which Kirby himself had to reimburse Wicks. Now Swann stood in his office.

'What are *you* doing here?' Kirby demanded. 'How did you get in?'

'Your front door was open,' answered Swann, 'and I am here to demand the release of a wrongly accused man.'

These were not the answers Kirby wanted.

'That door should always be locked,' replied an indignant Kirby, 'and what gives you the right to think that you can barge in here and demand anything?'

'I can demand it, sir, because my investigation shows him to be innocent.'

'I am the arresting magistrate and so this is *my* investigation. And even if this were not the case, I do not believe any of my colleagues, even Henry Fitzpatrick, would release a possible murder suspect simply due to your wild speculations and misinformed observations. In this city, Mr Swann, we deal in hard facts.'

'And the facts in this case being?' enquired Swann.

'It is really none of your business, as this investigation does not concern you. I thought I told Fitzpatrick to make that clear to you!'

'Yes, he did, but he is unaware of my presence here now.'

'Well, that presence is no longer required, good day to you.'

'You have a choice Kirby. You can either tell me what evidence you have on Mr Gregor-Smith, or I will leave this office and head straight to those occupied by the *Bath Chronicle*, to visit a journalist acquaintance I have recently made. I am certain he would be most interested to learn about this case.'

Kirby was fuming but did not show it. He took a manilla-coloured folder from one of the trays on his desk and opened it.

'In the case of the first murder, Gregor-Smith's residence is in very close proximity to the crime and …'

Swann shook his head in disbelief as Kirby continued.

'… further to this, both murders are described in his unpublished manuscript.'

'Those facts are merely circumstantial,' retorted Swann.

The magistrate opened a drawer and retrieved an item from inside it.

'Well, this was actually found on the body of the second murder victim,' Kirby said. He held up a piece of jewellery that Swann saw was a small mauve amulet with a silver chain attached.

'There is also an inscription engraved on it,' continued Kirby. 'It reads: "To Henry G-S, warmest love always, Lydia". Very touching, I am sure you will agree, but also very incriminating.'

Swann was not impressed.

'Gregor-Smith had already lost that amulet when I spoke with him yesterday,' Swann told the magistrate.

'Then I suggest it was located after you left his residence but he was careless enough to lose it again while murdering the clergyman. There is nothing I can do until he faces the charges he has been arrested for and Fitzpatrick would agree.'

'I wish to see Gregor-Smith. Where are you holding him?' said Swann.

'That is impossible, I cannot allow it,' replied Kirby.

'He is an innocent man. I demand it.'

'Again you demand it, sir,' exclaimed Kirby, as he stood angrily at his desk. 'Just remember where you are making this demand. You may have acquired a reputation in London and seem to be building one here, but in this city I have jurisdiction and what I decide is the law. Now, once more, good day to you, I have legal matters to attend to.'

Kirby strode over to the door and pulled it open. Swann remained by the desk for a moment before he left. He was not pleased at this turn of events but realised he had to bide his time. Nevertheless, as he went through the door, he said, 'You have not heard the last of this, Kirby.'

An hour later Swann sat opposite Gregor-Smith in his cell. In his jacket pocket was the forged letter, hastily written on Kirby's personal notepaper, which had allowed Swann access to the writer; the headed sheet requisitioned from Kirby's office as the magistrate walked over to the door, while Swann remained at the desk for the briefest moment, the signature copied from a fleetingly observed one at the bottom of a letter that was also on the desk. Even this letter, however, could not guarantee a completely trouble-free journey and Swann had tried several places where he thought the writer might be held, before finally locating him within the Grove Street prison. It was a shrewd move by Kirby, Swann thought, as he had entered the prison, as ordinarily its inhabitants consisted purely of petty offenders and debtors, not double-murderers. Swann had been taken to the rear of the building, on being granted access, and found Gregor-Smith in a cell within the recently built block which, although only two years old, had been left inadequately damp and completely uninhabitable through the regular flooding of the building.

'I will get you out of here,' Swann told the writer, 'do not concern yourself.'

'That is most kind of you,' replied a haggard-looking Gregor-Smith, 'but I fear my fate has been cast. Once the journalists get hold of the story there will be no one in England who will believe my innocence.'

'There will always be one person that believes it,' replied Swann.

'However well that is received by myself, I believe it may not be enough, as I doubt your powers to be such as to combat the entire press, the judicial system and the determination of the person carrying out these murders.'

'Is there anyone who holds a grudge against you?'

'I do not intentionally make enemies, Mr Swann. And although I do not quite understand why you are helping me, sir, I do appreciate it greatly,' said Gregor-Smith.

'I have my reasons,' said Swann, 'although the main one is that I know you to be innocent. It is now up to me to prove that and get you released from this filthy abomination of a prison before Kirby can make his next move.'

Swann now stood, little realising what the next forty-eight hours would bring.

CHAPTER FIFTY-ONE

'Kirby is right I'm afraid, Swann,' said Fitzpatrick, as they stood within the somewhat crowded art gallery in studious contemplation of a landscape painted by Mr Luchini. 'However much you may believe him to twist justice to serve his own means, this time he does have the law on his side.'

'I cannot believe how a man like that can hold office,' replied Swann disdainfully.

'Perhaps you may call me misguided, but I have always found Kirby to be a pleasant enough sort,' responded Fitzpatrick, 'not someone you would want at your side in the midst of battle possibly, but nevertheless a competent fellow in upholding the law and carrying out his duties.'

Swann did not answer.

'This painting is most exquisite, do you not agree,' enquired Fitzpatrick, tactfully changing the subject.

The landscape they had been viewing was one painted from the same spot on the top of Beechen Cliff where Swann had stood earlier that afternoon and along with several others, all of which looked down on the city from various locations on its surrounding hillsides, comprised *A Series of Bath Landscapes by Italian Master Visconti Luchini.*

'Yes, Mr Luchini has certainly succeeded in capturing the city in its full glory,' replied Swann.

As they continued their mutual admiration of the painting, Mary, accompanied by Lockhart, joined them.

'Mary, your teacher is an excellent painter,' said Fitzpatrick. 'Perhaps one day we may view such a creation from you?'

'I have given up landscape painting,' replied Mary, matter-of-factly.

'I do not understand,' said the magistrate, genuinely puzzled.

'The considered opinion, Henry, is that any artistic talent I may possess lies elsewhere.'

Before Fitzpatrick could respond, Swann's attention was distracted by someone at the far end of the gallery.

'If you will excuse me temporarily,' said Swann, 'there is an old acquaintance I wish to converse with.' He now crossed the art gallery floor and greeted a rotund man with a flush-red face.

'Jack Swann! If my eyes do not deceive me,' exclaimed a somewhat surprised but nevertheless overtly pleased Richard Huntley. 'What are you doing here in Bath, Jack? I cannot believe it is for the *Season!*'

'Your belief remains intact, my friend. It is my work which keeps me here at present. And yourself?'

'I have been ordered out of the capital by an overzealous physician and advised to take the waters here.'

'You are staying in the city?' enquired Swann.

'Good lord no,' replied Richard. 'I have taken up residence just outside it, in Bathford, if you know the place. As you may be aware, I always prefer to be on the periphery and in that way one is able to attain a better perspective of how things are. Rather than being in the centre looking out, therefore, I am on the outside looking in.'

Swann smiled. 'Yes, that sounds like the Richard Huntley I know. But how is your stay affecting your business, a top literary agent not based in London?'

'Even this far from my domain I am aware of everything that goes on within that world. This very evening, for example, after this preview, I am entertaining several influential people from the publishing world. You should come along, Jack.'

'I would sincerely enjoy your invitation, but I have a matter which consumes my attention and so I believe I would not make for very good company. You are aware of Gregor-Smith's arrest?'

The literary agent nodded solemnly.

'I have taken it upon myself to prove his innocence.'

'And what is the basis of your conviction?' asked Richard.

'Well, from the conversations I have had with Gregor-Smith …'

'You have spoken with him?' interjected Huntley.

'Yes, on two occasions,' replied Swann.

'Then I absolutely insist you must attend tonight. Mr Gregor-Smith is a most renowned recluse and there will be many people at my dinner table who would be equally interested to learn what he is like.'

'I appreciate your offer and ordinarily would accept it without hesitation but I cannot tonight,' said Swann. 'Perhaps, though, I could ask a favour of you.'

∽

Meanwhile, standing in the same place where Swann had left them, Fitzpatrick was engaged in conversation with Mary and Lockhart.

'I cannot understand why your brother is so convinced the writer is innocent,' said Lockhart.

'Well Edmund, have you not heard of a kindred spirit? My brother believes Mr Gregor-Smith to be wrongly accused. And that being the case, then he must do everything he can to prove his innocence. It was the same when we were growing up. When my brother was fifteen, there was an incident in which a servant from a nearby house was found with stolen goods in his bedroom. He was to be flogged and transported before Jack intervened. He proved the servant was innocent.'

'How did he achieve this?' asked Fitzpatrick.

'As my brother recalls it, he first had to find a reason why someone would do such a thing and so he looked around for the person to benefit most from the servant's transportation. With my brother's ability to converse with the servants on their level, he was able to gain their trust and glean the fact that the servant had a secret tryst with a domestic girl from an adjoining household. It was all very innocent and they were very much in love but their relationship had to be kept secret, as the two masters of the households did not like each other.'

'A domestic Romeo and Juliet,' interjected Lockhart, smiling at Mary.

'That's right, Edmund,' replied Mary, smiling back. 'So once my brother had this information, it was a case of finding out who had the most to gain from the broken relationship. He learnt there was another servant in the same household as the girl, who lusted after her, so with this information Jack was able to trap the real perpetrator of the theft.'

'So what did he do?' asked Fitzpatrick.

'He waited for the guilty servant to go out for the evening and then did the same to *him*. He confessed and the innocent servant was taken off the boat in Bristol, just before they sailed for Botany Bay.'

'A close call then, I would suggest,' said Lockhart.

'As my brother said at the time, it is better to free a man the moment before the hangman's trapdoor is opened, than the moment afterwards.'

As Fitzpatrick smiled, a man approached who he recognised as one of his night-watchmen. The man whispered in Fitzpatrick's ear and the magistrate nodded.

'Mary, Edmund, would you please also excuse me for a moment,' Fitzpatrick said and then crossed the room to where Swann remained talking with Richard Huntley.

'Gentlemen, I am sorry to interrupt your conversation,' said Fitzpatrick, before he addressed Swann directly, 'but Johnson has been found.'

CHAPTER FIFTY-TWO

Swann and Fitzpatrick entered the building where the suspect, Johnson, was being held and sat down in the sparsely furnished room, opposite the visibly shaken man.

'Do you know why you have been brought here, Mr Johnson?' asked Swann.

'No sirs, I returned to my lodgings not half an hour ago this evening and the next thing I knew, I was overpowered and brought here.'

'You have been brought here,' said Fitzpatrick, 'because of the murd …'

'Fitzpatrick,' interrupted Swann. 'I realise you have the jurisdiction here, but may I question Mr Johnson in my own way?'

'Of course. Please go ahead Swann.'

'Thank you.' Swann turned back to the suspect. 'So, Mr Johnson, can you think of any reason why you should be here?'

'None sir. I am an honest man and have committed no crime I am aware of.'

'And can you tell me your employ?'

'Yes sir. At present I work as a senior typesetter at Tozer Printing, which is on the Bristol Road.'

'And who else works there?' asked Swann.

'Mr Tozer employs several people in his firm sir, each with different jobs, from typesetters down to the printer's devils.'

'I don't think I'm familiar with the term "printer's devil",' said Fitzpatrick.

'It refers to the most menial of workers in the industry,' explained Swann.

'Ah, I see,' said the magistrate.

'And does a girl known as Lizzy also work there, Mr Johnson?' said Swann, resuming his questioning.

'Yes sir, she is a relative of Mr Tozer's or somethin' like that, I don't know.'

'She is actually Mr Tozer's niece. And when did you last see Lizzy?'

'The day before last, sir, we were both at work.'

'Can you recall the exact details?' asked Swann.

Johnson remained silent for a few moments as he attempted to think back.

'I left the premises at six o'clock. Lizzy was still there, as Mr Tozer wanted her to do some extra work for him.'

'And what was that work?'

'I honestly don't know, sir.'

'Is it unusual that Mr Tozer asks his workers to stay there of an evening?'

'No sir. If a job needs finishing then we stay until it is done.'

'And do you get on with Lizzy?' asked Swann, as he suddenly changed tact.

'Shouldn't that be *did*, Swann?' interjected Fitzpatrick.

From the brief glance Swann gave him, Fitzpatrick realised he had spoken out of turn and the question's tense was part of Swann's method. Johnson, however, seemed unaware of what had passed between the two men.

'Not really, sir,' replied Johnson, 'but if I can be honest, she is quite a slow-witted girl who is not always fast in her work. I believe Mr Tozer gave her the position through her relationship to him, rather than on any skills she possesses.'

Swann paused for a moment before asking the next question: 'Did you know that Lizzy was murdered two nights ago?'

The reaction on Johnson's face informed Swann quite categorically of what he needed to know.

'Are you familiar with the content of the latest manuscript by Mr Gregor-Smith?'

'Of course, sir,' replied Johnson. 'I have been typesetting it.'

'Lizzy was murdered in the same way as the first victim in that manuscript.'

'She might have been a bit slow and all but she certainly didn't deserve that,' said Johnson, having obviously now recalled the vivid details of the killing in the book. 'Who would do such a terrible thing?'

'That is what we are hoping to find out, Mr Johnson,' said Swann.

The realisation dawned on Johnson.

'You think I did it?'

'You are one of the suspects, Mr Johnson, but if you tell us the truth as to your whereabouts for these past two days and why you did not turn up for work, you have nothing to fear.'

Johnson seemed reluctant to answer.

'Mr Johnson, from your reaction to the news of Lizzy's murder I believe you to be innocent of it,' said Swann, 'but if you do not tell us where you have been since her body was found then you may be wrongly executed.'

'Well sirs,' said Johnson, seemingly now wishing to co-operate, 'I have been in Bristol these two days in the pursuit of new employment. It is for a typesetting position in a large Bristol company. I swear it to be true sirs.'

'And you were successful in securing this position?'

'Yes sir. I can provide the company's address and my cousin can vouch for my presence overnight, as I stayed with him and his family.'

'Please lift up your boots,' requested Swann.

Johnson looked puzzled momentarily but then did as he was ordered.

'Is this the only pair that you possess?' asked Swann, as he viewed the man's footwear.

Johnson nodded.

'And what made you apply for this typesetter's position?'

'It was my cousin, sir, the one I stayed with in Bristol. He told me about it.'

'No,' interjected Fitzpatrick, unable to help himself, 'I believe my associate means what is your reason for wishing to leave Mr Tozer's firm. Are you not content in his employ?'

'Thank you, Fitzpatrick,' said Swann, happy this time that Fitzpatrick had asked the question.

'If I may be honest sirs, Mr Tozer has, how can I say, certain troubles.'

'Oh,' said Swann, leaning forward, 'and what exactly are these "troubles"?'

'Mr Tozer is a good businessman, sirs. He has built the company up into a prosperous one and I have been with him from the beginning. He started from nothing and at its height had a turnover of several thousand pounds a year; especially after Mr Gregor-Smith signed on with the company. He has been our biggest seller for the past three years, almost outselling on his own the rest of the authors that Mr Tozer has on his books. The trouble is with Mrs Tozer, as she is not there anymore.'

'She has left him?' enquired Fitzpatrick.

'No, she is not right in the mind, they say.'

'And how did this come about?' asked Swann.

'No one knows. Mr Tozer does not speak of it and I am sure if he was to hear anyone else discussing it, they would be out of a job. All I know, and I would be most grateful to you if it was not repeated to Mr Tozer, in case my new position falls through, is that his wife has been taken to a place for those people whose minds are unstable, if you know what I mean, sirs. Mr Tozer is beside himself with anger.'

'But why would that make you seek another employment, especially one in a different city?'

'Well, they say because of his anger, his judgement has become untrustworthy and he has also got himself in debt, paying for his wife's treatment and not being able to run the financial side of the business properly. He had the opportunity to put another writer under contract recently but for some reason he was not able to obtain his signature. It was as good as signed, although I heard it was something to do with Mr Gregor-Smith, who was an acquaintance.'

Swann put his hand to his chin and thought for a few moments.

'Do you think that Mr Gregor-Smith could have carried out the murders?' asked Fitzpatrick.

Swann was again happy for Johnson to answer Fitzpatrick's question.

'I do not know Mr Gregor-Smith personally,' replied Johnson, 'I mainly know him by reputation and if one went by that, then …'

'Well, exactly,' said Fitzpatrick.

'Well, exactly what, Fitzpatrick?' asked Swann.

'Um, I do not know exactly,' responded the magistrate, a little sheepishly.

'I have only actually met him on a couple of occasions,' continued Johnson, 'when he has delivered his manuscripts, but at those times I found him pleasant and nothing like the papers make him out to be.'

'That is more exacting,' said Swann. 'Well Mr Johnson, we wish you every success with your new employment, you are free to go if my associate agrees.'

'I am not sure that Kirby would …'

'Fitzpatrick, it is *you* that is here, not him. Besides, as far as Kirby is concerned the murderer already resides behind bars, so I am certain he would not wish to have another possible suspect turn up outside the prison as well.'

'I see your point, Swann. Well, if you believe Mr Johnson should go free, then I will sign the papers.'

'Thank you, Fitzpatrick.'

After Johnson had been allowed to leave, Fitzpatrick and Swann stayed in the room to discuss the matter.

'So what convinced you of his innocence, Swann?'

'It was mainly from the way he reacted to the news of the girl's murder. Unless he is a fine actor, it showed in his eyes that he was unaware of it previously.'

'So we are back to Mr Gregor-Smith, then?'

'No,' said Swann. 'I still think, perhaps even more so now, that someone is trying to frame him and I am starting to believe I know who it may be.'

'Can I have a crack at it?' asked Fitzpatrick.

'Certainly,' said Swann.

'Well, I think it may be connected to the other writer Tozer was going to sign to his firm. It might be that Gregor-Smith in some way interfered in the deal and the other writer was angry.'

'Why would he do that?' asked Swann.

'If you are the best-selling author with a publishing firm, as Gregor-Smith seems to be,' said Fitzpatrick, warming to the task, 'you may not want any rivals to that position, even if this other writer is an acquaintance.'

'So you are saying that it is the writer who has sought revenge?' said Swann.

'I know it is conjecture, but nevertheless a possibility. Would you not agree?'

'It is certainly an interesting piece of deduction, Fitzpatrick,' said Swann. He did not wish to be drawn into further speculation, however, and so changed the subject. 'I meant to enquire as to whether you received any wine at your office yesterday?'

'Yes, indeed I did,' replied Fitzpatrick. 'A case of German hock arrived while I was away. There was no note with it though or explanation as to why it had been delivered or who it was from. I did wonder if you had anything to do with it and had intended to ask you about it at the first opportune moment.'

'I assume you realised the bottles do not actually contain hock,' said Swann.

'The thought had crossed my mind,' Fitzpatrick answered, 'especially as the initials *T.J.* were engraved on each bottle.'

'They were especially created for the cellar of Thomas Jewel,' said Swann, 'a financier living in Paris, as the initials testify. During the war with France he had kept a very low profile, but after the Treaty of Amiens had carelessly allowed his presence to become known. When the peace was broken earlier this year and war with Bonaparte resumed, he was forced to leave his home and consequently abandoned his beloved collection. Given the fact that the borders between our two countries were then closed, as you know, Thomas Jewel, on his return to England, began the process of covertly arranging transport of the contents of his wine cellar, using whatever means he could, and at the same time placing orders for new vintages. One such order was for half a dozen cases of Chateau d'Yquem, 1799. However, they never reached their intended recipient. Having been smuggled out of France under the guise of ordinary German hock, the consignment was shipwrecked off the Cornish coast, seized by the government as contraband and then sold at auction. The six cases were purchased by a wine merchant who then unknowingly sold them on to Pickwick at the White Hart. I fortuitously happened to help in the transaction and secured half of them, one of which was the case delivered to your office.'

'How did you come to know all this?'

'Largely through a recent article in a wine periodical, which reported Thomas Jewel's death, fittingly attributed to a broken heart through the loss of his cellar, and then a piece of deductive reasoning after seeing an unrelated advert in the same publication of an upcoming auction.'

'That is an incredible story,' replied Fitzpatrick. 'You never cease to amaze me, Swann. So to what degree am I in your debt for them?'

'Consider it a gift, Fitzpatrick,' replied Swann. 'In honour of our continuing friendship.'

'That is most generous of you, Swann.'

Shortly afterwards, the two men bade each other goodnight and Swann made his way back to Great Pulteney Street. On arriving at the house, he was informed by Emily that her mistress had yet to return from the art exhibition. Swann had left Mary at the gallery with Lockhart and although he was not overly concerned at present, decided that he would stay awake until he heard her come home. He changed into his night clothing and retired to the library, where the fire had recently been lit by Emily. Swann sat in an armchair watching the fire while contemplating the facts of his present investigation; he always found staring at the flickering flames conducive to deductive thinking.

As far as Swann was aware, there were only three people possibly connected to the manuscript from which the murders had been apparently copied; the writer, the senior typesetter and the publisher. Swann believed Gregor-Smith and Johnson to be innocent but this left Tozer as the prime suspect and Swann did not have a convincing motive at present. Fitzpatrick's suggestion that it might be the other writer was certainly intriguing, but given that Gregor-Smith had mentioned he never let anyone else read his work before it is published, it could be assumed that this possible rival to his best-selling status was ruled out as well.

Swann felt as if there was a piece of the puzzle missing and that once this was discovered, the case would solve itself. What that particular piece was, however, he did not yet know, but as he considered several possibilities, he found himself becoming mesmerised by the hypnotic, iridescent flames and his eyelids slowly began to close.

CHAPTER FIFTY-THREE

Wednesday 30th November, 1803

My dearest Aunt Harriet

I begin this letter with the most wonderously happy news. Edmund has this very evening offered a proposal of marriage and I have accepted. We attended an exhibition of landscape work by my art teacher, Mr Luchini, and afterwards Edmund escorted me for a late supper at a restaurant with which he has recently become acquainted. It was here, and during the final course, he produced an engagement ring and made his proposition.

He is aware that our going forward with this arrangement and the setting of an actual date for our betrothal is dependent on certain approvals; these I wish to come from my brother and yourself, my dear aunt. I hope neither of you will find any reason for objection, however, as I am beside myself with happiness.

In regard to Edmund's proposal, I cannot say I was taken completely by surprise by it, as we seem to have become closer lately, even though he has been in London on business often. Perhaps it is true what they say, that absence does indeed make the heart grow fonder.

This happiness at the prospect of becoming a wife may seem contradictory, given my new programme of reading, but I do not believe it to be so. I remember the talk I attended at your house last month and what your speaker, Catherine Jennings, felt regarding the subject of marriage. As she herself believed, the responsibility lies solely with the woman herself in so much as she should ensure in her own mind that the man she marries will not stand in the way of her continuing personal development. And I believe Edmund to be such a man, as he is considerate and willingly allows me to have my own opinion. At the same time I am secure in the knowledge it is not for financial gain I marry. 'The road of matrimony for financial reasons is surely the road to the spirit's dissolution,' I now hear Catherine's voice once more and like her I feel it is better a woman lives a financially impoverished existence than a spiritually impoverished one.

Do not think for one moment dear aunt, that I intend to abandon my reading on account of this momentous development; if anything I feel it will be enhanced. More and more I am coming to understand what you said at the funeral; that women are educated to the tastes of men, not for their own benefit, but mainly to conform to men's own ideas, tastes and fashions.

I therefore implore you to give your approval in this matter of marriage, as I do not wish to proceed without your blessing, although my hand shakes slightly as I write this, as I do not know what I will do if your answer shows you against it.

I then only hope Jack is as conducive as I will you to be. I have not yet had the chance to inform him of this joyous news, as on my return home from the supper I discovered him asleep in the library. I put a blanket across him, as he lay in the chair, and retired to my room to compose this letter.

If the truth is known, I am worried about him. I have not mentioned this in any of my previous correspondence, as I felt I did not want to betray his trust. Not that he has asked specifically for the matter not to be discussed outside the two of us, but as it is of a very personal nature I felt obliged to him. However, as I am now more and more concerned for his wellbeing, and you may be able to offer comforting words, I feel justified in disclosing these details.

Not long after my brother's arrival in Bath, he believed he saw one of the men responsible for his father's murder, twenty years ago. This is the reason he has remained in Bath since mother's funeral, although he had not discussed the man again until today. He announced that he had learnt of an artist who could age people through portraits of themselves. The examples he had observed were of those who had been painted as they would appear in the future, but my brother has commissioned the man to paint this man from his past as he would now look in the present. To undertake this, however, the artist required a sketch of how the man looked all those years ago and through my brother's description, I was able to complete a portrait of him. I do not know whether it bore a true likeness to the person, but Jack was more than satisfied with it. Whatever this portrait brings for him though, I hope it also brings peace, as the nightmares he has suffered since childhood has become regular of late and I have attended him several times since he has lived here.

I will end my correspondence here, but although I have asked for comforting words from you in the above matter, the ability to be able to disclose my feelings through the words on these pages seems to have brought with it some consolation.

Your most faithful niece

Mary

CHAPTER FIFTY-FOUR

A fresh fall of snow had greeted the inhabitants of Bath on their waking but whereas it had quickly melted two days earlier, this time it stayed for longer. By the time Swann was being driven out to Tozer's publishing company in the mid-morning, however, the majority of snow on the route out had been turned to slush by the multitude of vehicles which had passed over it earlier. Swann looked up from Fitzpatrick's carriage to Lansdown, and as he saw Gregor-Smith's residence in the distance, reiterated the promise made to himself, that he would ensure the writer's return there in the very near future.

Swann stepped out of the carriage on its arrival outside Tozer's premises and this time gestured for the driver not to wait. He went inside the building and was immediately confronted by the unmistakable sound of books being printed. On reaching Tozer's office, he found it was empty. He looked around and saw one of the workers he had interviewed two days before, next to a printing press. It was Johnson's nephew, William.

'Is Mr Tozer in the building?' shouted Swann, trying to make himself heard above the noise of the press.

'What did you say, sir?' William loudly replied.

'Is Mr Tozer here?' repeated Swann, but realised once more that he had not been heard. He tried again. 'Is there somewhere we can talk away from this noise?'

'No sir, I cannot leave this machine at the moment.'

'Where is Mr Tozer?' asked Swann, pronouncing his words precisely, so that William might hopefully lip-read.

'I do not know,' William shouted back, but pointed over to a co-worker unloading boxes near the rear door. 'That's Mr Skinner, he might know.' Before Swann could go over, however, William asked about his uncle.

'You do not need to concern yourself,' said Swann, 'your uncle is a free man.'

Swann now went over to the other man. The noise from the press was still loud but not invasive enough to forbid a conversation.

'He is not in all day,' replied the middle-aged Mr Skinner, on being asked the same question.

'Do you know where he is?' asked Swann.

'I would not like to say, begging your pardon, sir.'

'Ah, then I would assume he is visiting his wife.'

Skinner looked surprised.

'A co-worker has informed me of Mrs Tozer's condition and her residency at a particular institution,' explained Swann. 'It is certainly a tragedy what opium can do to a person's mind.'

The worker once again looked surprised but this time answered: 'Yes, it is.'

The information regarding the opium and Mrs Tozer's residency was actually news to Swann, but a hunch arising from what Johnson had mentioned the previous evening, and Kirby's showing him the amulet belonging to Gregor-Smith, had caused him to fabricate his knowledge of the situation. It was an old trick Swann had used on several occasions before; one ventured a piece of information as though you knew it to be fact and if the other person did not deny it, or in this case agreed, it was taken as to be proven true.

Alternatively, if it was not fact, Swann imbibed so much assurance in what he said that the person would usually then reveal the actual truth, as they believed him to be already 'in the know' and an 'equal' in knowledge. And once this connection had been established, more searching questions could be asked and more personal details gained.

'And Mr Tozer? I understand he does not partake of this drug?'

'That's right sir, at least not that I am aware, sir.'

'So where did Mrs Tozer acquire the opium, was it from Avon Street?'

'Oh no, sir, it was at those gatherings she attended.'

'Gatherings?' queried Swann.

'At that big house belonging to one of the writers we publish.'

'Oh yes, I forgot. Mr Gregor-Smith?'

Skinner did not respond.

'Can I ask how you came by this information?' continued Swann. 'Is Mrs Tozer's condition and the parties she attended common knowledge here?'

'I do not believe so,' Skinner answered. 'It was through a conversation I overheard between Mr Tozer and his wife a while back sir, before her present state of mind came on. I was working late and happened to be behind a stack of books near his office, when I heard shouting. Mrs Tozer was in his office and he was yelling at her, saying she was putting their marriage in trouble and that he knew about her secret liaisons.'

'Did she deny it?'

'Not so I remember it, sir. She did say something about enjoying herself and referred to their marital relations, but prudence dictates I do not repeat it here.'

Swann nodded his understanding.

'I then made a noise, sir. Mr Tozer came out of his office but I am sure did not see me. Afterwards, however, he closed the office door and I could not hear them anymore. I did look over once though, through his window, and saw him strike ... oh, perhaps I have said enough. Is Mr Tozer in trouble?'

'I honestly do not know, Mr Skinner, but thank you for all your information, you have been most helpful.'

Swann began to leave but then turned back toward the worker.

'One last question, if I may Mr Skinner. Remind me of Mrs Tozer's first name; Martha is it not?'

'No sir, it is Lydia.'

CHAPTER FIFTY-FIVE

A short while after Swann had arrived at Tozer's premises, a distinctive salmon pink-coloured carriage pulled up outside the house in Great Pulteney Street. In what had now become a regular occurrence on a Thursday morning, the driver knocked on the front door, waited until it opened and Mary handed him a letter, whereupon he then remounted the carriage and continued on his way.

Once the driver had finished his collection of the series of letters from various addresses in Bath, he made a circumvented route back to where he had originally left from earlier that morning; gathering on his return journey more letters from outlying villages such as Hinton Charterhouse, Norton St Philip, Woolverton, Rode and Beckington.

The carriage's destination was the Manor House, just outside the market town of Frome. The grand residence had originally been built from the proceeds of the thriving and lucrative cloth trade in the town, by a family who were one of its biggest employers. This particular family firm, however, had lost the majority of their fortune when war had broken out against the French a decade earlier and the seemingly insatiable demand by France for kerseymeres – a particular type of fine twilled woollen cloth – had ceased overnight. The house had fallen to disrepair until purchased by Harriet, Mary's aunt, who set about restoring it to its former glory, although she was finding it increasingly frustrating to deal with her unreliable and incompetent builders.

Once the driver arrived at the main doorway, he decided to bypass the various building works going on just inside and entered the house by a side entrance, which took him on an interminable route to Harriet's temporary office, located in the depths of the west wing. He then knocked on the open door and waited. His mistress looked up from a huge desk, behind which she had been putting the final touches to a thin pamphlet outlining possible uses of women in regard to foreign diplomacy. On seeing the driver she beckoned him in.

'Ah, my weekly correspondence,' she said, excitedly.

'Yes, Lady Harriet. All except one has responded this week.'

'Excellent,' she answered.

The driver placed the canvas satchel, in which he had secured all the letters, on her desk.

'Any replies will be ready by midday,' said Harriet.

The driver nodded and then took his leave.

Harriet put aside the document she was working on and opened the satchel. She tipped its contents onto the mahogany surface of her desk and began to sift her way through them. She picked up each envelope individually and attempted to identify its sender through the handwriting, which she had become accustomed to seeing most weeks. This was her 'circle' as she referred to them, her informant network through which she learnt all manner of information, from domestic disputes to illicit affairs, from personal revelations to business secrets. She had single-handedly created this network a few years beforehand, and although most of the contents of these weekly correspondences proved to be largely innocuous, on several occasions it had proved very useful, including one spectacular piece of good fortune earlier in the year, when a certain piece of information received this way had assisted in a matter of national security. She instructed her driver to collect them, as he had done this morning, for speed and secrecy. Although the contents of the letters would, in most cases, be harmless if they fell into the wrong hands, as they would be taken out of context, in her line of work one could not be too careful and so the more secure the lines of communication were, the happier she felt. She identified each handwriting specimen as a practical exercise to sharpen her observation skills, rather than a desire to know its sender before the letter was opened.

Harriet picked up the next envelope in the pile and studied the handwriting. It was one she had newly memorised, as the correspondent was a recent addition to the circle. She opened her niece's letter and slowly read the contents Mary had written the previous night. Immediately her expression changed to one of anger; the news of Lockhart's proposal being the catalyst. Beginning a relationship with Mary had already been in defiance of the stipulations under which he had been brought into the organisation, but for the sake of retaining the status quo it had been decided not to interfere. His marriage proposal, however, was going far too far and was completely unacceptable. She would give her approval for it though, after fabricating an initial meeting to meet Lockhart, and this would give her time to find a way to stop it, without of course jeopardising the operation.

Once her initial reaction had subsided a little, she reread the accompanying sections that followed the news and included Mary's thoughts on marriage. Her argument showed, in places at least, there was a maturity of understanding in regard to certain statements Ms Astell and several others had made over the centuries towards this subject, but nevertheless, Harriet could detect there was still a naivety about her general outlook.

Harriet now read the news about Jack and the portrait he had commissioned. If this was the same man she thought it was, whose image was being reproduced, it moved the entire situation to a new level. She had been saddened to learn the previous month that Thomas Malone had been murdered in Bath, but that was one of the hazards in this line of work; although not the most pleasant man she had ever met, he had nonetheless played his part admirably last summer and everyone connected with the operation, included herself, had been appreciative. That though, as far as *they* were concerned, had been the end of it. But now, with her adoptive nephew possibly close to stirring up the equivalent of a hornet's nest, certain preventative action might have to be taken. She did not want to take it that far – somewhere she had a begrudging admiration towards him – but that was the type of war they were involved in and better the sacrifice of the one for the many, especially when it concerned the country's security. Because, if her nephew was to find this man, the consequences would mean several months of planning being completely wasted and the contacts within that world, which had been so carefully established and cultivated over the last few years, eliminated. And it was, after all, her job to make sure this did not happen.

Once Harriet had finished reading Mary's letter, she took out a piece of paper and began to write her reply.

Thursday 1st December 1803

Dear Mary (my most appreciative niece)
Thank you for your most recent communication and regarding your initial news may I offer you my sincerest heartfelt congratulations.

I am most honoured that you would ask my approval of this betrothal and would not hesitate for one moment in giving it to you. My only reservation, however, is that as I have yet to meet your Mr Lockhart, I feel it would be remiss of me in my capacity as your closest blood relative, and doing you a disservice, not to reserve this approval until after such time as I have had the pleasure of the company of this gentleman. In the meanwhile, please peruse your diary engagements for the forthcoming period of time, so that the two of us might arrange a convenient date so as to discuss this matter in person.

In regard to your news concerning Jack and his commissioning of this portrait, I think you may be right to be concerned for him. I may be able to help in certain ways but first, I would be interested in seeing an image of this man your brother believes he is searching for. Would you be able to furnish me with a duplicate of the drawing you undertook for your brother and forward it on to me (without Jack's knowledge, of course) and, once the portrait is completed, sur-reptitiously make a drawing of this as well? These requests may seem to ask much of you, but I do believe that they are in the best interest of your brother.

I look forward to hearing from you again soon.

Yours

Harriet

Harriet sealed the letter and placed it in the tray for col-lection by the driver. She would work through the rest of the correspondence and answer those which required replies, later. Before that, however, was the requirement to now compile an urgent report to send to London, detailing what she had just learnt in Mary's letter. This was one of the reasons she admired her nephew. Why no one had thought of using portrait artists in this way before, she did not know.

They were so ubiquitous in the circles she moved in, and nearly everyone she knew within those circles had been the subject, at least once, but to use them to reproduce likenesses of criminals or other disreputable characters was a stroke of genius on his part. And with her niece's ability to draw a portrait from merely a description, she could become a very useful tool for Harriet and the Office.

CHAPTER FIFTY-SIX

Swann left Tozer's publishing firm and having dismissed Fitzpatrick's driver on his arrival, instigated his plan of returning to the city centre along the river. The watercourse was not far from the rear of the building and before long he was at the river's edge. Although the water at this part was heavily polluted and the path was muddy underfoot from melting snow, there was a tranquil ambiance to the area and this was why he had chosen to walk back. He tapped the place on his jacket, underneath which his pistol resided, and then set off at a stride; he wanted to benefit from the meditative element of the walk as much as he could but at the same time was prepared for any possible trouble that might be waiting along this isolated stretch of riverbank.

The River Avon was the heart of Bath and one of the main connections between the city and Bristol. It began its seventy-five mile journey in south Gloucestershire, before it curved and snaked its way through several counties and numerous towns and villages, before passing through Bath on its way to the mouth at the Severn Estuary in Bristol. At a number of places, further back on its route, the waters were pure enough to drink but on passing through the several urban conurbations, including Bath, subsequently became polluted from the volumes of waste pumped into it. It was a pleasant enough walk, however, and Swann enjoyed the restorative feeling that free-flowing water always gave him. Although aware there might be notorious black spots for robbery, the trees were rapidly shedding their leaves, becoming brown mulch on the ground and there was little foliage therefore behind which robbers could hide. And so Swann strode on with all the confidence one possessed when able to see clearly and with the added security of having a concealed weapon about one's person.

Across the river could now be observed the settlement of Twerton, originally known as Twiverton, which had grown up around the weaving trade during the seventeenth and eighteenth centuries. For Swann though, and other literary pilgrims, its importance lay in the fact it was, for a while, home to the novelist Henry Fielding, who, later in life, also became the founder of the Bow Street Runners, the organisation Swann had undertaken consultancy work for back in London. It was while in Twerton though, that Fielding had written his acknowledged masterpiece *Tom Jones*, a novel which contained, according to a later critic, one of the 'three most perfect plots ever planned' (the other two being those of *Oedipus Tyrannus* and the *Alchemist*). The novel's connection to the city of Bath, other than its author's one-time residency, was further enhanced by Fielding having based the character of Squire Allworthy on his friend Ralph Allen, while the fictional squire's estate was loosely reminiscent of Allen's own Prior Park, which in the words of the book was 'a most charming prospect'.

As the building which housed Tozer's publishing firm began to diminish into the background, Swann briefly reviewed the information he had been given by Skinner and secured it in his own mind in relation to the conclusion he was rapidly forming as regards to the murderer. But that could wait, because as he now walked on, the rooftops of the houses in the Avon

Street district became visible ahead in the distance. And as he walked closer, Swann's mind became engrossed elsewhere, namely London, in the year 1783. In his mind, he now saw the unblemished face of the Scarred Man and then the agonising scream as the white hot metal of the poker seared his flesh.

A noise behind him brought Swann immediately back into the present. He instinctively turned his head, but could see nothing except the bare-limbed trees, which stood impassive and silent.

Swann now found he was at the river-bank by Avon Street itself. He climbed his way up a steep grassy incline and on to the slush-filled streets. A fine snow was falling once more but the area would not see white settle on it again today. He made his way through the traders and the hustle-bustle towards Broad Quay and the artist's studio. Was he being followed? He had a sense of it but having looked around again, could still see nobody that was not otherwise engaged in their everyday business.

He entered the artist's building. The woman Swann had grappled with the day before was coming out of her doorway. She stopped momentarily when she saw him but then continued quickly on, as she left the dwelling. Swann, meanwhile, climbed the stairs of the building once more until he reached the top floor. He made his way across the floor to the artist's studio. He knocked on the door and then called out, 'Hello? I've come for the portrait.'

As last time, there came no answer. He knocked again and then tried the door handle. It was open once more and he went inside. The room was empty except for the easel on which stood the barely begun canvas which now depicted the two naked girls from the previous day, but entwined in a different position.

'Hello?' Swann called again.

Again, there was no response. The room was damp and cold and felt as if no one had been here for a while. Swann walked cautiously across the room toward a small partitioned alcove. The recess was covered by a curtain. He reached for it and then pulled it aside. The artist lay slumped against the wall, the chair he was sitting on having tipped and wedged him in, so he did not fall far onto the floor. In front of him was a small easel. Mary's drawing was attached at the top and below it he now saw the portrait. Swann involuntary took a step back as his eyes confronted those of the present-day Scarred Man. The portrait was unfinished but was complete enough to allow the features to be distinguished clearly. The man's nose was broken and down his right cheek ran the three and a half inch scar. In that moment, Swann knew this was the man he had passed on the street.

Swann lent forward and touched the artist to see if he was dead, but instead he sat bolt upright.

'Don't hurt me,' he shouted out. 'I didn't touch the girls.'

'No one is going to hurt you,' said Swann, holding the other man's shoulders to keep him seated. 'I have returned for this portrait. Remember?'

'Er, yeah, yeah, I remember,' said the artist, still drowsy. 'Let me get up.'

Swann stepped aside to allow the artist to stand. As the artist did so, however, he kicked the chair back at Swann. Momentarily taken by surprise, Swann now found himself knocked to the floor with the artist on top of him.

'You've come to kill me, I know it, I know it,' screamed the artist, as the two men grappled on the floor of the studio.

It took all of Swann's strength to push the other man away but in one swift movement the artist now lay with his back on the floor and Swann had the upper hand again.

'Listen to me,' said Swann. 'I have not come here to kill you. I have come for the portrait in the alcove, remember?'

Swann kept the artist pinned down until he saw in the other man's eyes a look of recognition.

'My balm, get me my balm,' said the artist at last.

Swann did not budge.

'Please, it is medication. It is over there on that table.'

Swann cautiously loosened his grip, stood up and retrieved the small bottle, all the while his attention focused completely on the artist still on the floor. He handed the bottle to the man, who uncapped it and inhaled its contents heavily. After a few seconds he repeated these imbitions and then held his hand out so as to be helped up. Swann extended his left hand but was ready with the right to administer a punch if needed.

'The balm stops the visions, but I didn't take it yesterday so I could do that,' the artist said, gesturing towards the alcove. He then looked back at Swann.

'I don't know who you are,' he continued, 'but stay away from that man. There is nothing but evil there. I have been with it all night.'

'Well, I thank you most gratefully for your work,' said Swann, stepping toward the alcove to collect the portrait.

'No! It is not finished yet,' said the artist. 'It will be ready for you tomorrow.'

'Will you be able to complete it now that you have taken your medication?'

'Yes, it is the vision I require and I have the awful memory of that now.'

'It is a great gift you posses,' said Swann, staring at the portrait again.

'I believe it to be a curse,' the artist replied. 'This ability to see people not as they are but how they will become.'

'And do you see that in only those you paint?'

'Towards the end I saw it with everyone,' he answered, as he raised the bottle, 'which is why I use this concoction to make it stop.'

'And have you seen what I become?'

The artist hesitated slightly. 'I did not meet you until yesterday, and have never met this other man, but all I will say is that he brings with him nothing except torment for your soul, that is until you have relinquished the need for the revenge you seek. Whatever it is this man has done to you, it is far worse what you do to yourself by pursuing him.'

'But you do not understand ... ' Swann started.

'However much this man has wronged you in the past,' interrupted the artist, 'for your own sake you must let this matter rest.' The man saw Swann was not to be persuaded and then shrugged his shoulders. 'As I've said, the portrait will be ready tomorrow.'

As Swann left the building he again had the sense of being watched. As before, he looked around but could see no one suspicious. He walked the short distance to Horse Street and then turned up it to head back towards the city centre. As he neared the bottom of Stall Street, he started to hear the indistinct voice of the newspaper boys shouting out the latest headlines. It was only as he neared them, however, that he could make out the words properly.

'Extra, read all about it. Gothic writer found guilty of horrible murders. To be hanged tomorrow at three o'clock.'

CHAPTER FIFTY-SEVEN

Bath, Thursday 1st December, 1803
I find myself increasingly agitated as I write this entry, due in part,
I believe, to my mind being brought to a heightened level of disquiet
as the numerous strands of my fragmented thoughts become seemingly
intertwined with one another.

Today I have looked once more on the face of the accomplice from
that night, this time through the artist's portrait, only now I have seen
him as he is, not as he was. In the twenty years that have elapsed he
appears to have become evil in his own right. I almost dare not admit
it to myself, even after all this time, but I believe there was a kind of
innocence I observed in his eyes on that first occasion, which may have
reflected the fact he had found himself involved in an unfolding situa-
tion beyond his control. Having recently discovered that Sean Malone
came to England, after killing a man in cold blood, the same year he
murdered my father, I wonder if the Scarred Man journeyed with him
from Ireland or if they met in London? Wherever their association
began though and whether it remains to this day, it has been forever
imprinted in my own mind through the actions of that night, and
the mark the Scarred Man received from my father has become the
reminder of how they came to be so inextricably linked.

What of the artist's words to me though, concerning my continued pur-
suit of them? Is he right in what he said, does he really have a gift to view
the future? If not, how was he aware of my search and why was he able
to so disturbingly capture the evil that resides in the face of the Scarred

Man? Does he know of him? How accurate is the portrait? All I know is that an innocent man, Gregor-Smith, goes to the gallows tomorrow and I feel I have failed him as there is no more I can do. With this portrait though, I feel it will enable me to continue my search for the Scarred Man, and ultimately Malone, and in this way, I will not fail my father as well.

I am shaken to the centre of my being as I continue to write, remembering the pure face I looked upon twenty years ago, and have held in my memory ever since, to now become so distorted into evil. For I did see something pure within the Scarred Man that night; it was for a moment only, but it was there. As my father inched his way forward to the fireplace, the Scarred Man wrapped around his legs in order to stop him, he turned his head towards me and in the brief moment our eyes met, I saw everything. The Scarred Man believed he was there to rob the house and had been informed by Malone it would be empty, so there would be no trouble, and being young and naïve, he believed him. Malone, however, already had evil in his eyes, I saw that too, and was prepared to commit the ultimate act as merely part of his nature. But the possibility to do something other than pursue the criminal life existed in the Scarred Man's eyes and it was the deprived circumstances of his surroundings which no doubt led him to be at the house on that night and be party to the consequences of Malone's action once there. All that has now changed though, and the years which have since passed have altered the Scarred Man in a most Faustian way, with Malone his Mephistopheles, as they go about their devil's work, together or separate.

It is not the same for everyone though, in the sense we are all shaped by circumstances out of our control and events that happen as much to us, as because of us, then live out our lives influenced by the consequences of them. In my situation, what would I have become if my father was not murdered? I certainly would not have been adopted by the Gardiners and therefore would not have enjoyed the privilege and wealth it has brought to me. And yet, somehow ironically, I have spent these resources in pursuit of the very men who were the cause of it in the first place.

As for Gregor-Smith, would he have become something other than a writer if his life had been different, if his father had not committed suicide? And if that was the case, then he would not have written the book containing the murders which have now condemned him to death. And what of the artist? Was there an event or incident which caused his visions to manifest in the first place and, if that had not happened, would he have become something other than an artist, in the way the Scarred Man might have transcended the criminal life and redeemed his soul if robbery had not become murder? Yet all these random events which have happened to others, these separate existences which are all outside my own, have all conspired together to shape my life and bring me here, to this moment, to this situation, to this fate.

CHAPTER FIFTY-EIGHT

That night Swann's recurring nightmare began again and once more he found himself in the Gardiner's London residence on the night of his father's murder. It proceeded as usual, with Swann seated at the table staring at the empty cup. At the sound of the vase smashing, he stood and made his way to the doorway in the same manner he had done so hundreds of times before. There was his father grappling in the hallway with the other man, followed by their tumble into the front room and then the few steps it took him to reach the entrance to witness the scene unfold within.

The Scarred Man lay on the floor writhing in agony after being struck by the poker. Only this time, however, the face he clutched took on the appearance of his present-day portrait. His accomplice appeared at the doorway, but instead of Malone, his features were now those of Wicks. No, this cannot be right. The thought resonated deep within Swann's psyche; there was something wrong, something terribly wrong. In his nightmare he saw that the features of his father had become those of Gregor-Smith. And it was the writer who went sprawling on to the floor and waited to receive the fatal stab wound to the heart.

The nightmare then became a series of images, flashed in rapid succession, as Swann's recent present merged with his distant past, through recollected events from the days and weeks since he arrived in Bath, before his all-too-remembered past then distorted into an horrifying, imagined future ... He was chasing Tyler, the first criminal Swann encountered in Bath and the man who had tried to kill him, down a long passageway, one whose end continued to stretch infinitely out in front of Swann until he suddenly found himself alone in a deserted street ... A man with a covered face now rushing towards him and as much as Swann tried to reach out to grab the man, as he passed within touching distance, could not ... The artist sitting behind a canvas and as he painted, imploring Swann to stop seeking revenge. And then the portrait itself which, once the artist had turned it around, Swann could see was an aged portrait of himself, the features harrowed and grotesque ... then the scene shifting to the Gardiner's drawing room where he was informed of his adoption, only now Fitzpatrick stood in the place of Mr Gardiner and Harriet in that of her recently deceased sister. As the young Mary reached out her hand to hold Swann's, she became her present-day version and before they could grasp one another, Lockhart snatched Mary's hand away ... the scene shifted again and now Swann was leaving the artist's building with two masked men behind him. And then, back on the top floor, standing in the doorway just in time to witness them beside a battered and beaten artist. The two men turned towards Swann and he saw it was Wicks and the Scarred Man, the latter holding his own portrait aloft, so his companion, after unsheathing his cutlass, could slash it to pieces. Once destroyed, Wicks raising his cutlass once more, this time to administer the fatal blow to the artist, but as he thrust the blade downward, Swann saw the victim's features become those of his own father; and so the final scene of his recurrent nightmare, which had always been mercifully omitted previously, now unfolded in all its terrifying revulsion … finally, looking on in disbelief and shock as his father's killer straightened up and Swann saw his own harrowed and grotesquely aged features reflected back at him. At that moment, however, Swann bolted upright in bed as he awoke to his usual cry of '*Noooooooooooo!*'

'It is all right Jack,' said Mary, as she reassuringly stroked her brother's arm, summoned to the room by his screaming. 'It was a bad dream, just a bad dream.'

CHAPTER FIFTY-NINE

After Mary had returned downstairs to her own room, Swann spent the rest of the night sleeping fitfully or meditatively pacing up and down his bedroom floor; his mind intently focused on his present investigation. By first light he believed he had pieced together a version of the truth which only required one missing piece; yet that piece's absence could cost Gregor-Smith his life, as the writer was due to be executed later that day.

Around the time of Swann's normal departure to the White Hart, he had gone to the front door of the house to check for the letter he was expecting. There was nothing. He had checked with Emily, but she merely confirmed there had been no correspondence received. He was still optimistic and had therefore decided to postpone his morning visit to the coaching inn until later. Swann now sat in the drawing room, staring out on to the street in anticipation, when Mary entered.

'Ah Jack, there you are. I have wonderful news to share with you. I did not feel it appropriate to do so last night and there have been no other suitable occasions since its occurrence.'

'What is it, Mary?' asked Swann, a little distractedly, his attention still focused outside.

As Mary was about to speak, Swann raised his hand to stop her and then leapt up from his chair.

'One moment, sister, someone has arrived at the front door and I believe they carry with them a most important correspondence.'

As Swann reached the main door, he saw Emily had already taken charge of a letter. She handed it to him.

'It is addressed to you, sir,' she said.

Swann thanked her and took the letter. He turned it over to look at the back. It bore the seal of Richard Huntley, literary agent.

'This is the letter I have been waiting for, Mary,' said Swann, on his return to the drawing room. He picked up a jewel-encrusted letter opener from a small table and slit the top of the envelope.

'Can it not wait, Jack?'

'Ah, as I expected,' he said, having taken out the letter and quickly read it. 'This is a letter from the acquaintance I conversed with at the gallery. It contains very important news. I must leave immediately.'

'You are not going now, Jack, there is something I require to ask you?'

'I am afraid it will have to wait,' he replied, as he put the letter in his pocket. 'An innocent man's life is at stake. You can ask me later, after I have saved a man from the gallows.'

Swann hailed down the nearest carriage, once outside the house, and the driver headed off in the direction of the address he had been given. Ten minutes later, the carriage stood outside Fitzpatrick's Camden Crescent residence, while inside, the magistrate was getting himself ready in order to leave with Swann.

'So what is this news that calls me from breakfast?' asked Fitzpatrick, as they emerged from the front door and entered the carriage.

'I have heard from my literary contact and he sends the answer to a question I asked him at the gallery.'

'But where are we going now?'

'We are heading to Tozer's publishing. I believe the murderer of both the girl and the priest to be Mr Tozer himself!' Swann announced.

'Tozer!' exclaimed Fitzpatrick. 'And how did you arrive at that notion?'

'This letter I have received this very morning from Huntley is very revealing. He is the literary agent I was conversing with at the gallery. What he does not know in the literary world has little worth and so I asked him to make certain enquires on my behalf. Our Mr Tozer is, indeed, in great financial debt, which we knew, but what we did not know is that Gregor-Smith has recently signed a publishing deal with another company. The same company the other writer, who was possibly going to sign with Tozer, has joined as well.'

'But surely these are not reasons enough to commit murder?' said Fitzpatrick.

'Perhaps not, but I believe Mrs Tozer to have had an illicit liaison with Gregor-Smith at some time in the past, and during this period attended several parties where they partook of opium. Gregor-Smith's constitution is strong, while Mrs Tozer's was not, and it affected her mind so much so that she now resides in an institution. With his publishing business in ruins, his bestselling writer leaving the company and his wife apparently driven mad by the very same, that is perhaps more than enough reason to commit murder and frame the man he holds responsible.'

'That is certainly a potent reason for murder Swann, but that means he killed his own niece!'

'I realise this, but sometimes the desire for revenge will make men go to any lengths, Fitzpatrick.'

'What do you intend to do once we get there.'

'I shall confront him with what knowledge I have and I want you to bear witness to his replies and reaction.'

Fitzpatrick nodded once more.

The carriage now reached the premises of Tozer Publishing and as it turned the corner into the yard, Swann could see the owner unlocking a small side door in the main building. As the carriage pulled up alongside the publisher, Swann and Fitzpatrick jumped out. Tozer turned to face them.

'Gentlemen, really, are you never to allow me to conduct my business without constant interruptions? Well, I am sorry, but I cannot allow you to talk to any of my workers today.'

'We have not come to talk to your workers, Mr Tozer,' said Swann. 'We have come to talk to *you* and I would suggest that we do so in your office.'

'I have nothing to say wherever we may be,' answered Tozer defiantly, as he carried on about his business.

'We are aware of your troubles,' continued Swann, 'both your financial and more personal ones.'

'You have me at a disadvantage then, sirs. What are you talking about?'

'I do sympathise with you,' said Swann. 'Your wife's mind has become unstable, your bestselling writer has signed with another publisher and you are not far from losing your business. And I would suggest that these were also the reasons behind murdering your niece and the clergyman, in order to implicate Gregor-Smith.'

'You are talking utter nonsense, sir,' said Tozer, looking Swann directly in the eyes. 'I am merely a publisher of books, not a murderer, this is most …'

'Mr Tozer,' Fitzpatrick interjected, 'there are only two people who had access to Mr Gregor-Smith's manuscript, and Mr Johnson's alibi has been confirmed.'

'But you have forgotten the writer,' exclaimed Tozer. 'It is him! Did they not find his amulet at the murder scene?'

'How do you know it was an amulet?' Swann asked the publisher.

'It was in the newspaper report,' replied Tozer.

'The report only gave mention to a personal item, not an exact description.'

At this, Tozer turned and ran off along the side of the building.

'Make sure everyone stays inside, Fitzpatrick,' shouted Swann, as he ran off after the publisher.

Swann reached the corner of the building just in time to see Tozer climbing a metal ladder attached to the side of it. As Swann began to follow the publisher up the ladder, Tozer reached the top and clambered onto the roof of the building. A few seconds later, his head appeared again and threw down a wooden pole towards Swann. It narrowly missed him, however, and he carried on to the top regardless and then hoisted himself over. He now saw the publisher at the far end of the debris-strewn roof, trying frantically to open a door. It was locked.

'There is nowhere to run, Mr Tozer.'

Tozer bent down and picked up one of the metal pipes that lay around. 'Stay where you are,' he shouted, waving it in the air. 'I do not deserve this. It is Gregor-Smith who should suffer.'

'It was through him that your wife became addicted to opium?' asked Swann, sympathetically.

'Yes, the opium sent her mad, and it was him who did it.'

'But to seek revenge through murdering your niece?' said Swann, as he edged a little closer.

Tozer saw this, however, and waved the metal bar furiously.

'I said stay where you are! I was only protecting Lizzy, she was going to be his next conquest.'

'I do not understand,' said Swann.

'When Gregor-Smith delivered his manuscript here last week, I saw the way he looked at Lizzy and she at him. He would have seduced her in the way he did my wife and got her addicted as well. She would have suffered the same fate as my dear Lydia and I could not allow that to happen.'

'What about murdering the reverend?' Swann replied, as he took another step closer.

Tozer threw the pipe at Swann's head, but missed.

'I'm not going to prison; who will take care of my wife and my business?'

Tozer began to run towards where the metal ladder was attached, but Swann wrestled him to the ground. The publisher wriggled free, however, and was able to carry on back across the roof towards the ladder. Swann picked up another metal pole and threw it at the legs of the fleeing man. It made contact just below the back of the knees and caused the publisher to stumble. Tozer tried to regain his balance and for a moment looked as if he had done so, but then tripped and fell through a skylight on the roof, shattering the glass as he went through it.

Swann swiftly made his way to the skylight and looked down. Below he saw Tozer dead, his twisted body impacted on one of his printing machines. In that moment, Swann felt sorrow for him. He had not seemed like a man with evil intent, merely one whose circumstances had overtaken him.

'You heard everything, Fitzpatrick?' asked Swann, as he saw the magistrate bending over the dead man's body.

'Yes,' replied the magistrate.

'Good,' replied Swann. 'So I suggest we now return to the city and release an innocent man.'

Fitzpatrick looked up and nodded solemnly.

CHAPTER SIXTY

'Thank you once again Mr Swann, I do not know how I can ever repay you,' said Gregor-Smith, stepping into the carriage that would take him back to his residence in Lansdown.

'You might reconsider your decision not to have your manuscript published,' said Swann, handing the thick sheaf of papers to the writer. 'Despite the tragic events surrounding it, I believe it would be a great loss to the reading public to do otherwise.'

'That is most kind of you, but my mind is set. Like Dante, I have had cause to consider this midway point of life and realise through incarceration within my own inferno, however brief, and with the prospect of imminent execution, that I too have strayed from the True Way and from hereon in have pledged myself to celebrate life and no longer sensationalise death. In doing this, I may even leave England and move to the Continent. I have always been particularly fond of the lake at Geneva. I am therefore indebted to you Mr Swann in ways you will never know. If you would care for the manuscript yourself then you are most welcome to retain it.'

'Thank you, I am deeply honoured,' said Swann, as he took the papers back.

The two men shook hands and the carriage drove away. After Swann and Fitzpatrick had made their own farewells, Swann headed off towards the city centre and began to walk down Horse Street, towards the artist's studio in Broad Quay.

Now the murder case had been solved, and Gregor-Smith freed, Swann could once again concentrate fully on his search for the Scarred Man.

As Swann neared the end of the street, he noticed George and Bridges ahead, in conversation with a stallholder. Good, thought Swann, if they were to come with him now, he could show them the portrait and they could carry on their investigation immediately. As he approached them, Bridges saw him and signed to George to finish talking.

'George, Bridges, the very men,' said Swann, genuinely happy to see the pair.

George turned and Swann saw he had acquired a second black eye.

'Not another encounter with Wicks' men, George?' asked Swann, concerned.

'No, sir,' he replied, sheepishly.

Bridges, who now stood behind George, gestured a woman's outline to Swann, then followed it with the signs for husband and punch. Swann smiled but chose not to tease George this time.

'If you care to join me, gentlemen,' he said, 'I am on my way to collect an item that will be of interest to you.'

The two men nodded and followed Swann down to the river and along to the building that housed the artist's studio. Once inside they climbed the stairs to the top floor, but as they reached the final few stairs, Swann could see the door was ajar. The three men stood outside and prepared themselves for possible trouble. Bridges then cautiously pushed open the door and they quietly entered the room. The studio looked the same as it had when Swann left it yesterday; there were no signs of disturbance, although for once the large wooden easel stood canvas-less in the middle of the room.

'Perhaps he went out into town?' whispered George.

'He never goes out,' replied Swann.

The men crossed the floor to the curtained partition. Swann gestured with one hand for them to ready themselves as he raised the other hand to pull back the covering. He brought it back in one swift action and as he did so, the sight which greeted them caused Swann to look on appalled as the body of the artist was revealed. It hung from the low ceiling within the small alcove.

'What do you want us to do, Mr Swann?' asked George.

Swann did not respond as he stared in disbelief at the scene that confronted them. A rope was tied tight around the artist's neck and beyond his limp corpse, still perched on the small easel as it had been the day before, was the obliterated portrait.

'Mr Swann?'

'Oh … yes … we had better bring him down.'

George and Bridges moved forward and, under Swann's instruction, cut down the body and took it into the main part of the studio, where they laid it on the battered chaise longue, which been the backdrop to so much of his work. Swann stayed at the alcove entrance, still looking on distraught at the ruined painting; the canvas had been ripped to shreds and the Scarred Man's features completely obliterated. There was nothing Swann could do. It seemed as if the visions had finally proved too much for the artist and had caused him to take his own life, but before that act he had destroyed the final creation which they had informed.

'What do you want us to do now, Mr Swann?' asked George.

'All we can do is to inform Fitzpatrick,' said Swann dejectedly, 'so he can organise the disposal of the body.'

Swann left the portrait where it was and then covered the artist's body with the green material from the back of the chaise longue. He then gestured to his two companions that it was time to leave and in doing so, they closed the door. They then retreated back down the stairs and came out of building, into the sun-deprived day. They turned left and headed back towards Horse Street. As they reached the thoroughfare though, Swann spotted Wicks on the opposite side of the street, intently watching them with a malicious, self-satisfied expression on his face.

'The artistic temperament, eh Swann?' Wicks shouted. 'One minute he is painting a portrait, the next minute, he is taking his own life.'

At the sudden realisation of what had really happened, an angry Swann began to cross the street towards Wicks. He had only gone a few steps before he found himself held back by George and Bridges.

'Mr Swann, don't,' implored George. 'Now's not the time or place.'

'You are right, George,' said Swann, as he relented. 'But do not think you will get away with this, Wicks. Your time will come.'

A despairing Swann turned towards the upper town and headed back there, accompanied by his two companions.

Once the three men were out of sight, another figure stepped out from behind a wall and stood next to Wicks.

'You've done well Wicks, I will not forget this,' said the 'friend' from London, who looked exactly as he had been portrayed by the deceased artist in the now destroyed portrait.

CHAPTER SIXTY-ONE

Bath, Friday 2nd December, 1803

I write this entry in the knowledge that all is not lost in the way I believed it to be and having had the time to reflect on the matter, I do not feel as despondent as earlier with regard to my quest to find the men responsible for my father's death. This renewed sanguinity has come about, in part, through the remembrance of an occurrence during the walk I undertook in Lyncombe Vale yesterday afternoon. There was a moment when I had cause to stop and while doing so, concentrated upon the immediate surroundings. My view focussed on a tree and as I gazed at its bare branches I found myself envisaging its appearance throughout all of the seasons; the onset of spring bringing with it blossoms bursting forth in an accord of colour – the whites, the yellows, the pinks – along with tiny leaves and green shoots, accompanied in their awakening by the chaffinch's melodious refrain and the other wonderous songs of spring. And then, as the leaves unfurled from their protective bud casings, I saw their continuous enrichment by deep-entrenched roots, providing them sustenance through to the full maturity of summer. The time when heavily laden branches, fruit ripened to the core, bask in the endless warmth of long halcyon days, before the first signs of autumn appear, to herald the returning of the leaves back to the soil and donning of the tree's bare exterior to carry it safely through the cold of winter, though replete in the knowledge this is but one part of nature's ongoing cycle and that spring will arrive once more and the cycle begun again.

And so I must always remember, as I continue my search, whenever I may feel as if a winter lies within myself, through external events happening outside my control, this feeling does not exist in isolation and is merely part of a whole, as inside me there is also a spring, with its anticipation of new life, the acceptance of autumnal decay and an endless warmth emanating from an invincible summer.

It still remains that the portrait of the Scarred Man is destroyed and its creator dead, but I now realise I require neither image nor artist to continue in my search for him and, ultimately, Malone. I have the memory of the Scarred Man's present-day appearance firmly etched in my mind from when I saw the portrait, and although it was unfinished, I am confident in my ability to provide Mary once more with enough detail for her to sketch another true likeness, with which I can then furnish George and Bridges. I will broach the subject with her tomorrow, as I believe she sleeps now.

There are several questions which remain to be answered, however. What led Wicks to be interested in the portrait and subsequently become directly involved, for I know he was involved, as my intuition tells me the artist did not commit suicide or destroy his own painting? In that respect, as the bad dream I had last night, in which the artist was murdered by Wicks, has come true, does this mean he is also connected in some way with the Scarred Man? If so, is that why George and Bridges were involved in their hostile encounter with Wicks' men a few days ago, as they made enquires, and why Wicks paid his visit to the Fountain Inn? But how did Wicks find the artist? As the landlord did not know where he resided, I can only assume my instincts were correct and I have been careless enough to allow myself to be followed; this must not happen again.

The main question that waits to be answered, however, concerns myself and whether or not to continue my quest of finding the Scarred Man. This doubt has arisen through the artist's words which have returned to me again. 'However much this man has wronged you in the past, for your own sake you must let this matter rest,' I hear him say. But I cannot let this matter rest, I cannot. Although it saddens me to know my actions in pursing the Scarred Man have caused the death of the very man whose words these were, I do not feel guilty, I must not feel guilty, because I know to do so would cause me to question every action I have undertaken and encumber any future ones. Every decision we take, every act we perform, contains within it a consequence, though these, of course, are not usually seen until later. If Gregor-Smith had not had a liaison with Lydia Tozer, or introduced her to opium, her husband would not have sought revenge and carried out the murders. Yet should Gregor-Smith be held accountable for those subsequent actions through his own? As we cannot ever fully comprehend what consequences our actions will elicit, tragic or otherwise, I believe we can only proceed with good intentions and aim to stay pure in the actions we carry out.

And so this is what I must do in regard to another revelation of the day: that of Lockhart's proposal. Mary informed me of her 'most wonderous' news on my return home this afternoon. I gave my immediate approval, in response to her request, as I did not wish to bring disharmony into the household at this present time. In the months to come though, between this present time and the date they will soon set for their betrothal, I will do everything within my power to discover the truth surrounding the mysterious Lockhart and then act accordingly. And so I am to remain in Bath for the foreseeable future. Nothing has changed since my initial decision those few weeks ago, other than that I have the additional reason of finding the connection between Wicks and the Scarred Man.

As I sit by the bedroom window, in the early hours of the morning, looking out upon the darkened streets of the city, I feel as if one chapter of my life is closing and another is soon to begin. What will the future hold? Am I really as close to finding the men responsible for my father's death as I feel myself to be? Certainly all the clues I have investigated during these past years, the potential leads, the possible sightings, the alleyways of hope, the passageways of despair, have *finally proved worthwhile through the chance conversation I overheard in London, which brought me to Bath in the first place. And even though the murdered Malone was not the one I sought and I have yet to encounter the Scarred Man again in person, since two days after my arrival in Bath, the fact that Wicks is possibly involved with the Scarred Man leads me to be optimistic.*

Whatever may be yet to come though, I have now arrived at the realisation that if I was ever to cease my quest, without the proper satisfaction of an appropriate resolution, I would be denying an integral part of myself which has been shaped by the events of my past and to which I must remain true in the future. In that way, the two are so inextricably linked that I believe one cannot exist without the other and where the past informs the future through experience, the future can enlighten the past through acquired insight. Therefore I must not only remain authentic in myself to the experience of this past future, but also to the possible insights arising out of the future past.

About the Authors

David Lassman is a scriptwriter, author, journalist and lecturer. He has appeared many times on television and radio, including BBC's *The One Show*, Radio Four's *The Today Programme*, *News at Ten* and *Good Morning America*. He currently teaches at City of Bath College and runs the Bath Writers' Workshop. David was born in Bath and now lives in Frome.

Now a full-time writer, Terence James is an award-winning editor (*Murder of Shirley Banks*, *Dangerous Music*) at ITV. Throughout an illustrious career he has held various roles on prestigious television programmes such as *Man Alive* (BBC) and *The Avengers* (ITV) as well as feature films at Elstree, Pinewood and Shepperton studios. He was born in London but has lived in Bath for more than forty years.

The Regency Detective series of novels are being written in conjunction with the development of a television series of the same name. The project is based in the city of Bath and has the backing of the Bath City Council, Bath Film Office, Bath Tourism Plus, The Jane Austen Centre and several other organisations in and around the city.